The Marionettist

The Marionettist

Brooks Pettit

Library of Congress Control Number: 2012914801

ISBN:	Hardcover	978-1-4797-0073-8
	Softcover	978-1-4797-0072-1
	Ebook	978-1-4797-0074-5

This book was printed in the United States of America.

To order additional copies of this book, contact:
Xlibris Corporation
1-888-795-4274
www.Xlibris.com
Orders@Xlibris.com
119883

This book is dedicated to my wife,
in all respects my muse and inspiration

"Once in a while you will stumble upon the truth, but most of us manage to pick ourselves up and hurry along as if nothing had happened."
Winston Churchill

"It is now life and not art that requires the willing suspension of disbelief."
Lionel Trilling

AUTHOR'S PREFACE

My boundless appreciation to John and Kelly Pettit, whose initial encouragement, goading and misguided suggestions engendered this undertaking. They are deserving of both gratitude and apologies; gratitude because this book has kept the author occupied and out of trouble for several months, and apologies because, for a number of reasons, they bear some responsibility for what follows. Also, it is undeniable that this book would never have been possible had it not been for the forbearance of my wife (see dedication), who wishes to remain anonymous.

The sole purpose of this book has been to provide entertainment for and bring pleasure to its author. If by chance any credulous, indiscriminating family members or friends wish to read it, the author and his extensive staff wish to thank them, wish them good luck, and request that they refrain from sending donations or directing critical comments towards either the book or the author personally.

If the length or the content of this book becomes daunting, the author understands and sympathizes should the reader decide to jump ship at any point and involve him or herself in something meaningful. In that event, however, you are encouraged to move directly to the Epilogue (which is really not a epilogue at all, but more of a denouement). This will allow you to circumvent the majority of drivel contained in the intervening pages, and move directly to the more significant, more enjoyable and considerably shorter pages of the précis. *

If even that becomes intimidating, the Appendix might be more appealing. It contains a number of entertaining photographs and renderings which, for those who prefer to eschew the written word, may be enjoyed without bothering with either the epilogue or the book itself.

Those who depend upon an obligatory torrid sex scene or two to make a book worth reading may be faced with profound disappointment in the following pages. Under the guidance of certain understandable personal restraints, such as accountability and propriety (to say nothing of common decency), and given the possibility that this book might fall into more fastidious hands than those of my direct family, it was determined at the sole discretion of the author that decorum should take precedence over debauchery. It is hoped that this decision will not impact too severely those whose tastes run more in the direction of "Lady Chatterley's Lover" or "Fifty Shades of Grey."

A note of caution to the reader; several of the allusions in this book are clan-inspired or family-oriented. As a result, some references may seem inane, superfluous, humorless, or frivolous to the uninitiated. The author assures the reader that nothing could be further from the truth, and that in fact every reference, however elusive or obscure, is saturated with wit, substance, and significance.

Finally, to those who may harbor a fondness for political correctness, this disclaimer is offered. Some elements in this book may not be suitable for those who are members of, sympathetic to or sensitive about any of the following organizations: The Baptist Church, the Episcopal Church, Judaism, the Air Force, the Army, the Tea Party, the medical profession, the University of Florida, the Occupiers, Hispanics, the Irish, Algerians, Cubans, Columbians, WASPS, any Police Department, the Hemingway Society, the town of Weed, California, the city of Portland, Oregon and the states of Florida and Texas. In a word, no effort has been made in these pages to capitulate to accepted standards of propriety. If you suspect that you may be susceptible to that benchmark of indifference, the author respectfully advises that you proceed with suitable deliberation and vigilance.

All characters, names and details in this book are historically accurate and based entirely on fact—unless, of course, they are entirely fictional, which is quite often the case. The exercise of separating the factual from the fictional is left to the discretion of the reader.

The author, August 2012

*This book was self-edited, which should suffice as both an explanation and a defense.

It was the trivial, petulant act of a child. A young boy, a box of matches, a Christmas tree and "Young Frankenstein" had unaccountably and darkly joined forces to create a spectral event. Together they had started the initial flames, so small at first, but so alarming to the boy with the match.

How many times had he been told never to play with matches, he wondered for years after? "You're too young for that kind of film, Henry," his mother had repeated as his older brother and sisters left for the movie. He felt the familiar resentment of a child who cannot change his age, but is confident of one thing; that at seven he's not too young for "Young Frankenstein," "The Godfather," "The French Connection" or a legion of other films considered too adult for those his age.

With that knowledge he carried out his very small act of rebellion. He broke the cardinal rule and lit the match, watching it flare between his fingers, drawing back from the powerful tang of sulfur in his nostrils. But he held it too long, fascinated by both the flame and his transgression, until it burned his fingers.

If only he hadn't lit the match. If only he'd thrown the match, and not dropped it. If only it hadn't fallen into the snow—that ubiquitous snow. And if only his mother hadn't been so eagerly determined to overdo every aspect of Christmas, much as he loved it when she did. The 9-foot tree so perilously close to the ceiling that it caused the angel on top to dip her head as if in prayer; the profusion of gaudy, hastily wrapped gifts scattered under it; the overabundance of decorations around the room—and the snow. There was so much thick, fluffy snow. If only there hadn't been so much snow.

Eight rolls of cotton batting had been needed to recreate his mother's child-like vision of snow under the Christmas tree. It surrounded the tree like a deep, feathery, white halo. And how it flared when the match touched it.

Responding to his panicked screams, his mother rushed into the room and saw the futile thrashings of a seven-year-old trying to put out the flaming cotton. She pushed him back, shrieking at him to leave the room and began a hopeless dance of her own to stop the flames from spreading. If only she hadn't been wearing a long, chenille robe and cotton bedroom slippers.

He stood in the doorway screaming soundlessly as the flames, livid and angry, rose about her feet and swiftly swallowed her body. His voice returned and he screamed his throat raw, while each of his other senses seemed shocked into cruel, vivid focus. He saw, and smelled, and tasted it all until his father thrust him aside. Then finally, and mercifully, his senses left him.

She had lived for a time, and wished she hadn't. She forgave him endlessly through her pain as he stood beside her bed, looking dismally at the floor. Even then, weeks later as he stood in her room, the sight and sounds of his mother on fire and the stench of her burning flesh were revived in his memory. He watched as her world became first a haze of narcotics, then was overwhelmed by the hopeless agonies surgery and rehabilitation. And then she gave up and died. She had tried, she had forgiven him, but his father never could. His youthful Christmas gift to his mother, and her subsequent, unending legacy to her son, was a perpetual horror of the smell and torment of fire. His gift to his father was to result in a lifetime of passive rejection.

* * *

Two police officers were standing close by the car in the parking lot. They were surrounded by a small but growing group of nervous onlookers, shuffling their feet and stealing awkward looks at one another and the burned-out car. The revolving lights from the fire trucks played erratically over the car, casting a series of dancing, vaporous shadows over the scene. The car was a mottled, colorless gray, made glistening with water from the fire hoses that were now coiled haphazardly on the pavement beside it. Water dripped from the bottoms of fenders and wheel wells. All four doors and the trunk were open, as if passengers had hurriedly fled before the car became fully engulfed. Inside the springs of the seats stood out in skeletal contrast to the surrounding metal of the car. There were spiral traces of smoke in the air that disappeared quickly into the early light of the dawn.

Near the body was a stocky man in plain clothes with the unambiguous look and carriage of a plain-clothes detective. The Crime Scene Investigator pulled up behind an ambulance that had been parked diagonally across the street in an effort to block any through traffic. A tow truck driver with spikey blond hair stood quietly nearby, hands in his pockets, lighting a cigarette, apparently unaware of the incongruity of his action. It was shortly after six in the morning.

The investigator stopped his car, but the smell reached him before he set the emergency brake. He opened the door of his car reluctantly and stood looking at the two officers and the detective. He didn't have to leave his car to know that he had arson and a dead body. He fought to control the urge to return to his car and leave. Sam would be on the way, there was no helping whatever was in that car, and there was always a migraine or the stomach flu to be used as an escape route. He simply wasn't sure he could force himself into the teeth of that terrible stench again. Every impulse urged him back to the car and the relief of air conditioning. He paused, reached back into his car and, retrieving the mandatory flashlight, walked as steadily as he could toward the silent men waiting for him.

Henry Louis had been investigating crime scenes for more than seventeen years. In that time he'd made many friends and few mistakes. He was very good at his job, and was recognized as one of the best investigators the Midland department could send to the scene of an accident or a suspected homicide. He was a stocky man whose red, blotchy complexion bore testimony to an affinity for bourbon and cigarettes. He mourned the days of a hard, flat abdomen, and lamented the small paunch that had accompanied his middle age. He'd cut quite a figure in his youth, he was convinced, but his current lifestyle and habits had betrayed him. Still, Louis was a contented man, respected by his friends for his humor and his professionalism, happy with his recent divorce and confident of his perpetual bachelorhood.

Louis greeted the two officers, the younger of whom looked pale and queasy. "First body?" He asked. The older officer answered for him. "It's his first call. He just out of the academy. Guess they figured he'd have to get his feet wet someday," he said mechanically.

"Congratulations—and welcome." He addressed the young man. "It gets easier after a while, son." He'd always hated it when older colleagues had addressed him as "son", but found that he had carelessly and inevitably fallen into the habit a few years before.

He turned to the detective. "What have we got here?" he asked, and reached out his hand.

The detective shook his hand and introduced himself. "Chavez, Jesus Chavez," he said simply, "but just call me Raul." Then he turned his attention back to the body. Chavez was a short, stocky man who had unsuccessfully stuffed himself into a worn, rumpled suit, and as a result had the appearance of a badly made bed.

"Body in the trunk," he said simply, and led the way across the wet pavement to the car. "Body couldn't have gotten itself in there, for sure. If this isn't a homicide, I'll eat my hat," he added.

"What hat?" Louis asked, looking for humor in response. The man was both bald and bareheaded.

"The one I left at home," Chavez answered. Louis wasn't sure if the man was being humorous or not. "Take a look at the car and the body. The doors and trunk were shut when the police got here. This guy would have had to work real hard to do this to himself." Louis decided that humor might not be Chavez' strong point.

Louis turned from the detective, looked briefly at the car in passing, then leaned into the trunk and looked at the body.

"Jesus," he said, recoiling. "I should have known better than that. No breakfast this morning," He pulled a handkerchief from his pocket and held it over his nose. "Classic crispy critter," he said aloud in an effort to conquer his revulsion with careless professionalism. He was aware that his voice was betraying him. Swallowing hard, he continued to no one in particular, "No need to hurry. He's not going anywhere. I could have taken the scenic route."

Despite the early morning light and the dull, sallow glow from a streetlight nearby, Louis could see that hurrying to the scene to prevent forensic contamination had been unnecessary. Standing a few feet back from the open trunk, he took a deep breath and considered the scene in front of him in its entirety. After a moment he shook his head reflectively.

Television had turned his job into celebrity stuff. In truth what he did most often fell under what he called the tedious pursuit of the obvious. Criminals were, by and large, a pretty incompetent lot. They frequently left clues by the bucket-full, witnesses, fingerprints, footprints, DNA, weapons, and most important, motives. Most often they left their motives behind in plain sight, which made police and forensic work straightforward and uncomplicated. The exploits shown on the most popular television shows were heroic enough, but incredibly embellished and inflated. "Aha" moments were rare and generally unnecessary in this business. The evidence to solve the crime was most often right in front of you, if you looked carefully enough. It did make for a good, engaging hour in front of the tube, however, he had to admit.

He looked more closely at the body and was immediately overwhelmed by both the smell and his memories. He managed to murmur "Hmmm" louder than was necessary, more an effort to appear composed and nonchalant for the benefit of the onlookers than an exclamation of interest in the scene in front of him. Then he rose, returned to his car and retrieved his rubber gloves and camera. As he turned back to the ruined hulk of the car, a small, noiseless puff of black smoke issued from somewhere beneath it. The onlookers, who had increased in number during the last few minutes, recoiled a few feet.

Louis walked slowly around the car and took photographs from several angles. Chavez followed him patiently, saying nothing. The detective stopped at the trunk, took a deep breath, muttered "Jesus, Joseph and Maria," then leaned closer inside. His eyes widened and his bronzed skin turned waxen. Louis feared the man might collapse, adding another installment to an already bizarre chronicle. He took him by one shoulder, turned him away from the trunk, and said quietly, "Detective, would you ask these people to move back, please?" Chavez gratefully complied, moving towards the crowd with his arms spread wide chanting, "back, back, back," over and over as he walked. Louis suspected that one or two "backs" would have been sufficient, and decided that the detective was using the moment to distance himself from both the car and body in the trunk.

With the onlookers more distant, Louis turned back to the scene and began taking photographs, carefully documenting the car and its occupant from each angle. He took several more photos of the area surrounding the car. He automatically counted off a total of thirty-four photographs, the majority taken of the body in the trunk. These photos, he reflected, were in many ways superfluous to solving the case, but they would be needed as evidence of the scene itself as matters progressed. Crime Scene and police detectives would have possession of the car and the body. They could take all the time they needed looking at each. The additional photos were required simply to record the relative positions of the car and its surroundings, and to document the scene when the automobile and its passenger were removed.

"Well, what do you think?" Chavez asked, returning after an apparently adequate respite.

"I think you won't have to eat your hat," Louis answered without looking up or smiling. "And I think it would be a real challenge to climb into the trunk of a car, pour accelerant all over yourself, set yourself on fire and shut the trunk again."

Chavez looked at him with confusion etched on his smooth face. "What makes you think that he shut the trunk . . . I mean that the trunk was shut *after* the body was set on fire?"

"Look at this," Louis said patiently, obviously enjoying his role as instructor. "The body is on its back. The areas from his waist to the top of his head are badly burned, but there's very little damage to his extremities. His arms and legs are pretty much in tact, and you can even make out the color of his shirt and trousers." Louis used the pronoun "he" because by now it was obvious that the corpse was male.

"So?" said Chavez, now clearly intrigued by either Louis's observation or his explanation.

"So, whoever torched this poor guy was an amateur. My guess is that he poured gasoline over the face and upper torso of an already dead guy, tossed in a match and slammed the trunk shut. He was probably worried about the flare-up creating an audience, even this early in the morning. It's a cautious move, but the action of a real amateur."

"How do you know that?" Chavez asked, clearly confused by Louis's description.

"When the guy shut the trunk, he stopped the circulation of oxygen around the body. Without oxygen to feed it, the fire burned itself out before it consumed the whole body. Fires will search for oxygen, and this one couldn't find enough in the trunk to sustain it." He realized he was speaking of fire as if it were alive and predatory.

"It looks like this one burned through the back seat in its search for oxygen, and eventually ignited the body of the car. Paint burns, you know," he added a bit pedantically. "A pro would know that, which is why this has amateur written all over it. If he," he paused, "or she had left the trunk open and chanced the flare up, that corpse would be unrecognizable except maybe for a couple of teeth and a belt buckle."

Chavez bronze face again turned ashen and he nodded.

"And because the person who did this is an amateur, we've got a real good chance of identifying the body," Louis concluded, turning to face the two policeman across the empty parking lot. He intentionally directed his question to the younger policeman. "Were you guys here before the firemen?" he asked in a voice loud enough to be heard across the empty lot.

The younger policeman seemed to have been struck dumb and answered the question with a blank stare. The older policeman answered for him.

"We got here just before they did," he answered. "Maybe two minutes, no more."

"Did you move anything or touch anything? Louis asked as he walked closer to the men.

"Not a thing until the fire was out. Then we opened the doors to see if there was anyone inside." He looked uncomfortable, realizing that he might have contaminated a crime scene. "We were just thinking that someone could be alive, you know. It could happen," he added defensively.

"You can smell a burned corpse two blocks away, for God's sake. Why open the trunk?" Louis asked, trying not to sound too accusatory.

"Sean told me to check it out," the younger policeman stammered having recovered some of his composure and most of his voice, "so I punched the trunk lid button when it had cooled down a bit."

"Next time, don't," Louis said and turned to the older man, "You're Sean." It wasn't a question.

"I guess I wasn't thinking," the man said. "It looked like any other old deserted wreck that someone had torched for the insurance money," he said, looking down at the pavement.

"I guess you weren't," Louis said, and then finished the thought under his breath; 'amateur hour at the crime scene.' He shook his head in disbelief, then turned and looked at the car more closely. Right out of 'The Gang That Couldn't Shoot Straight,' he thought to himself, trying as he said it to remember the name of the author. Once again he leaned down to look at the corpse in the trunk. The smell stung his eyes and constricted his throat. "At least we've got a shot at finding out who this poor bastard was," he said with more bravado than he felt.

Two things were apparent; the man had been murdered, and whoever had murdered him had done a hasty, careless, unprofessional job. All three were factors in Louis's favor. He looked up into the flashing lights of the police cars to see his partner pulling his battered red Oldsmobile up beside the two police cars. "Meet Sampson," he said evenly to Jesus Raul Chavez, "and please cover the body."

* * *

It was just past seven in the evening on January 11th when the two men left the parking lot. They took no notice of the pickup truck, engine idling quietly at the top of the hill. Tires shrieking, it suddenly roared to life. Lights on, engine howling, it closed the distance from the top of the hill to the two men crossing the street at astonishing speed. The taller man, with surprising quickness and agility, wrenched his shorter companion off his feet and back to the sidewalk as the truck raced past them.

"That person tried to kill us, Sherwood! He barely missed us." The shorter man was struggling to regain his composure on the sidewalk.

"Did you hear it? A Hemi, no doubt about it," the man called Sherwood said.

"I beg your pardon?" his friend answered.

"A Hemi—a Dodge Ram Hemi. You can tell by the sound of the engine. It's a dead give-away",

"We were nearly killed and you're classifying the make and model of the vehicle responsible for it," the smaller man said incredulously, carefully brushing off his trousers. "For heaven's sake, Sherwood." Even short of breath his accent was clipped and had a slightly exotic inflection.

"He wasn't trying to kill us. He was trying to scare us."

"Well, he most certainly succeeded. And you make it sound as if you know who the perpetrator was. Is this a common occurrence, if I may ask?"

"I do know who it was. Well, I don't really know him, but we've crossed paths before. He's harmless. At least I'm pretty sure he's harmless. And it is a fairly common occurrence. Come on. I'll explain. It may cost you a couple of hours and a beer or two," the man called Sherwood said as he led his shorter friend across the street.

"Cost me?" The shorter man answered, emphasizing the pronoun as they crossed the street.

The two men entered Harry's Seafood Bar and Grill and carefully shouldered their way through the crowd to a table at far end of the room. The taller man's name was Sherwood Tualatin. His shorter companion, Archer Brownlow, occasionally addressed him using just his initials, laying blame on the cumbersome and unwieldy nature of his friend's name. Sherwood simply didn't break down easily into a catchy nickname. Brownlow, on the other hand, steadfastly resisted Sherwood's counter-efforts to devise a similar label for him. Archer's name had been inherited from his great-grandfather, an austere and distant Presbyterian minister from Knoxville, Tennessee. Tradition, family lineage and propriety mattered greatly to Archer. In this area, as in a number of others, he differed markedly from his conspicuously gawky friend. Nonetheless, and despite his insistence to the contrary, Sherwood persisted in calling him 'Arch' or even 'Archie' which, from a practical standpoint, Archer decided was infinitely better than either A.B. or Brownie, which had in the past come briefly under consideration.

After they had ordered, Archer spoke quietly to his friend across the table from him.

"I have one question before you explain to me exactly what happened out there. Do you have any concept as to what the weather is outside?" The pronunciation and accent were decidedly elegant, something Brownlow maintained he had unconsciously cultivated in his late adolescence.

Sherwood nodded distractedly. "Of course I do."

"It's February, 50 degrees, dark and raining, and you're wearing short pants and a short sleeve shirt. You're in your summer uniform. When are you going to finally let the weather make an impression on you, my friend?" He asked this seriously, but with affection in his voice.

Whenever the legislature was in town, Sherwood's schedule was shifted as determined by the unpredictable whims of the frantic, overworked hotel day manager. On this day, before meeting with Archer, he had been arbitrarily assigned the early afternoon shift. This involved the busiest period of the day, when the late sleepers were checking out, and the exhausted politicians with their entourage of toadying lobbyists checked in. The shift lasted until 7:30 p.m. when, if matters were under control, his day ended. As was his preference, for any number of reasons, Sherwood had elected to dress in his summer uniform that afternoon.

He looked down at his brown polo shirt and shorts. "It's drizzling, not raining, 50 degrees isn't cold, and it reminds me of Oregon. What's more, it could turn hot at any minute. You know Tallahassee weather." Still distracted, he continued to concentrate on something distant.

"Very well, the shorts and shirt will do, then, but the white socks—trust me, Sherwood, they make you look like the president of the ham radio club in junior high school." Only with Sherwood was Brownlow able to express himself without feeling he had overstepped the natural barriers of polite discourse that he held in such high regard. Not unlike Miniver Cheevy, Archer was the product of another century.

"The tie, Arch. Do you wear the tie to bed too?" Sherwood replied, re-focusing his attention on his friend. Brownlow was seldom without a necktie knotted neatly and securely at his neck.

"Only when I anticipate that I may have a particularly formal dream," Archer countered, and Sherwood smiled in spite of himself.

"In any event, this is Wayne's Legacy," Archer added, carefully adjusting the knot of his necktie. "I think of him each time I tie it."

"Who was Wayne, and what was his legacy?" The two men had been friends for some time and the name had never come up before.

"Wayne worked at a very fashionable men's clothing store in Knoxville," Archer answered. "He was a small man, he dressed fastidiously, and he took it upon himself to spruce me up a bit when I was a teenager. For some reason he seemed to like me. I was fifteen and not terribly likeable at the time. I also had no appreciation for my appearance or for a great many other things, for that matter. My father sent me to Wayne when I was accepted at Episcopal, and Wayne not only dressed me, he encouraged me to value and appreciate neatness and good taste. He made an enormous impression on me when I was a teenager, which was no easy task, believe me." He paused, absorbed for a moment in his memories. Sherwood interrupted his thoughts.

"Obviously, but why do you call your necktie Wayne's Legacy?" he asked.

"Not the tie, Sherwood, the knot. You don't understand. I was rather unskilled at knotting my necktie properly when I met Wayne." The word 'rather' was drawn out with an unusually long 'a', and the last syllable was hard to distinguish. Archer's accent showed every characteristic of having a faintly British heritage.

"He was, simply put, one of the nicest and most patient men I'd ever met at that juncture in my life. It was strange. He had always worked as a salesman in a clothing store, and yet he had the presence and the taste of a member of the Beacon Hill elite." Sherwood looked at him, and saw that Archer was again adrift in nostalgia, and perhaps in Beacon Hill as well.

"Beacon Hill elite?"

"Boston Brahmin, my friend. Saltonstall, Winthrop, Lodge, Peabody, Cabot . . . Shall I go on?" Archer had ticked them off effortlessly.

"Anyway, this Wayne made that big an impression?" Sherwood asked, aware that he had entered an alien world of the New England elite.

"Wayne was a quiet, patient gentleman who did his job very well," Archer said, returning to the present. "I came into the store one day and felt that I was in very good order. I was wearing one of the jackets he'd sold me, a white button-down shirt, regimental striped tie, wing-tip cordovan shoes and grey flannels. He took me aside very quietly, and explained that my tie was all wrong. He didn't use those words. There was also no suggestion of criticism in his words. He simply suggested quietly that it could be done better. So Wayne taught me how to tie a necktie so that the knot was perfect every time." Again he fingered the knot thoughtfully. "And there it is." He said, back in the present again.

"I guess I still don't understand why you call it Wayne's legacy. There must be more to it than that."

"Wayne died. He was a young man—perhaps our age—and I hadn't heard about it. I went into the store after my preparatory school graduation ceremonies and asked for him." The 'o' in the word 'preparatory' was effectively swallowed. "The owner said that he'd died. Just like that—'Wayne died'. Then he asked if he could help me find anything. I walked out and never went in the store again."

"I get it." Sherwood said. "Wayne's legacy."

"That is indeed Wayne's legacy. I think of him each time I tie my necktie, which, as you know, is my custom once a day. But the most interesting part of the story is that I was subsequently elected the best dressed in my senior class at Episcopal—thanks in no small part to Wayne's influence."

"And of course Episcopal then catapulted you on to great achievements."

"You might find a number of people who would dispute the notion that I ever reached any significant level of achievement, Sherwood. But I think we might consider returning to the discussion of why we were nearly killed by a pickup truck tonight."

"A Lamborghini might have been better?" Sherwood had noted the icy contempt in his friend's voice when he had used the term 'pick-up truck' when describing the vehicle.

The waitress came for their order, and both men ordered beer.

* * *

Archer had attended a private school in the suburbs of Knoxville where a necktie, short hair and a rigorous program of study were the standard. "Man is fashioned through the Rigors of Athletics and Study," was the motto of the Episcopal School of Knoxville, which also translated into an obligatory and strenuous sports program as a part of every student's day. Archer's description of the school and its motto had always reminded Sherwood of the slogan "Arbeit macht Frei", which had solemnized a very different kind of institution, but he avoided mention of this to his friend.

As it was a sports-oriented institution, Brownlow was herded from gym to field in hopes that something would fit his inclinations and physique, not necessarily in that order. Every such effort ended in total, disheartening failure. But hard as he tried, Archer Brownlow was unable to entirely avoid the athletic program, though he did sidestep its more arduous aspects by becoming soccer manager in the fall of his sophomore year. In the winter term he joined the basketball team as its shortest member and most dependable benchwarmer.

Finally in the spring he was allowed, in part because of his academic achievement and in part because of stunning athletic ineptitude, to take a season off. This was not well accepted by his classmates, but it did allow him time to develop a series of curious interests and hobbies, interests that he actively pursued into adulthood.

The beer arrived with a check, which both men eyed until Sherwood finally picked it up with a deep sigh. "I guess this is on me. I seem to be the one who got us here."

"Thank you. Now, if you would, please enlighten me as to why we are here and why we were nearly killed out there a few moments ago," Archer said, returning to the matter at hand as their drinks were served. "As you can imagine I tend to take an interest in learning what's behind every near-death experience I'm a part of, although I am disappointed that I saw neither a bright light nor my life flash before my eyes tonight."

"You want to know what happened out there, and why I said no one was trying to kill us. The only answer is that I'm not entirely sure. It's happened before, any number of times. My guess is that they're trying to scare me. I'm afraid that's the best I can do, Archie."

"Whoever they are, they certainly did a bang-up job in my case." He turned and looked around the bar, which was rapidly filling up with customers. "This may not be the appropriate place to discuss this, Sherwood. Too much company. I'd suggest we go elsewhere and you can fill in the gaps in detail and more seclusion."

Sherwood's eyes swept the room and he nodded at his friend. "Finish your beer and we'll go to my place. It's not far. But I'll warn you, it's a pretty elaborate story, and if I tell you you'll be involved, and I'm not sure you'll thank me for involving you."

"If it has anything to do with what almost got us both killed out there, I expect I ought to hear about it, don't you? We can worry about my thanking you or not later."

"O.K., but I warned you. It's complicated, and it could be really hazardous to your health. That sounds kind of like the warning label on a bottle of rat poison, doesn't it?" Sherwood said smiling slightly and leaning closer. "But I mean it in all seriousness."

Sherwood paid the bill and the two men left their beers untouched on the table.

* * *

When he was born, Sherwood Leland Tualatin was a surprise and a delight to his parents, Edna and Leland Tualatin. His name was pronounced "two-all-a-tin" by all except, of course, his classmates later on in grade school. There he suffered stoically through both "Woody" and "Wally" during his adolescence. He found preferred Woody because it had a more robust ring to it, but disliked the "Toy Story" connection when it was pointed out to him.

As a child he often wondered how his parents had come up with the name Sherwood. He soothed himself by fastening onto the notion that it related to the English folklore hero Robin Hood and his preferred place of hiding, Sherwood Forest. He even relayed this conviction to a few classmates, convincingly a sufficient number that it resulted in a temporary de-escalation in their harassment of him.

He was born to parents who differed vastly in nearly every aspect of their backgrounds, experiences and educations. It was not so much a couple at odds with one another, but simply two people of very divergent ideas and styles.

His father, born in 1947 in Buffalo, Texas, had an interesting and somewhat checkered past. Christened Leland Cooley at birth, as a young man he had developed what he considered an inconsequential dossier of legal misunderstandings with both the Federal Government and the local authorities in Texas. It was rumored that he had been connected with a network of militia movements in the state as an impressionable young man in his early twenties. In 1967, apparently with the certainty of an arrest warrant looming, he reached what to him was the only logical conclusion. Arrest, he was convinced, was imminent, as was the draft, which in fact concerned him a great deal more than jail. He therefore decided it would be best to take his leave of both Texas and the land of his birth, and in the late summer headed north with Vancouver, Canada, as his destination. He was in good company.

Leland ran out of money in Weed, California, where he worked briefly as a part-time salesman in a hardware store. The town's name may have been purely a coincidence, but given the tenor of the times, it claimed the very center of the counter-culture in the area. That fact also ideally suited the young man's newly acquired lifestyle and inclinations. As something of a rootless vagabond, a nomad with few options and fewer prospects, he found himself happily adrift in the moment. Shirtless, shoeless, surrounded by peace signs and pot, he spent a number of weeks in a happy haze of what the locals called Maui Wowie.

He might have stayed in Weed for some time but the town, true to its name and celebrated for its readily available supply of cannabis and other far more potent mind-altering chemicals, eventually drew the attention of the authorities. Once again Leland, in a rare moment of lucidity, pictured himself squarely in their sights. Facing a clear fight or flight situation, without hesitation he chose the latter. With a borrowed backpack, shoes and shirt, he resolutely continued his enforced exodus to the north.

His next stop was initially to be a brief one in Portland, Oregon. He needed to earn enough travel money to enable him to continue his flight to Vancouver. Upon his arrival he unexpectedly found himself in a city that had as its unofficial motto "Keep Portland weird." The appeal was both immediate and visceral, and he decided to do his part to personally champion the motto. He settled into life in the city at once, feeling equally at home with the counter-culture and the redolent aroma of pot fumes that scented the downtown areas.

Leland realized that both the law and the draft had a fair chance of catching up with him, even in Portland, Oregon. He therefore decided to change his name and to shave off the early stages of a handlebar mustache, which he had been cultivating since seeing a re-run several months before of "Magnum P.I", starring Tom Selleck. He needed a new beginning and a new name to go along with it. He was at the time, for obvious reasons, not in the most imaginative frame of mind, and he failed to devote even a shred of reasoned thought to that relatively simple task.

Fumbling through the City of Portland yellow pages one afternoon in a comfortable cloud of marijuana, he found what he determined to be a worthy candidate. Under "UPS Stores" was a listing for UPS Store #2755 on Tualatin-Sherwood Road in Sherwood, Oregon. The name had an immediate appeal to Leland's pharmaceutically muddled brain. Deciding that it would be especially difficult for someone to track him down with such an unusual name, he resolved to take the name Tualatin as his own, and unconsciously save Sherwood, which he also was partial to, for later use. (Subsequently, as a clever and inquisitive teenager, his son would research his family name. He found that the Tualatin was a Native American Indian band, also called the Atafavelati. Tualatin, he was to learn, was also roughly translated as "sluggish or lazy", something he was never comfortable sharing with his father).

Leland Tualatin had found a new identity and soon after a new job as well. Being without marketable skills, he managed to find what he expected to be temporary employment with a tree service just north of the downtown area. In order to keep the job and avoid any further brushes with the law, he determined to leave his lifestyle as a fugitive behind him. He flushed enough marijuana to require a plumber to unblock the toilet. He was forced to pay the man a usurious fee for the house call in return for his silence. For years after he had difficulty recalling the moment when he watched the last of his stash disappear in a rush of water without tears coming to his eyes.

After two years of hard work and devoted service, he became one of the company's best ground men (Leland despised heights, and had always feared that if the army had gotten its hands on him, they'd have made him a paratrooper). It wasn't long before he was promoted to crew manager, a job which brought with it both responsibility and a substantial pay increase. He had in the process managed to accumulate a small balance in his savings account and rent an even smaller house twelve miles north of the city. In his rental house, with a regular, healthy paycheck and an agreeable job, he settled comfortably into a new and gratifying reality.

It was at this time the he met Edna Sturgis, the woman who was to become his wife. The sheltered daughter of an evangelical minister and his serene, repressed wife, the little girl's name had been chosen from the Old Testament. In the Book of Tobit, Edna was the wife of Raguel and mother of Sarah. Having heard this obliquely referenced in a substitute pastor's sermon one Sunday, and after a brief squabble, both her parents agreed that the name was suitably decorous and of appropriate theological significance for their child, should she be born a girl. Zebadiah had been her father's choice had things gone the other way.

Edna grew up both sheltered and secluded, as befitted the daughter of an evangelical minister. She was rigorously home-schooled, and the only social environments she was familiar with were home, family and her father's small church with its tiny, loyal and vocal congregation. She had no brothers or sisters. She did, however, finally manage to convince her protective parents to let her have a dog for company. They dutifully scoured the dog pounds, and finally decided on a small, friendly creature of undetermined heritage.

Edna named the dog "Doodles". At that point no one in the family had undertaken an examination of Doodle's underside to determine the dog's gender. When Leland finally and gingerly devoted himself to the task, the dog was immediately renamed "Dude". Energetic, with tail perpetually wagging and possessed of boundless good will, Dude became Edna's constant companion and confidante.

"Edna sounds a little old for a child," her mother had suggested quietly when the question of her name was still under discussion.

"The name is from the Bible," her husband answered brusquely. "If it's good enough for the Bible, dadgummit, it's good enough for me. The minute I heard it I sensed the Lord had sent me a message. He as much as told me that Edna was right name for the child if it was a girl."

"There are other names in the Bible, dear," his wife countered a bit lamely. "There's Rachel, and Sarah, and Eve . . ."

"It's Edna. The minute I heard it in the sermon the other day, I knew it was ordained, woman. It's Edna, and that's the end of it."

And indeed that was the end of it. But as neither parent was familiar with the origin of the name, little could they have known that the name in Hebrew translated as "pleasure" or "delight". The Book of Tobit was part of the Catholic and Orthodox biblical canon, and a foreign text to either of the child's biblically immersed parents. And there would come a time when Edna would come to embody the meaning of her name in a sense that would nearly unravel her father, who lived his life according in the strictest and most puritanical of Christian values. The fact that its origins were Hebrew, which her father learned much later, would only add additional flame to the fire.

When she was still quite young, it became apparent that Edna had an extraordinary intellect. She spoke at a very early age and had a prodigious vocabulary, although she seldom exercised it. Obedient, quiet and subdued, she excelled at the homework her parents assigned her, and finished it with astonishing speed and ease. Her abilities were evident to both parents who, despite urging from interested members of the parish, steadfastly resisted efforts to involve her in programs for gifted children outside of the home. She grew up in her mother's image, but for a small, imperceptible rebellious spark that flickered and began to glow quietly beneath the surface.

At the age of eighteen, Edna could be recognized by her long, styleless dresses of indeterminate shape and color, her flat shoes and her hair pulled back into an austere ponytail. Since reaching the age of six she had displayed no skin above the wrist or ankle, and she wore blouses that buttoned severely under her chin. She had spent her nineteen years in a completely submissive and deferential posture to her parents and their church, but the world, with all its pleasures and problems, had approached quietly, and was alarmingly close to her doorstep.

She met young Leland Tualatin quite by accident on an unusually warm October afternoon while waiting for her parents in front of the neighborhood farmer's market at Shemanski park. The two spoke only briefly, but Leland was smitten and Edna intrigued. When he suggested that they meet again at the same location the very next day Edna agreed, surprising even herself in the process. After a very few, very clandestine and highly charged meetings adjacent to the farmer's market, Leland proposed marriage, and in a moment of what can only be termed hubris, she accepted.

Leland had in the interim, to some degree at least, immersed himself in the Bethany Evangelical Free Church. Arguably his interest was fueled more by his secular attraction to Edna than by purely theological sentiments. In any case his transitory conversion had its desired effect, and her parents, if not enthralled with the man who would be their son-in-law, were at least somewhat placated.

Another possibility is that Leland sensed that the authorities had again taken up his trail from Texas to Portland, and he believed that it would be far more difficult for them to unmask him as a fervent, clean-shaven parishioner in the pews at Bethany.

The spark that had glowed so quietly in Edna for nineteen years burst into full flame. They eloped seventeen days later, after locating a bourbon-soaked Justice of the Peace in downtown Portland near the Japanese Gardens. It was an inauspicious ceremony, and as they picked their way through the huddled homeless on the rainy streets outside, Edna thought that perhaps her good judgment had deserted her at precisely the wrong moment.

It was an unusual union from several perspectives. A tall, outgoing but physically inelegant groom and a 19 year-old celestial, serene young woman walking hand in hand through the cold drizzle of downtown Portland. But Edna saw in her new husband a man of both substance and mystery, a man who knew the world—or at least the west coast. She also found in him security and a promise of excitement, for in those days Leland could give the appearance of youthful confidence and even gallantry. In short, she felt she had found in her new husband not a single trace of the fervent, evangelical pastor who had so dominated her childhood and adolescence, and that thought alone may have carried the day.

Although it took several months, the couple eventually won the tolerance if not the support of Edna's parents. In that pursuit they agreed to return and become faithful members of the flock, a promise easily made but not easily kept. Edna's new found freedom and introduction to a wider world of Portland society were simply too appealing to the young woman. Their church visits subsided after only a month or two. Not long thereafter, they learned that they were not unexpectedly expecting an addition.

* * *

At birth Sherwood Tualatin weighed seven pounds six ounces and measured slightly more than twenty-three inches in length. But for his ears, he was the kind of infant that any visitor would have said was perfectly presentable—an "adorable little bundle", his mother called him. In truth, he more closely resembled a pale, wrinkled, hairless white rodent, but to his parents he was simply exquisite. He was born on December 7th, 1971, in a small, modest two-bedroom house twelve miles north of the city of Portland, Oregon. It was a memorable event on a memorable date in history.

His parents were completely blind to Sherwood's unusual physical features, so dazzled were they by the general package they had fashioned. Leland, who saw himself as the family historian, read tirelessly to the tiny infant, relating stories of the family's fabled but unsubstantiated exploits during the Civil War. It didn't seem to bother him that Sherwood was only a few days or months old, and presumably possessed neither the vocabulary nor the intellectual capacity to understand his father's epic accounts. Edna, however, provided an essential balance with her quiet wisdom and sensible approach. The child was soon was teetering in a delicate dance between his father's energetic fabulism and his mother's intellectual practicality. It was to be this balance that became both the bane and the salvation of the young boy's adolescence.

As Sherwood grew into his early teenage years, he experienced an incredible growth spurt. At fourteen he was, despite his ears, a standard issue adolescent, complete with a devastating case of acne. The ears, a neighbor noted dryly and out of earshot, were sufficient to impede the boy's progress, particularly in a stiff breeze. They were to become a trademark.

A scant year and a half later he had added more than eleven inches to his height. Even taking into consideration normal adolescent awkwardness, Sherwood cut a nearly impossible figure—tall, lanky and ungainly. By now it had become apparent that both his name and his physical attributes were equally unusual. Well over six feet tall and with a remarkably elongated neck, his arms had grown so long that he was forced to abandon the search for shirts with suitable sleeve lengths. As a result he was inclined, if not forced, to wear short sleeve shirts despite the weather in order not to call attention to his unusual wingspan. Unconcerned with the effect this caused, he also typically wore short pants, white socks and low cut boots, which served to emphasize both the length of his legs and his bony knees.

Sherwood had also taken to holding himself exceptionally erect, so much so that he often seemed to be just on the verge of toppling over backwards. He adopted this physical attitude during grade school, when shorter classmates, in an attempt to draw themselves up to his height, would thrust their faces directly under his chin and wetly recount their evaluations of his appearance. This posture further served to create the impression that he was trying to gain distance between himself and the person opposite him, which was indeed what had triggered it in the first place.

Some schoolmates found in this posture an expression of arrogance, which was augmented by the fact that he smiled infrequently, and then only as if it were a compulsory exercise. With ears that stuck out at nearly straight angles and a strange, loping gait, he gave the exaggerated, unwieldy impression of a large, flightless bird on the ground. For these and other reasons, his classmates in the ninth grade dubbed him "Lurch", which he accepted gravely and with the passive tolerance he had inherited from his mother.

His early years in school had been difficult for Sherwood. When he wasn't peeling the ever-present "kick me" stickers off his back, a smaller and more agile student would tie his shoelaces together outside the classroom as another engaged him in conversation. Unsuspecting, or perhaps uncaring, Sherwood more than once toppled like a giant redwood in the school corridors. This was met with the characteristic hoots of appreciation from adolescents, grateful that it was Sherwood, and not they, who were suffering the humiliation.

In contrast with his physical inelegance, however, he was blessed with a prodigious intellect, which, of course, served to make him an even easier target for the less gifted youngsters in his class. In later years these same classmates would describe him in the yearbook as "studious, intense, creative, with a mind capable of a kind of corkscrew thinking."

None of these qualities were to endear him to his less academically refined contemporaries at the time, however. As if to make matters worse, he was pathologically imaginative, a boy with the mind of an adventurer if not the body. He sat dutifully in the classroom hour after hour, his long legs cramped under a tiny desk, instinctively raising his hand at every question from the teacher, again significantly increasing his chances of harassment by his contemporaries. He was, predictably, the kind of student whose hands, trousers and desk were always ink-stained, but whose homework was always neat, precise and of high quality.

In Portland as a youth, Sherwood first became fascinated with the archeological lore in the area. He took advantage of every opportunity to go on class field trips in search of local Indian artifacts. Once, it was said, while living on Pop Tarts in a small tent outside the city limits, he discovered a new species of mole that had taken refuge in his sleeping bag. It lacked the propellex, or extra thumb common to other species of moles. He brought it home, fed it nuts and earthworms, and won a science prize for his find in the 9th grade. This fascination with discovery and research was to remain with him during his days in school and college. But again, it gained him little recognition among his classmates, who called the little creature he'd discovered "Lurch's rat."

Sherwood's life in Portland was permanently interrupted by a fortuitous act of nature. In late November of 1985, when he was fifteen years old, hurricane Kate slashed through Cuba, Florida and Georgia, causing more than five hundred and thirty million dollars in damage. In the immediate wake of the destruction inflicted by the hurricane, Leland recognized an opportunity to give both his son and his family a fresh start. He sought employment with several tree service companies in Tallahassee, Florida. Countless trees had been blown down in and around the city, destroying power lines and the paralyzing the city's electrical grid.

On November 20th in the Portland Gazette, Leland read the following quote by Alan Katz, a well-known attorney in the Florida's capital city. Katz was reported as saying: "If I wanted to live like this I would move to Guatemala," a statement which was unlikely to ingratiate him to either the state department or the Guatemalan people. Katz was, years later, to become the Ambassador to the Republic of Portugal under president Obama. It was reported that Guatemala was never under consideration.

Leland saw both the quote and the situation in Tallahassee as an economic opportunity and an invitation. If the populace was this vocal in expressing its concern over the state of affairs, it was a clear indication that an experienced tree specialist was needed. In addition, the climate in Portland had worn on him. The constant rain and drizzle either slowed business, stopped it entirely, or made the work outside unpredictable and dangerous. Perhaps ever the dreamer, in Tallahassee he could visualize only pleasant winters and temperate summers.

He made a number of calls to businesses in the city and was offered immediate employment by two of them. He had never felt so much in demand in his life. He decided on Cricket's Tree Service on Fitz Lane purely on the basis of its location on a state map that he had purchased. Before his move he had found a reasonably priced rental home on Old St. Augustine Road through a local real estate broker. The house was old but adequate, and Cricket's was less than three miles from his new residence.

As Leland had hoped and anticipated, with distressed homeowners clamoring for action, the local supply of electricians was not up to the demand. He notified his landlord in Portland that he was moving, packed up his wife, son and possessions, and the great cross-country adventure was underway. The family left their Portland home just after Thanksgiving, and drove across the country in their 1977 Chevrolet station wagon. After four days, one flat tire and three crowded nights in Super 88 Motels, they arrived exhausted and excited in Tallahassee.

* * *

Leland Tualatin worked diligently for Cricket's for more than three years. Not long after he began, he had established himself as an extremely able and experienced worker, and soon handled the majority of on-site management for the company. But after two years of applying himself unrelentingly to his work at the cost of time spent with wife and son, he saw no more promotions or meaningful raises on the horizon. At the age of forty-one he envisioned himself at the same job and essentially the same salary for the next twenty-five years. The thought left him deeply depressed and in need of another strategy.

Acting on a bit of a lark, he leveraged himself and his family into near bankruptcy and established his new business. He called it "Tualatin and Sons Tree Service." He chose "Sons" because he felt in its plural form it conveyed greater legitimacy to his fledgling operation, despite the fact that Sherwood was his sole male progeny and neither old enough for nor marginally interested in the tree service business.

Nonetheless, Leland rented a small building, bought cast-off, second-hand equipment, and proudly hung a large sign out front announcing that Tualatin and Sons was open for business. He also managed to locate a very willing, hard-working and very illegal alien to became his only employee. Perhaps predictably given the devastation of the storm, the business picked up steam immediately, and soon was flourishing with two additional illegals on the payroll.

Sherwood, meanwhile, entered his new high school as a junior. A bit withdrawn and considered a loner, his academic success gained him accolades but very few friends. His adolescent classmates referred to him as "Jughead", a dated nod to the cartoon character Jughead Jones in the Archie comic strip, and a not-so-subtle allusion to the size of his ears. He responded with patience and a feigned air of dismissal. He found that by adopting the appearance of detachment, he softened the sting of the sophomoric barbs that were aimed at him. While he succeeded to some extent in defusing the taunts, he failed to discourage them completely.

Eventually his ability to deal with his outcast status and the persistent teasing of the athletic contingent of his classmates impressed a handful of his more enlightened contemporaries. He made several friends, each of whom invariably fell into the intellectually-gifted-but-socially-unpopular category. He joined the Science Club as a sophomore, and in the 11th grade founded the History Club, which was dedicated specifically to the study of the Confederacy before, during and after the Civil War. In this pursuit he was a tireless researcher, historian and enthusiast.

Meanwhile Leland, from his perspective as a underemployed tree company owner and manager, had sensibly advised Sherwood to concentrate on electrical engineering and management in school. After his second year of high school, Sherwood qualified for and was accepted by Tallahassee Community College as a first year student. At the end of his second year there he applied to several colleges, was accepted at most, and decided to attend Florida State. His decision was made on the basis of two factors. The first was that Florida State would keep him closer to the source of his historical interests generally, and specifically to the termination point of Jefferson Davis's flight south. The last days of the Confederacy had become his obsession. The second was the announcement that the football team had succeeded in recruiting a number of outstanding incoming freshman football players. Strangely and completely out of character, Sherwood had become an avid football fan in his six years as a resident of Florida's capital city.

At Florida State Sherwood majored in electrical engineering, and eighteen months later graduated near the top of his class. In the interim period, although still the ungainly specimen of his younger days, he had cast off the better part of his social artlessness and become an accepted, if atypical, member of his class. He was even invited to join Phi Delta Theta, which was crudely referred to as "I Felta Thigh" by nonmembers. If not exactly flourishing in that environment, he was acknowledged and ultimately managed to establish a number of close friendships in the fraternity.

When Sherwood wasn't buried in his course work or watching A.C.C. football, he tirelessly pursued his study of the Civil War. No doubt in response to the frequency of his father's anecdotes, he found himself increasingly fascinated by the final days of the conflict and Jefferson Davis's flight to the south. Leland's never-ending accounts of his family's history of dedication and heroism during the conflict had become a central point of interest. Numerous members of the family, Leland recounted, had storied connections with the Confederacy during the War of Northern Aggression, a phrase that had become his father's endless incantation at home.

Leland tirelessly recited the story of Jefferson Davis's flight from Richmond, Virginia on April 2nd, 1865 to Irwinville, Georgia, where he was to be finally captured more than a month later. The senior Tualatin fancied himself a direct relative of John Reagan's, who had served as Jefferson Davis's Postmaster General for the duration of the war. There seemed precious little historical evidence to support this assertion, but Leland insisted on its accuracy. If believed, Reagan was but one of several honest-to-goodness Confederate heroes in the family tree.

When queried, Leland tended to become a bit tongue-tied trying to explain how the name Tualatin, with such a distinctly northwest Indian flavor, fit into Civil War lore. For obvious reasons he had carefully avoided bringing Buffalo, Texas and the name Cooley into any discussions of the family past. Nonetheless Sherwood, despite his tendency to be critical of many things his historically-animated father told him, or anyone else for that matter, decided there must at least be some basis of truth to the story.

Perhaps inevitably he made the decision to pursue the end of the conflict and Jefferson Davis's flight as his avocation. Almost as an afterthought, he sent out a number of applications after graduation, limited them to local organizations and agencies, and was shortly offered employment with the city as an electrical engineer. His career path, for the moment, looked assured and secure.

* * *

The scorched hulk of the automobile, now identified as an aged Chevrolet Nova, was put carefully on the back of a Jerr-Dan roll-bed truck and removed from the scene. The body was left undisturbed in the trunk, to be examined in the condition it had been found at the scene by Crime Scene Investigators and forensic scientists when it arrived its destination. The trunk was carefully taped shut, lest a cavernous pothole were to dislodge the corpse from its temporary coffin and bounce it unceremoniously down the street.

Weeks cringed visibly when Louis launched into a vivid description of the consequences, and exactly what would happen to their passenger should such a thing occur. When his description finally ended, Weeks wrapped several extra layers of duct tape around the trunk, firmly securing it to both rear fenders and the bumper. If the body went adrift, so would the trunk, frame, fenders and most of the rear portion of the car. Nonetheless, he decided on a circuitous route home, one chosen to avoid any chance of having to follow closely behind the tow truck. Despite Sam's precautions, Louis could not shake the image of a charred body bouncing down the road, bits and pieces breaking off and scattering from sidewalk to sidewalk. The image pursued him all the way back to the lab.

The examination of the crime scene had been extensive and singularly disappointing. Starting from the location of the burned out vehicle Louis, Weeks, Chavez and the two other policemen worked in grids, then fanned out to cover an area of more than a hundred yards from the where the car had been found. Other than an overabundance of used condoms, beer cans and cigarette butts, the search proved fruitless. Neighbors were questioned, all sleepy and nursing cups of coffee, but none had seen or heard anything unusual. Silence and uncooperative witnesses were the norm in the crime-ridden areas of Midland, but this neighborhood was a blue collar, middle-class, country, flag and apple pie kind of area. It was not a neighborhood that displayed any tendency to shy away from 'the man,' and therefore the investigators naturally assumed that the crime had occurred without witnesses. Save for an early riser or a worker returning from the night shift, there was no help to be had on that front.

It quickly became apparent that any evidence would have to be found in the car, the trunk, or connected with the identity of the dead man. The problem was that fire created nearly insurmountable problems for investigators. Fire brought with it as a necessary consequence water, and water not only diluted clues, in many cases it washed them away. The combination of fire and water was the bête noire of arson investigators and forensic scientists alike.

As they drove home, Weeks suggested to his partner that the identity of the victim would be their best avenue to solving the crime. The face had been badly disfigured, but clothing, fingerprints and dental impressions were potentially all factors in their favor. Louis agreed tacitly but didn't answer. He quietly thanked whatever gods were responsible for the existence of amateur murderers.

* * *

The meeting took place on February 14th in a large, lavishly paneled conference room on the top floor of First Capital Bank building in downtown Midland, Texas. Before the meeting opened there was an undercurrent of low chatter from two dozen or more men talking quietly, cautiously. The only lighting in the room was soft and indirect, and seemed to emanate from low on the walls and beneath the table. It had the effect of nearly concealing the faces and identities of the men seated around the table. Though they were well known to one another, they were often best able to recognize a speaker by his voice or the shadowy outline of his frame. The pewter wall sconces had been turned off.

The subdued lighting reflected weakly off the walls of the room, which were lavishly paneled in pecan wood. The huge oval table around which the men were seated was burnished Philippine mahogany, and though brightly polished, showed the distress marks of countless meetings. Six water pitchers were evenly spaced on the table, and each man had a glass and napkin at his place. There was no food on the table. The chairs were high back leather swivel chairs that reclined comfortably. Every man around table, however, kept his chair rigidly upright and leaned forward attentively. Neither food, tobacco nor coffee were allowed in the room.

A large, heavy set, florid man with sparse, iron gray hair and a brush haircut sat at the head of the table and waited until the others around the table had fallen silent. He wore a dark navy blazer that was stretched alarmingly at the shoulders, an open collar, neatly pressed khakis and polished cowboy boots. His face conveyed both patience and forbearance as he watched the other men.

He had the ability to silence a room using nothing other than the force of his own personality and a modest frown. His size was a contributing factor, but far less so than his reputation. Ham-fisted and thick-bodied, he gave the physical impression of profound solidity. And while age and good food had softened the edges of his physique somewhat, he remained a formidable and imposing figure. He was a quiet, composed man who hadn't found the need to threaten or raise his voice for years in order to assert the unmistakable impact of leadership. Jesse Don Bowen was, in the simplest terms, a man whose presence in a room conveyed a sense of stability, authority and confidence.

When the low chatter had quieted, Bowen rose with difficulty, gripping the edge of the table for support. He stood, favoring his left leg, and said quietly, "The Flame and the Sword will come to order." He smiled humorlessly at the faceless men in front of him and sat down, grimacing as he slid his left leg straight out in front of him. In his meetings Bowen used no gavel, required no minutes, permitted no motions from the floor, countenanced no interruptions, and allowed questions only when he himself opened the floor.

"Your man failed again yesterday, Five," he said tonelessly. "How many times is that?" He directed the question at the shadowy figure of a tall, well-dressed man across the table wearing a bow tie.

That's what Ralph seems to do best," the man answered, his face partially obscured. "Fail, that is."

"He's been well paid for nearly six months," Bowen said quietly, "and his job hasn't been a particularly demanding one. Are you sure he has no idea why he's doing this and what's behind it?"

"I'm sure", the man addressed as Five answered. "As in most things, he's clueless as far as insight is concerned. He's got barnyard smarts, but it doesn't extend much beyond that."

"So one might guess. Please ask him to come in", Bowen said.

The man left and returned shortly in the company of a rather hulking, disheveled man with a protruding stomach, overly long, greying hair and a startling comb-over. An offensive puff of chest hair jutted from above the open third button of his shirt.*

"Metzger", Bowen said quietly. "I'm afraid you're off the case and off the payroll. We appreciate your efforts, but your approach obviously flawed. There'll be a small severance bonus, but as of now you're on your own. And remember, you know nothing about us. You don't know that we exist."

Ralph Metzger paused for a moment, either unsure of how to respond or perhaps pondering the meaning of the word flawed.

"Sir," he finally managed, "that guy just doesn't scare. I damn near ran him over a half dozen times and he's got so he almost doesn't hurry to get out of the way anymore. It's like he knows I won't hit him. Maybe I could clip him a little bit next time, you know, draw a little blood and show him we're not messing around? Just nick him, you know?"

"There's no 'we' anymore, Metzger. There's only you. Please remember, you don't work for us, and you never did. You're an independent contractor and that's the only connection you have with the organization. You've been paid in cash—well paid in cash," Bowen emphasized, "and as far as we're all concerned, you're just a lousy driver who endangers pedestrians. Please remember that. It would be very dangerous to forget it."

"Yes sir. But give me one more shot at it. I'll have him soiling his pants, guaranteed."

"Metzger, Be a good fella, take your bonus and move on to your next endeavor. You aren't working for us on this one anymore." Bowen spoke politely but with the rigid tone of a stern parent.

Metzger lowered his head, exhibiting even more the breath-taking extent and complexity of his comb-over. "Yes sir, thank you, but if you need me again, to do anything, I'd be more than . . ."

"I'm sure you would, Metzger, I'm sure. Au revoir", Bowen said curtly.

After the visitor had left, a small figure at the end of the table who was referred to as Seventeen raised his hand. Everyone in the room except Bowen was referred to by number, from one to twenty. It was a security measure that had been in force since the group had first been organized. It had served its purpose well for over a hundred years.

"What is it, Seventeen?"

**See Appendix 9, included only in special limited editions*

"How did we ever end up with this guy? Who found him, and whatever did he have to recommend him?" Seventeen's most distinguishing feature, his bald head, reflected the half-light in the room weakly.

"Name and the reputation. Metzger came to us purported to be a disciplined, efficient killing machine, if you remember. We felt that we'd hired the better part of the British Secret Service right here in Midland. So we signed him on. And there was the German thing, too. You haven't forgotten what his last name means in German, have you? It means butcher. That had a nice connotation to it. Metzger the Butcher," he said almost nostalgically.

Ralph Metzger had been born to first generation German immigrants in 1952. His parents brought much of their heritage with them, and when their first son was born they named him Rolf, which, according to its German origins, meant "famous wolf". Rolf, who had a beefy, lurking physical presence even as a teenager, discovered during those years that he had a compensating aptitude for persuasion and merchandising. He cultivated those talents with the attentiveness of a dedicated gardener. As he scrambled awkwardly into adulthood he became a consummate lobbyist and salesman, and he learned to depend upon those skills as an adult. He believed that he could sell salt water to a sailor with enough time, and time often seemed to be on his side. He also legally changed the spelling of his name to 'Ralph', which, although not particularly prepossessing in and of itself, at least diminished the combined Teutonic impact of his first and last names.

Hardly a well-honed killing machine, Ralph Metzger had originally made his living convincing guileless senior citizens to invest their savings in real estate, which in many cases was shabby, overpriced and often lacking intrinsic value. Having been chased out of Cleveland by the authorities after numerous complaints from his tapped-out clients, he relocated to Midland, Texas, where he spent the next several months re-creating himself. He sat with beady-eyed intensity, hour after hour in seedy downtown watering holes, convincing anyone naïve enough to listen that he was a loaded revolver with a hair trigger, a hired gun extraordinaire. Somehow he managed to convince a handful of his unsophisticated listeners of his fabricated talent, and as a result developed an entirely undeserved reputation in an underworld of squalid bars.

One person whom he convinced of his authenticity would lead him to an outcome that would stun even Metzger. A few weeks following what he believed had been another innocuous series of inventions about his abilities with a quiet stranger in one of Midland's less refined bars, he was approached by a member of Bowen's group. In the course of one conversation, Ralph managed to elevate his former tawdry real estate career to a new and far more exciting level. No more angry customers and persistent lawyers, he had now managed to sell himself as a legitimate hired gun, and a promising, lucrative new career lay ahead of him.

"What now?" number Fourteen, a paunchy man with an immense double chin above his bolo tie asked.

"Now we call in Sanjay", Bowen answered.

"Sanjay," someone repeated softly and gratuitously, "Jesus." Otherwise, the name left the men in the room in solemn, hushed silence.

* * *

When he first met Archer Brownlow, Sherwood was working as a concierge at the Governor's Inn on South Adams Street in Tallahassee, a job that seemed completely incongruous to his friend. Sherwood explained to Archer that, for several reasons, this vocational incompatibility was both comfortable and enjoyable for him.

"I can't quite put my finger on it, but it's almost as if I've done this kind of thing before. I enjoy it, and somehow the job seems to come naturally to me. It could be that hotel work has a family history or something." In response Archer was tempted to make an offhand comment about the perils of karma, but the seriousness of Sherwood's demeanor dissuaded him.

As a concierge Sherwood's duties, as advertised by the Inn, were ". . . to arrange automobile services, babysitting, delivery of meals, pet-sitting, grooming or walking services . . ." One of the appeals the position held for him was that it involved meeting strangers and giving them information and advice about the city. His manner and bearing were professional, and his unusual physical qualities seemed not to work against him. Although he maintained a reserved distance from his hotel clients, he was seen as helpful, gracious and approachable by all but the most disagreeable snowbirds from the north.

None of his duties troubled him except dog sitting, an assignment which mercifully occurred infrequently. On one occasion he had sat on the floor of a room on the 7th floor for three hours, trapped by a Neapolitan Mastiff, whose owners had promised Sherwood that the dog was a pussycat. For three long hours the dog sat, staring at him menacingly through drooping lids and drooling copiously.

"Burple[1]," which was the beast's name, had been so labeled because in the right light his coloring reflected a blue and purplish hue. Burple weighed 154 pounds, and though he never growled he sat, unmoving and silent, and with surprising ease effectively blocked every attempt Sherwood made to reach the bathroom door. Sherwood had never observed a large, ponderous dog with the ability to shuffle sideways with the agility that Burple exhibited any time Sherwood tried to move. He was forced to finally capitulate and sat immobile in the corner, mesmerized by the progress of the long strands of saliva that Burple produced from beneath his massive jowls. Even more fascinating were the occasions when the dog violently shook his head, loosing the saliva with alarming velocity in unpredictable directions.

When they finally returned, Burple's owners cooed baby talk to the dog, patting him and congratulating him for taking such good care of the nice babysitter. As Sherwood reached the door, he turned in time to see Burple shake his head and loose a final, ropey salvo of saliva east and west across the room.

* * *

As they walked silently through the drizzle from Harry's to his apartment, Sherwood, with his height advantage, looked down at his shorter friend. It struck him that no two friends were less alike in terms of lineage, education or upbringing. Sherwood's youth had been a confusion of surnames, schools and social stumbling. Archer, he knew, had been set on a straight, smooth and expensive path to easy street—an ordained journey. In terms of life's unmerited advantages, the two men were studies in contrast.

Archer Gannaway Brownlow was, in anyone's vocabulary, an eccentric. In contrast to his friend, he was far shorter in stature, but was possessed of an elegant, almost regal carriage. Also unlike Sherwood, he seemed to exude high levels of energy even when he was relaxing. He had prominent, chiseled features and a tangled mane of curly, dark brown hair. His bearing was erect and his mannerisms refined. During the process of his education he had effectively discarded any hint of a southern accent, and managed to adopt inflections and intonations that were a combination of a British and a 19th century Ivy League elocution. Those in the northeast might have referred to it scornfully as 'Long Island lockjaw', but in truth Archer's

[1] See Appendix 1

accent was far more polished than that. While it indeed had an inflection reminiscent of an Oxford experience, lurking subtly behind was the slightest suggestion of a southern lilt. His accent was a charming if affected adjunct to his individuality. Archer knew it and played it well. Sherwood had always wondered when, not if, Archer would graduate to the 'jolly good', 'beastly weather', and 'tally-ho' stage.

Archer dressed impeccably and expensively, and was most often seen wearing a white shirt and a 'Wayne's Legacy' necktie, despite the inconvenience of the southern climate. As a result of that he was often taken to be haughty or arrogant. Occasionally, though not always, that observation proved quite accurate.

Archer Brownlow was the scion of a very prominent Knoxville family, and was intensely proud of his heritage as well as his family name. His great-great-great-grandfather, for whom Archer was named, had been an austere Methodist minister who had gone on to a distinguished if unconventional career in politics after the ministry. William Gannaway Brownlow[2] was a man who boasted that he was "never neutral", and his uncompromising and radical viewpoints made him one of the most divisive figures in Tennessee political history. At the onset of the Civil War, he fired broadsides at abolitionists and secessionists alike, claiming that both groups were essentially on the same side. Once Tennessee seceded, Brownlow shifted his relentless attack to the Confederate government. He was arrested in Knoxville in 1861, eventually to be released to Union lines in March of 1862.

Despite the efforts of his opponent's to rig the vote against him, Brownlow was elected Governor of Tennessee at the end of the Civil War. His policy of enfranchising former slaves brought him into conflict with the newly founded Ku Klux Klan and its leader, Nathan Bedford Forrest. A man of unwavering conviction and tireless energy, Brownlow invariably managed to set the political agenda and, to a great extent, disarm his political enemies in the process. And somehow during that process he converted large numbers of former adversaries into friends.

Although not officially recognized until July of 1866, Tennessee was nonetheless the first former Confederate state to be officially readmitted to the Union. This was in large part the result of Governor Brownlow's unflagging determination. He resigned from office in 1869 to accept appointment to the United States Senate by the state legislature, a practice

---

[2] See Appendix 2

commonly in widespread use before the ratification of the Seventeenth Amendment to the United States Constitution. He died in 1877, still pursuing his preferred calling as a newspaperman, a vocation that had originally propelled him into political office. Because the Governor had carried the nickname "Parson" during his lifetime and career, Archer Gannaway Brownlow had inherited not only his famous relative's passion and energy, but his nickname as well.

Young Archer was born and raised in the toney enclave of Farragut in West Knoxville. Early in life he learned the catchphrase "There's west Knoxville and there's the rest of Knoxville". Poverty and crime, it was said with some accuracy, recognized the border between the two. Archer was also the beneficiary of a tidy fortune, thanks to the tireless efforts of his grandfather, a prominent Knoxville planter.

Well-supported by unearned wealth, he lacked nothing of his forebears talents except their athleticism and physical stature. In his adolescence and teens, he chased doggedly after a conventionally acceptable existence. He unsuccessfully tried swearing and telling racy jokes, but in the one instance had difficulty putting the appropriate adjective in front of the noun, and in the other he invariably made shambles of the punch line. He even eagerly if ill-advisedly tried his hand at football. At his prep school early one fall he stood anonymously in a line as helmets, shoulder pads and other foreign-looking paraphernalia were being handed out to his enormous, bulky classmates, a fair number of whom would move on to division one colleges after graduation. When he reached the coach, he was met with a pause and a sympathetic smile. He was promptly taken aside by a compassionate assistant backfield coach who, after explaining how important the job was, advised Archer that he could become team manager.

There followed two miserable years of sweaty locker rooms, sweaty players, sweaty coaches, crowded showers and noisy reprisals that followed lost opportunities on the field. Added to that were the taunts from impatient players when the Gator-aid and towels weren't supplied quickly enough. But Archer persevered, dreading every game and practice, and eventually won a number of friends on the football team for his energy and determination. It was a task he hated, but pride prevented him from quitting. It was in the classroom, however, that he found his calling.

Archer was a scholar, and was to distinguish himself academically at Episcopal and later at college. But independent schools being what they are, and over-privileged boys being what they are, he, like many before and after him, suffered through the ruthless verbal barbarism generated by his adolescent male classmates.

He first endured the ignominy of being referred to as 'Short Fuse' in the shower room during his first year at Episcopal. This, he incorrectly assumed, was in reference to his temper, which in truth was quite mild. Only weeks later did he learn from a sympathetic friend that the reference was a physical rather than an emotional one. Being unaware of any way to alter the situation, he took to showering at the end of the day when the shower room, still heavy with steam, sufficiently restricted visibility or was vacant. Later in life he was to reflect that this kind of juvenile male brutality ended mercifully by one's junior year, at which time the equally steamy pursuit of adolescent females was entering into full swing. He often marveled at the smoothness of the transition.

At Episcopal Archer immersed himself in scholarship and excelled in nearly every subject. His only serious misstep was not of an academic nature but a social one. As something of a lark, he founded and was subsequently elected president of an organization he named OPEC. OPEC stood for *Over-educated Protestant Elite Caucasians*, and while it did initially attract a few members, it was quashed relatively early in its infancy.

When word about the organization leaked out to the school and its constituents, it not only brought down the wrath of the parents of scholarship students, but of the board of trustees as well. The president of MetLife Knoxville, one of the larger employers in the city, happened to be African-American, and also happened to be a prominent board member at Episcopal. Archer was forced to both disband the organization and to write a letter of apology addressed to board members and parent body as well. Though only fifteen, he was thoroughly mortified, and vowed never to find himself in a similar position again.

At seventeen, considerably matured and enrolled at Emory College in Atlanta, he majored in Psychology and carried a minor in Philosophy. It was a crushing academic load, but he managed it with apparent ease. While he did involve himself in the social scene at Emory, he nonetheless maintained an aura of privacy and remoteness, and for all intents and purposes acted more the part of an onlooker than a participant.

His classmates regarded Archer as a brilliant, unconventional, social and academic enigma, traits which to some degree he shared with Sherwood. However, the rigor and schedule eventually did him in. He simply lost interest in what he now saw as a colossal waste of time-philosophy. Energy had turned to lethargy, and the gifted scholar had now become an academic vagrant. An unmotivated Archer decided that a change of scenery would be of benefit, and he moved to Tallahassee to see if that city's graduate programs would fire his curiosity and ignite his interest.

Like his friend Sherwood, Archer inherited both clarity of insight and imagination from one if not more branches of his family tree. Now forty-one years old, he was seldom seen without his recently acquired reading glasses, which he wore low on his nose and were clearly an a unnecessary decoration. His vision was excellent. He had spent countless hours fine-tuning his head movements so that reading and distance vision had become a series of well-orchestrated, bird-like progressions. It had been a difficult adjustment at first. He tended initially to look through the magnified lenses at objects in the distance and over them to read the printed page. But after much practice he was well satisfied with the result, secure in the thought that it lent him an appropriate air of scholarly focus and intensity.

Archer Brownlow was a man who kept both busy and to himself. While in Tallahassee he took no meaningful steps towards a career, but eventually developed interests and hobbies that were to become consuming passions. It did not appear to the outside world that he was, in the accepted sense of the word, gainfully employed. Opinion on this was divided, some who knew him saying he was a black sheep of the family because he had never worked, some saying he was the only smart one in his family because he had never worked. This small tempest swirled around him apparently escaping his notice, or at least his interest.

Unmarried, nocturnal and allergic to children, Archer had at some point in his earlier life become something of an amateur lepidopterist. He also found time to build strange, intricate floor lamps, which often sparked alarmingly when plugged in, or leaned precariously when set upon the floor. Being suspicious of electricity to begin with, he finally decided to build all his future projects without bulbs or plugs. These unusual traits taken together gained him a reputation that he savored. He was regarded as a gifted but harmless eccentric, and people generally left him to his own devices.

Archer met Sherwood at a poorly attended lecture on "The Impact of the Civil War on the Southern Psyche." Like a man too long afloat, he was seeking an academic life ring of sorts, hoping to find some interest that would stimulate his intellect. He quickly became captivated with the subject, and he and Sherwood often found themselves in animated conversations in the hallways during a lecture break. The connection between the two was immediate and became securely cemented by their shared interests.

Archer was of a personality that was at once friendly and distant. While he could appear to be an almost obsessively shy person, he took an immediate and almost paternal interest in this relatively recent transplant from Portland. They spent hours talking about whether Longstreet or Lee was responsible for the debacle at Gettysburg, if Stonewall Jackson was a superb general or a driven zealot, if Nathan Bedford Forrest redeemed himself by his actions after the war, and if the Union started the conflict to occupy the South or simply to fatally disrupt slavery, the cotton trade and the economy. Together they presented stark physical studies in contrast when they were together, the one tall, lanky, creative and clumsy, the other shorter, studious, aimless and intensely intellectual. But both men shared the unburied and unspoken indignities of having been persecuted by their classmates during their formative school years.

Although Sherwood shared none of Archer's other unusual interests, fascination with the Civil War bound them inextricably. They studied nearly every aspect of the conflict, discussed it endlessly and nearly living it. It was this passion that was to carry them in a direction that was to prove both intriguing and dangerous, a direction which neither man could have foreseen.

* * *

Archer trailed a step or two behind Sherwood as two men entered the small building and climbed the stairs to Sherwood's apartment on the third floor of the three-story complex. He had always struggled to cope with the exaggerated length of Sherwood's stride, and found himself taking two steps for every one of his friend's. Agility was admittedly not his strong point, and he found he had to sacrifice speed for safety in his effort to keep pace.

When they entered the apartment they were welcomed by Sherwood's dog, Dillinger[3], who greeted them noisily inside the door. A stubby, vastly overweight pug who snorted and wheezed like a locomotive, Dillinger was Sherwood's unlikely and only live-in companion. She was brindle in color and sausage-shaped with a leg at each corner. Her name, Sherwood explained, resulted from the staccato rat-a-tat sound made by her stumpy little legs and toenails as she raced across the floor to greet him. It reminded him of a machine gun. It didn't bother him that Dillinger was a female.

---

[3] See appendix 3

Archer liked the dog but found that, in his experience, Dillinger had a significant shortcoming. She had developed a lustful propensity for his right leg, or his left leg, depending upon which was closer at hand. Sherwood patiently explained that this was normal, and that Archer should perhaps even be complimented by such a favorable show of affection. The Parson, however, regarded it as both indecorous and borderline dissolute, the former being to his mind even more objectionable than the latter. He found it was best dealt with by avoiding sitting almost entirely, or by maintaining a fairly constant, agitated state of motion. When sitting was the only option, he crossed one leg over the other and swung the topmost leg constantly. In that way Dillinger had far more difficulty gaining suitable purchase on the leg, and generally gave up the chase after a few minutes.

Given her undersized legs, Dillinger had to be helped up on the bed each night, where she slept snoring and whistling noisily until hunger finally overwhelmed her and she pawed Sherwood awake at dawn. This and her tendency to snuggle close to his pillow in the early morning hours he bore with the tolerance of a confirmed bachelor. He endured her flatulence, however, with far less grace.

"She reminds me a bit of your ex-wife, Willow," Archer said with a quick, mischievous grin. Sherwood wasn't sure which of Dillinger's characteristics brought that to his friend's mind.

"I simply meant in terms of the wheezing and barking and all," Archer clarified.

"Willow as an error in judgment, caught, corrected and peacefully resolved," Sherwood answered good-naturedly. "And I was a victim of misleading information. Remember, she insisted that she was a big fan of American History, the Civil War, red wine and the classical music for starters. It was a good story, but pure fiction. I was young and impressionable, and no matter what you say, she didn't share Dillinger's particular deficiencies. "However," he mused, "she did tend to fill most of her time in a state of permanent collapse in the living room with the drapes drawn and Waylon Jennings' tapes droning on the stereo. She carried the practice of depression to new heights—or depths, depending on your interpretation."

Archer looked at the worn damask curtains hanging at both living room windows. Sherwood sensed his question.

"Those are the only positive things that came from the marriage, and about the only thing she neglected to take with her. She either forgot them or left them behind on purpose, as a kind of sobering reminder, I suppose. I've never bothered to take them down, and they do provide a bit of privacy."

"Sherwood, with a name like Willow, you really might have used your imagination," Archer said by way of being provocative, but recognizing that the footing was becoming tricky, he turned the subject away from Willow abruptly.

"I didn't mean to dredge up old memories. I think perhaps we should get back to the man in that truck outside of Harry's tonight."

Sherwood sighed. "The man in that truck has been doing this for weeks. It's become a kind of a game—he pretends to try to run me down, I pretend to dodge, and we both go home happy. At least I go home happy—I presume he does, too. But it's gotten so predictable that it's almost boring." He turned and led Archer into the small living room. Dillinger followed obediently behind, legs churning, making minimal headway.

The apartment was on the top floor of the building, chosen for both its light and its privacy. It was a sparsely furnished but comfortable three bedroom apartment, the second bedroom being used as an office, and the third room filled to overflowing with Civil War maps and memorabilia, old buttons, belt plates and numerous, largely unrecognizable excavated artifacts. He referred to this as the annex, no doubt an unconscious association with a museum annex.

There was no disorder here, only the appearance of it. In fact everything was numbered or labeled, and Sherwood could locate any individual artifact without resorting to his notes. There was a long rectangular table in the middle of the room and several smaller tables against the walls. Note pads were placed on each table, pages filled with notations and sketches. Every time Archer entered this sanctum he was astonished by its precise orderliness. Only one table looked to be in disarray, and that was covered by artifacts still-to-be catalogued and stored in soon-to-be designated boxes and trays. Sherwood's interest in Civil War artifacts was second only to his interest in the fall of the Confederacy and Davis's flight south. His job allowed him to pursue both with a mind uncluttered with the debris of work-related problems.

Archer was inexorably drawn to the annex and its contents. He was overwhelmed by the sense that he was in the presence of history—tangible relics with an almost spectral connection to the past. He paused by Sherwood's collection of Civil War buttons, carefully arranged in trays, each identified and catalogued. He picked one button from an open tray on the table in front of him. "You've told me how valuable some of these buttons can be. How much, for example, would this button cost on the open market?" he asked, indicating a button from the state of Virginia.

Sherwood walked over and examined the button more closely. "You picked a good one. It would probably cost close to $6,000, if the market was strong. Otherwise you might be able to steal it for between $4,000 and $5,000. But that's just the beginning."

"Just the beginning. And that means?" Archer asked.

"Well, the most expensive button ever sold, to my knowledge at least, sold for over $49,000. It was a Confederate Adjutant General's button, quite rare." He stopped and looked at Archer with a smile.

"$50,000 for a bloody uniform button." Archer said shaking his head. "And I thought Impressionist art was pricey."

Sherwood had always known he'd hear the word bloody from his friend eventually. Archer turned from the buttons and surveyed the entire collection that filled the room.

"Speaking of all of these," he gestured to the tables covered with artifacts, "how is your book coming along? These are the things you're writing about, if I'm not mistaken," Archer said.

"Not so well, I'm afraid. It seems I can read well, but I flat out can't write—not well, anyway. The problem is that I know what good writing is—really good writing, I mean, but I can't even come close to it."

"What is your paradigm of good writing? Shakespeare, I suppose, or Tolstoy. I trust you're not comparing yourself to the literary giants of the past."

Sherwood laughed. "Not so lofty. I'm talking about Conroy, Fraser, Eugenides, even Hemingway. They have style, their sentences are lyrical, their descriptions vivid. That's the kind of work I envy."

"Hemingway was as lyrical as an oyster, S.T. He was a self-promoting hack who developed a cult following and struggled with more than two syllable words—make that one syllable—but I can agree with the others," Archer interjected, hoping for an energetic disagreement about Hemingway's talents. Not eliciting the hoped-for response, he continued.

"You, my friend, tend to compare apples and oranges. You're writing non-fiction and comparing it to works of fiction. You're writing a treatise about certain aspects of the Civil War and comparing it to 'The Grapes of Wrath.' Those kinds of comparisons never work. And I'd add as well that you're not trying to write the great American novel, at least as I understand it. You're writing to a relatively small, committed audience, and not vying for a spot on the New York Times bestseller list, unless I'm badly mistaken."

"I'd guess you're not a fan of Hemingway's," Sherwood suggested with amusement, rising to but not taking the bait.

"Hemingway has a great deal in common with Wagner. He could write a good story, but that's not the definition of good writing. Wagner was a fine symphonist, but his operas were prolonged, extravagant, thundering bores—except perhaps for 'Die Meistersinger'. But you mentioned lyrical prose and vivid descriptions, and I'd submit that's about as far from Hemingway's work as a topless bar is from the ballet."

"That may be," Sherwood quietly, "but it doesn't solve my problem."

Archer softened. "As in the opera, one must remember that the audience is on your side, not waiting for a bungled line or a missed high C—unless you're Pavarotti, of course. The audience wants you to win, S.T. I'm sure your book will be very fine indeed."

"You know, Arch, sometimes I just want to drop the whole thing. It's a terrible mess to bring it all together, and it often doesn't seem worth it."

"Persevere, my friend. It will make you a proud author in the end. They say that if you write a book, plant a tree and build a boat you've lived a full life. I say that having done none of the three, but given sufficient time, tools and instruction, one never knows. Now please remind me of the book's subject. It is a bit esoteric, and I'm afraid I've forgotten it."

"The book is about the significance and impact of uniform accouterments on the morale of Civil War soldiers from 1861 to 1863," Sherwood said modestly. "As a matter of fact, that's most likely going to be the title."

"And a catchy one it is, but you have indeed made my case," Archer noted dryly. "You're not expecting an endorsement from Oprah's Book Club. At least I expect you're not. I may read it, but that's because, just like you, I'm a devotee. Otherwise this is pretty dry stuff for the average reader. You're not competing with Shakespeare or Faulkner, wouldn't you agree? And in addition, your audience is sure to be somewhat limited—in number only, I mean. I repeat, they'll be cheering for you, not researching your errors." He paused, looked thoughtful. "Unless one of them happens to be Dean Phelps, my senior thesis advisor in college, which is extremely unlikely. That was a long time ago. Anyway, you are writing to the choir, or singing to the choir, whatever the applicable maxim is. We're all believers, and we aren't expecting James McPherson or Bruce Catton. You know your subject and, of course, you don't have to worry about character development, plot lines or dramatic tension. You're doing pure historical research and reporting. Why compare yourself to the authors of the classics?"

"Because I know what a good piece of writing is, and this isn't it. You know, there are times I wish I were writing fiction and not chasing names, dates, and battles around and trying to keep them all in their chronological and historical order. It gets tedious sometimes, and I'm sure I'll botch the whole thing up in the end anyway."

"Count yourself lucky, my friend," the Parson responded. "Fiction is not so easy. Indeed, non-fiction appears to me to be the easier path. Do the research, follow the names and dates, put them in the proper sequence and it's done. Believe me, fiction presents a considerably greater challenge," he said, shaking his head and smiling.

"Come on, Arch. You start of with 'It was a dark and stormy night . . . 'or 'It was the best of times, it was the worst of times . . . 'or how about 'Call me Ishmael'? Then you throw in a torn bodice here, a lustful glance there, a strand of golden hair brushed delicately from a lustrous brown eye, a bit of creamy, white skin,—sprinkle enough of that around and you're off and running." Sherwood was clearly enjoying himself.

"It's not so easy, my friend. Fiction can be the bane of one's literary existence."

"You write fiction, then?" Sherwood asked with surprise.

"Not that I'll admit to." Archer responded. "And if you ever bring it up I'll deny it."

"Why, for heaven's sake?"

"Let me put it this way. I've tried, and because I'm uncommonly stubborn, I'll probably keep trying. But consider this. In fiction you have the freedom to create your own characters and situations—true. You then move them from chapter to chapter without any compass except your own imagination. The characters are, of course, of your own manufacture. Their success or failure is entirely dependent upon your ingenuity and, even more important, your diligence in keeping them consistent. For example you, my friend, would present an interesting challenge in that regard. Let's just say for the sake of argument that I create a character named Sherwood Tualatin. In that character I also create your distinguishing physical features, your personality, mannerisms, peculiarities, foibles, and so forth. Should I betray any of those characteristics in my work of fiction, you, as a character are finished. I like to call that tonal schizophrenia. If I introduce you as a witty and amusing character, kind of a bigger-than-life Oscar Wilde or Mark Twain or Dickensian fellow, you'd best remain witty and amusing and Dickensian throughout or you become unbelievable. And not only do you become unbelievable, but the entire book is undermined as well. That, in my opinion, is the great challenge to the writer of fiction, and I haven't even mentioned plot. I suspect that keeping the Battle of Chancellorsville and its individual combatants consistent is not particularly taxing, but fictional characters—that's another story, so to speak." Archer looked almost weary as he finished.

"A lot went on at Chancellorsville, Arch, but give me an example of a consistent character."

"My great pleasure. In my opinion, Bugs Bunny is one of the most consistent characters in any form of entertainment," Archer responded. "He's brilliantly cast-quick on his feet, always slightly irreverent, witty, sly in a transparent way, and always likeable even when he's outrageous. He's never out of character. In addition he's always so far ahead of his adversaries when it comes to reasoning or deduction, to say nothing of repartee, that it's embarrassing. Just think about how disarming the words 'Eh, what's up, Doc?' are. Those words simply shout 'simple-minded rabbit without a clue,' when in truth he already has his next three moves planned. Devious, perhaps, but endearing nevertheless, and consistently so. I suppose you might not want your son of to emulate him, but Bugs Bunny is not only extraordinarily consistent, he also ranks very high on my list of literary and cinematic heroes."

"I take your point, and I'll have to pay more attention on Saturday mornings," Sherwood answered with a grin, realizing that Archer was at least in part quite serious. "I guess like a lot of other things, fiction looks as if it's more fun from the other side of the street. The only answer is to write trash. Then nobody cares about character development or consistency. Just as long as there's a serial killer, a flawed detective, some bloodshed and a couple of good sex scenes . . ." Sherwood smiled as he finished.

"Even that takes a degree of talent and diligence, I'd suggest, or it can also become tedious," Archer said.

"I won't even try to argue with that," Sherwood said. "But let me tell how I'd approach the writing of fiction if I were you. As you know, I'm a fan of Charles Dickens. Dickens structured much of his writing so that there was a distinct variation in mood and substance from one chapter to the next. Now, allow me a touch of hyperbole, and I'll assure you that the basic premise is accurate. Dickens would set one chapter on a dismal day and describe the filth and squalor of the streets of London and the impoverished lives of the miserable creatures who lived there. The next chapter would be set in the English countryside and bathed in sunlight, crowded with privileged women in hoop skirts with parasols and young peacocks following them around hoping to be graced with a dropped handkerchief. One critic referred to his style as streaky, like the layers of fat and lean in a piece of bacon.

Now I would try to emulate Dickens but approach it differently. I would write one chapter in the morning, fueled only by coffee and orange juice. The next would be written in the evening with the benefit of two or three glasses of good Pinot Noir. I think the result just might even surpass Dickens. Not only that, but I'm sure it would make the process a great deal more pleasurable for me as the writer." He sat back with a satisfied smile and waited for Archer's response. He hadn't long to wait."

"That may be the most positive counsel you've provided me since we began this discussion. And wherever it might lead from a literary perspective, it does afford a natural segue into an even more agreeable neighborhood. Taking up where you and Dickens left off, why don't we enjoy a decent glass of wine in your study. You have some gaps to fill in, and to anticipate your next question, a delicate red with a forward nose and hints of oak and mocha would be fine."

Sherwood's face broke into a broad grin before his friend had finished.

Without waiting for a reply, Archer continued. "I should add, if it's drinkable. Incidentally, I have some curious news for you that may ruin your whole evening. There is another Sherwood in town."

"That's very funny, Archer, but I've never met another Sherwood in my life. I seem to be the only one in captivity. Now let's . . ."

"I'm quite serious, S.T. He is an older gentleman and he lives right under your nose—right around the corner, I should say, in a retirement community. His name is Sherwood DeForest."

"Humor was never a strong point of yours, Arch. Next you'll tell me his wife's name was maid Marion, and his friends were Little John and Friar Tuck," Sherwood said struggling with an uncooperative cork.

"I didn't expect you to believe me. If you let me use your computer later, I'll log on to the retirement community's site and download the resident's list. Proof in black and white," he said emphatically.

"Not the time, Arch. We've got some important ground to cover here," Sherwood answered. The cork made a moist, unsatisfactory plop as he drew it from the bottle. He looked apprehensively into the neck of the bottle, then poured two generous glasses of suspiciously dark red wine.

They moved to the study and Sherwood unceremoniously unseated a rangy, tattered cat from the most comfortable chair in the room.

"Get down, Torpid[4]," he said and swept the cat gently to the floor.

Archer looked up and asked, "I've neglected to ask you this before, but how did you ever come up with the name Torpid for a cat?"

"Because I couldn't come up with a name that described him any better. That's what he is and that's what he does. He's dormant and motionless. I could hardly have named him Frisky. Look." Sherwood pointed at the cat, which had taken what looked to be permanent residence on the small couch by the door. Torpid was settled into the cushion in what looked to be a state of semi-permanence, his breathing being the only thing to distinguish him from the cushion.

"He's old," continued Sherwood, "he can't hear too well, so he lives happily in his own little world. He'd been de-clawed when I found him, and I think that took a lot of the pizzazz out of him. He got outside once and tried to climb a tree. You should have seen the look on his face. He made it up maybe two feet and just slid slowly back down. That was the first time in my life I ever saw a cat look embarrassed. In any event, life for Torpid pretty much consists of sleeping, eating and generally ignoring me when I'm around."

"I still maintain it must make it a bit awkward when you call the cat, 'here, Torpid, here Torpid.'" It doesn't flow terribly well, now, does it?"

"You don't call a cat, Archer, and if you do, you don't expect a response. When was the last time you saw a cat race to the door eager to welcome you home, tail wagging? That's a dog's forte. You name a cat for purposes of identification only." He turned and walked through the room, pointing at each item as he identified it. "Chair, vase, television, microwave, Torpid. That's the only reason you name a cat—to distinguish it from other household objects."

Archer shook his head smiling, and the two men sat down in wing chairs facing one another in Sherwood's diminutive study. Sherwood poured them each a glass of Malbec with an undistinguished looking label. Archer turned his head and strained to read it—'Dona Paula Los Cardos Malbec'. With knitted brows he lifted his glass apprehensively, swirled the wine carefully, delicately breathed in the aroma and then swallowed, head cocked slightly to the side, expectantly.

"It might be best if this discussion doesn't take too long. This wine . . ." He made a face and shook his head solemnly. "Pungent. It needs some fresh air. I think I can make out a grape skin or two adrift on top of my glass."

---

[4] See appendix 4

"$7.99 a bottle. One drinks what one can afford," Sherwood commented with a smile. His friend had prodigiously lavish taste when it came to wine. "If you let it gasp for a few minutes before you drink it, the stuff isn't all that bad, particularly if you swallow fast enough. Anyway, when we're here we'll drink the mouthwash, when we're at your place, we'll drink one of those rare vintages of yours. That should more than balance out my Malbec." With Dillinger finally subdued and rasping noisily in the corner, he suggested they return to address his friend's concerns about near death and Dodge Hemis.

* * *

Near dusk on May 16th, Henry Louis sat with his partner and detective Chavez in front of a projection screen in a small laboratory annex of their offices in Midway, Texas. The room was dark but for the projector and the glow of Louis's cigarette. This time Chavez was dressed in a suit that fit him far better, but reflected badly on his taste in clothing. It was muted dung-brown in color with regularly spaced squares of green plaid in the background. It brought to mind a picture Louis had seen of mannequins in a men's department store in the 1950's, a dated caricature in checkered plaid.

"Jimmy Breslin," Louis said quietly to no one in particular, surprising himself. "He was the one who wrote 'The Gang That Couldn't Shoot Straight.'"

"Out, Louis, put the goddamn thing out," his colleague Sampson Weeks said pointing at the cigarette. "It took me years to kick that crap. I still do battle with it, and you aren't helping the situation a bit. Anyway, in this room there's no smoking, supposedly," he added acidly.

Louis walked to a sink in the corner, turned on the water and doused his cigarette.

"Look at the photo of the car, Sam", he said, purposefully not responding to Weeks. "First of all, the keys aren't in the ignition, and second the guy in the trunk was wearing a Rolex watch. That means this couldn't have been a robbery gone bad, or whoever did this would have dumped the body and taken the watch and the car—or at least the watch. The car wasn't worth it. They obviously killed the guy before he was put in the trunk and then the car was torched."

"'They,'" said Chavez, "Why 'they'?"

"Just a form of speech," Louis replied patiently. "Most likely a he. Women aren't usually into this kind of stuff. Anyway, they either wanted this guy to be really, really dead, or really, really dead and unrecognizable. Just look at his face, or what's left of it. It's a mess. Somebody just plain didn't like him."

Weeks interrupted. "Most people just plain don't like most of the people they murder, Louis. Grant me that and I'll agree with you that this is overkill in capital letters." The photographs on the screen were disturbing.

Sampson Weeks was a large black man whose first name fit him well. The sides of his head were shaved close, he had a tuft of short, coarse black hair on top, and a small, well-trimmed mustache. Well over 6'4" and weighing 265 pounds fresh from the shower, he had shown promise as an offensive lineman during his junior and senior years in high school. Lack of natural quickness and a gentle personality were not in his favor, however, and he chose a college with no football program and never looked back.

While Weeks was himself a veteran investigator, he was junior to Louis in terms of experience, a fact that his partner enjoyed pointing out. Weeks neither resented Louis's mild gibes nor envied his partner's senior position. He was a man with a well-defined sense of himself, and although he was unwilling to let Louis know it, he was perfectly content to play a slightly junior role. The two partners got along exceptionally well, both possessed of dry senses of humor and the ability to adapt to one another's moods and idiosyncrasies.

Louis turned to Chavez, who stood quietly beside the desk. "Hey, Jesus. My guess is you do the usual suspect thing now. First the wife or a family member, they're always good bets. Then a girlfriend—or boyfriend, if there is one. Check on drug use, life-style, enemies, relatives with grudges, relatives without grudges, the whole scenario." Louis hated the word scenario but could never come up with a substitute. "And last but not least, look for a business acquaintance who may have been screwed over by the victim. If all of those come out clean, or if they don't exist, it's square one again."

"It's 'Hay-zoos'. You pronounce the J like an H—'Hay-zoos,' and remember, I like Raul a whole lot better," Chavez answered quietly, not realizing that Louis was fully aware of the correct pronunciation of his name.

"Anyway, you got that right. That's basically the drill," Chavez continued. "You start with the people closest to the victim, then work your way out. We don't have a lot of manpower or resources, but we'll chase down anyone connected with this guy and find out as much about them as we can. My partner has already followed up on the obvious leads, and the wife simply doesn't have a motive. No affairs, exemplary life style, solid marriage, and no witnesses that we can find. We've got shit for clues, and we haven't been able to come up with anyone yet who had the slightest reason to kill this guy."

"Other than you, Chavez, Midland doesn't have many qualified investigators, to say nothing about manpower," Louis said brusquely. "With that group you got over there, if something doesn't break pretty quickly, the case could go cold in a hurry."

"Correction." Chavez voice had taken on a professional edge. "First of all, my partner's at least as good as I am, and a case doesn't usually go cold for at least a year, or until you've run out of clues and interviewed every possible suspect." Chavez paused, his eyebrows knitted in a slightly confused frown. "But in this case, we don't have any suspects."

"That's my point exactly," Louis answered. "Tell me more about the wife."

"She's got an alibi you couldn't crack with a jackhammer. She was visiting her mother in Schenectady and reported her husband missing the minute she got home. No sign of a struggle, only a few clothes packed and no note. She called friends, asked the children, but all anyone knew was that he was on a business trip. She has dozens of people who'll back up her story."

Louis continued to probe. "Could she have gotten to Midland between her visit to her mother and the time she reported him missing?" He was testing the thoroughness of the detective's work.

"No time," Chavez answered immediately. "She got off the plane, took a taxi home, walked into the house, and no lights, no husband, no nothing. Then she called. Lasansky worked that part hard. She's clean, believe me."

"Who's Lasansky? Louis asked.

"My partner. He's been a detective for twelve years and my partner for four. He's a good man."

Weeks seemed not to have heard the conversation going on the other side of his desk.

"Nothing on the body except a Rolex," he mumbled more to himself than to be heard. "No identification at all." Then he turned to Chavez.

"Your guys find anything around the car we can work with? Something in the parking lot the guy might have dropped or discarded? We came up empty."

Chavez' answer was discouraging, "The department's been over the scene several more times. The scene gives us nothing. You've got what we've got—the car and the body."

"The coroner's got the body, we've got the car," Louis corrected. "We're going the coroner's next. We may find something on the body. There's usually something," he said with an unusual hint of optimism.

"We start from scratch," Weeks said. "We'll start with missing persons, the teeth, such as they are, fingerprints, and DNA. We'll search the database and see if we get a hit on any of it."

"Which will take weeks." Louis slipped the word in, pleased with his timing.

"When are you going to get tired of using that one, Henry," Weeks said shaking his head. Chavez scratched his bald head and looked bewildered, the play on Sampson's name having sailed right over the top of it.

* * *

Archer plunged right in, "As I understand it, this person whom you've never met is terrorizing you, and you have no idea why this might be happening"?

"Sure I do", Sherwood answered as they settled into two chairs in the living room. "At least I'm pretty sure I do."

"Well?" asked Archer impatiently.

"As you well know, I've spent a fair amount of time studying the last days of the Confederacy in 1865—you and I have talked about it a lot. You also know I've followed Jeff Davis's flight south from Richmond after the capital of the Confederacy fell."

"How could I not?"

"Well, you've never asked me why I've stayed in Tallahassee as a concierge to the Governor's Inn after all that time I spent studying electrical engineering in college." Archer started to interrupt, but Sherwood stopped him.

"You'll understand in a minute." He produced a dog-eared, coffee-stained slip of paper on which a brief message was printed. The words were blurred but precisely formed, evenly and carefully spaced. Brownlow read:

> *"If it is your intention to work your mischief against the name and reputation of the president of the Confederacy, and therefore besmirch the ideals of the Confederacy itself, be advised that you will pay for this indiscretion with both your reputation and your life."*

Archer looked at it for a minute before he responded. "This is like something from the pen of Thoreau or Emerson. The language sounds like it was written in the 19th century. I even have the feeling I may have even read it somewhere," he mused.

"It doesn't seem like the language of a pissed-off redneck in a trailer park, does it?" Sherwood replied, enjoying a brief foray into the kind of language sure to disconcert Archer. Then he bent his stork-like frame over the table, took a pen out of his pocket, carefully smoothed out a napkin in front of him and began to sketch. When he'd finished, he had produced a crude sketch of the eastern part of the United States from northern Virginia to mid-Florida. He pushed it across the table to his friend. "This is what I think is at the bottom of the whole business."

Archer looked at the drawing briefly, followed a line drawn from roughly Richmond Virginia to the Georgia-Florida border, and looked up quizzically. "What's this supposed to mean?" he asked.

"This is Jeff Davis's route from Richmond to Irwinville, Georgia in 1865 when the Confederacy collapsed. He and his family and a few loyal friends and Confederate officers were captured there," Sherwood said, pointing to a small dot on the map. "That's as far as he got."

Archer looked at the map more closely and then asked, "What does this have to do with the attempt on our lives out there tonight?"

Nearly two hours later Archer rose, stretched his arms yawning, a preface to leaving. Sherwood offered to walk him to his car.

When the two men reached the sidewalk the streetlights, dimmed by a cold drizzle, reflected dimly off the surface of the street below.

Unnoticed in the gloom, the dark shape of a pickup truck, engine idling, edged away from the curb. The truck roared from a dead stop to more than sixty miles per hour and was thirty yards away before the two men saw it. This time the truck swerved directly at them. Had it not been for their moderate intake of alcohol ensured by the poor quality of the evening's wine, they might not have been able to avoid a painful confrontation with the pickup. As it was, the vehicle's driver appeared to be the more impaired of the three.

While both Archer and Sherwood found themselves on the sidewalk shaken but unhurt, the pickup driver overcorrected frantically, lost traction and slid, tires squealing, passenger side first into a mailbox. The mailbox, torn loose from its moorings, bounced twice and finally clattered to a stop less than three feet from Archer's left leg. The truck itself came to a jarring halt against a streetlight. The engine shuddered, coughed a hairball of black smoke from its exhaust pipe and died. The streetlight trembled but didn't budge from its moorings.

The two men picked themselves up and trotted towards the smoking vehicle. It was a dark blue Dodge Ram, and although the engine had died, Sherwood would have bet his last pair of white socks it was a powered by a Hemi. The driver was making dazed and futile efforts to open his door, but the truck had folded itself neatly around the streetlight on the passenger's side, thereby bending the frame and, without the services of the jaws of life, appeared to have made both doors inaccessible.

"I suppose we should be used to this by now," Archer said acerbically. "If you'd excuse me, I'd like a word with this fellow." Archer picked up a three foot, jagged piece of body molding that had sheared off the truck in both hands. He had surprising strength, despite a decided lack of exercise and athletic ability. He was also for the moment exceedingly and uncommonly angry, and adrenaline was controlling his actions. He swung the twisted metal at the front windshield of the car, shattering the glass where he struck it and creating a ragged three-foot oval hole from which radiated a symmetrical spider web of glass. The pickup shuddered in response.

"O.K., A.J., climb out," he ordered, completely out of character. Then, with considerable effort, he once again regained the familiar Brownlow composure.

"You drive like my dear old grandmother played rugby, my friend. That was quite an unfriendly thing you did just now, and it could have been hazardous as well. I think you might consider coming along with us. Please clean some of that detritus off your face and have we'll have a nice, long chat together somewhere quiet. You'll find us both of a friendly nature but very curious. I expect that you will be able to satisfy some of that curiosity." Archer ended his sentence on a temperate note, leaving Sherwood astonished that his friend could have regained his equanimity after such a unsettling event.

"A.J.?" Asked Sherwood, as they guided the obviously tipsy Ralph into the back of their car.

"You can't be so out of touch with the world around you that you've never heard of A.J. Foyt, the NASCAR driver?"

Sherwood looked at his friend in surprise. The Parson apparently was a fan of NASCAR. He tried hard to form a picture in his mind of Archer in a crowd of onlookers at a NASCAR event, dressed in his white shirt, necktie, half glasses, grey flannels and penny loafers. The image failed to materialize.

They stood on the sidewalk and spoke together quietly for a moment, Ralph nervously trying to eavesdrop. After a brief period of deliberation they decided to escort their new companion to neutral territory, where neighbors were few and privacy would be assured.

* * *

The three men drove to a seedy motel on the corner of Monroe Street and Thomasville Road, Sherwood at the wheel, Ralph Metzger silent and sullen in the back seat. Archer leveled his best scowl at him, hoping the expression was intimidating. It wasn't, but Ralph failed to even notice. He was lost in his own thoughts, and seemed unaware of what was going on around him. He spoke only once, blubbering "my truck" in a quavering voice.

When they reached the motel, Archer abandoned his scowl, went in and rented a room for one night. He chose a location at the far end of the building in the back, the quietest and most private room the motel had to offer. He was pleased to note that they would be working with the added assistance of a considerable level of traffic noise from the commuter traffic on Monroe Street.

When they entered the room, Sherwood silently led Ralph to a scarred wooden chair in front of an equally scarred wooden desk and sat him down abruptly. He instructed Ralph not to move until he returned, and left Archer in charge. The glower, effective or not, returned.

Sherwood went quickly to his car, opened the trunk and dug out a roll of duct tape and an old battery charger, which he always kept in his trunk. His father had told him years before that there was very little that couldn't be accomplished in life with a roll of duct tape, a roll of paper towels and a screwdriver. For the moment he had no use for the screwdriver.

When he returned to the room, Ralph sat dazed in the chair, head down and despondent. He offered no resistance as Sherwood wrapped the tape loosely around the man's hands, feet and chest, as he had seen done in countless movies. Despite the lack of pressure from the tape, Ralph began to hyperventilate. It was apparent that he'd graduated from his natural tendency to be faint-hearted and was closing in on an anxiety attack. This gratified Sherwood. It would make their work much easier. He turned to Ralph and spoke slowly and, he hoped, menacingly.

"Start at the beginning, leave nothing out, and we can deal with this like adults. Otherwise we have some helpful incentives in store for you that you might not enjoy." The Parson was standing beside the table holding the old 12-volt battery charger with two clamps attached.

"These," Archer said pointing at the clamps, "we use in case of reticence on your part." Ralph looked confused.

"Reticence would mean lack of directness or candor on your part. In other words, you lie, we incentivize you," Archer explained, unsure how it had occurred to him to use the word 'incentivize'. It was certainly not a part of his customary vocabulary.

Hearing those words, Ralph's vacant expression registered an unusual degree of comprehension.

"The clamps we can attach just about anywhere imaginable. And please don't entertain the illusion that twelve volts just creates a little sting or a tingle, my lead-footed friend. It not only hurts, it can kill you, and, depending on where we attach these," he waved the clamps ominously, "it can be one of the most lengthy, painful and insufferable events a man can endure—insufferable means unbearable," he explained in response to the man's bewildered expression.

Suddenly all became clear to Metzger. Archer had in his last sentence used just the right amount of emphasis on the word "man" and Ralph, understanding the intended destination of the clamps, paled noticeably. All he could manage was, "Aw, c'mon, fellas."

"We'll start with your employers. We know you're employed. You don't have the creativity of a flounder, and dreaming up this kind of thing is way out of the range of your aptitude. Forget I said aptitude," Archer continued preempting further confusion. "You're just too dumb."

Ralph sat motionless, just staring. In response Archer stepped closer with his clamps, moving them with a swaying motion like a pair of miniature cobras. Ralph followed them with his eyes, and for a moment Sherwood was concerned that the man was approaching a state of hypnosis. Then Ralph broke his silence with a torrent of words and perspiration.

"They'll kill me if they find out. If you tell anyone, I'm dead, or worse. They'll kill you too. What do you want me to do?" He seemed on the verge of tears.

"You might, for a start, consider buttoning the front of your shirt," Archer said caustically. "That look may work on the cover of GQ Magazine, but on you it's positively repugnant."

Ralph only response was a look of total bewilderment.

Sherwood maneuvered the conversation back to Ralph's concern about his personal safety. "If you're that worried about what they might do to you, just get out of Dodge," he suggested, for the moment unaware of the brilliant double-entendre he had crafted involving towns and trucks. Archer suppressed a chuckle and tried to reclaim his menacing glower.

"Hire yourself a good mover," Sherwood continued. "If you're married, get a divorce, give your dog to a neighbor if you have either one or the other, and change your name to something nice, maybe Irish, like O'Connell, or Dugan or something. Maybe try the witness protection program. Understand that your problem is not our business—and try not to worry too much about us." This last was said with a note of sarcasm. "Believe me, we'll take care of ourselves. You just start now, at the top, and don't stop until you get to the point where you met up with your stationary friend the telephone pole and us. If you deviate from the truth, we'll know it, and my electrically talented friend will start doing what he enjoys doing the most."

Archer was momentarily astonished by his friend's eloquence, syntax and originality. As a philologist he was particularly impressed with Sherwood's almost poetic choice of words. But the truth be told, Archer had never purposefully injured another human being, and even avoided stepping on bugs, a legacy of his grandmother's remonstration that an ant could be a transmigrating soul. Also Sherwood was, after all, the electrical engineer in the group, and rightfully should have been wielding the power source. Nevertheless, both men had agreed that Sherwood's chances of terrorizing Metzger were minimal. His curious looks and physique would work against him.

Although he had not requested the job, nor was he qualified for it, Archer set about his task as earnestly as he knew how. He certainly had made use of electrical outlets and changed light bulbs in the past but always cautiously, and he had steadfastly refused to delve any more deeply into that world of invisible, searing, crackling energy. Even now, as he waved the clamps menacingly in front of Ralph, and despite the fact though he knew full well that the battery charger's switch was turned off, he was as nervous as if he were about to make contact with the third rail in a subway terminal. He lowered his voice and assumed what he hoped was a sinister tone.

"Remember, we'll put these wherever we have to, and I can promise it will mess up a variety of your bodily functions," he warned, hoping his tone sounded more ominous than he felt.

Ralph responded slowly and nervously, but cooperatively. He began his story in muted tones, his voice unsteady. As he spoke he seemed to gather both strength and steam, and the words finally tumbled out on the heels of one another. It was as if he was easing his soul, if indeed a soul lurked in that unlikely exterior. It almost appeared that he was embarking on a final confession, and he had decided he might as well not pass over anything that might come back to haunt him later. He looked the clamps, then directly at Archer. "O.K., but this is just between you, him and I." He said.

"You, me and him, Metzger." Archer said with ill-disguised distaste. Grammatical errors were like fingernails on a blackboard to him.

"Huh?" Metzger looked at him uncomprehending.

"Never mind," Sherwood interjected. "Go ahead."

"Have you ever heard of something called 'Group Twenty' or the 'Flaming Sword'? Ralph asked. He looked as if he anticipated a negative answer to his question.

"Neither," Archer answered. "Enlighten us please, and try not to dangle too many participles."

"Huh?" Ralph said, clearly perplexed, returning to what seemed to be the most reliable word in his vocabulary.

"Go on, Metzger," Sherwood broke in again, trying to keep his captive from losing direction. "Just give us the whole story, and quickly."

"I'll give you all of it—at least all that I know, and some that I shouldn't—but it's got to stay here." A long pause followed. "Group Twenty is a very, very hush-hush organization, and their symbol is a flaming sword. They call it 'the flame-bladed sword'. I looked it up on Google—it's called 'Flammenschwert' in German, and there's some real interesting junk in there about it. Anyway, I wasn't ever supposed to know this stuff, but I overheard two of the Group talking in the can when I should have been waiting outside. I was sworn never to go to the can when any of the Group were in there, you know. Anyway, they all have a tattoo of the sword, these guys do, right here under their arms about as close to their armpits as you can get, I overheard them say. It's a requirement for the members. Must have hurt like hell. Anyway, the thing's hidden from pretty much everybody except when they wash their hair in a public shower, I guess. Maybe their wives know." Ralph smiled weakly at his own attempt at humor.

"The point, my friend, get to the point, if you please. What does all this have to do with us?" Archer interrupted.

"I don't really know," Metzger answered. "All I know is that I was hired to harass you—you know, scare you, chase you off, but not necessarily kill you. That's what I was paid for. They said the killing thing might have to come later."

"So tonight were you scaring us, trying to chase us off or kill us?" Sherwood asked.

"I was just trying to keep my job. They fired me today because they said I wasn't doing what I was supposed to do, you know—whatever that is. Anyway, I figured if I roughed you up a bit it might run you off and I'd get my job back. The pay's out of sight, you know. So I thought if I bounced you off the side of a building . . ."

"So you were acting on your own," Sherwood suggested.

"Yeah. They didn't know anything about tonight. They figure I'm past tense, you know. Terminated this morning. Anyway, this Group Twenty, as they call themselves . . ."

"How long have you worked with them?" Archer interrupted.

"I dunno, maybe five, six months," Ralph answered.

"And why are they after Sherwood?" he continued.

"I'm not sure, exactly. They think he knows something, something that makes them very nervous. They really take it seriously. They meet once a month, and they usually call me into every meeting. Every time the topic of conversation is what to do about your friend. And this isn't the end of it, I can promise you that. They want him off the case, and knowing them, they'll find a way to do it."

"What else haven't you told us?" Archer demanded.

"Only this. I know they're involved in something very big, and they think your friend is in the way. What I can't tell you is what your friend knows, and why what he knows is so dangerous to them." Archer was subconsciously counting the number of 'knows' Metzger had managed to shoe-horn into his last few sentences.

"Who is in this so-called Group Twenty?" Sherwood asked.

"I don't know. They don't use names, they use numbers. Number One is a big, beefy guy, looks like he could have played pro football, or something. He's in charge. He's a military type—has a bad leg and walks with a real serious limp. When he talks, everyone listens. The other ones call each other "Nine", "Fifteen", "Five", like that. Only one of them has a nickname—'Shylock'—they call him that sometimes. He has a number, too. I think it's Nine. I guess he's the one who handles the money or something. And they sure seem to have a ton of money to handle," he added with emphasis.

"Someone with a real name must have put his imprimatur on your activities. It's that name that we want."

"His what?"

"You don't know what imprimatur means?" Archer asked, conceivably feigning surprise. "Perhaps you should look it up."

"I know I never heard it used in the real estate racket," Ralph answered earnestly.

Sherwood intervened. "It means to be given permission. Someone gave you the instructions. Who was it?"

"Like I said, they use numbers, I guess to protect their identities, and I wasn't about to ask. Something about those people—I'm not sure what it is—if you ask too many questions, or the wrong question—well, you just don't. You answer their questions, and only ask about things that have to do with what you're supposed to be doing. Other than that, they shut you down. That's all I can tell you—numbers and Shylock," Ralph said, more sure of himself now.

The Parson took a step forward. "Come on, Metzger. I know verisimilitude when I hear it, and you're either lying or stalling. We want all of it—names, nicknames, where you met, all of it."

Ralph looked completely confused, obviously struggling with the six-syllable word that had just been thrown at him

Suddenly Sherwood walked behind up his captive and said, "Lean your head forward, Metzger. You know what comes next."

Ralph looked even more distraught than he had before. "Why?" he said lamely. With obvious distaste Sherwood put his hand on the back of the man's head, pushed it forward and roughly pulled the collar of his shirt away from the back of the man's neck.

"I thought so. There it is", he said without surprise.

On the back of Metzger's neck, well below the collar line, were two small, nearly overlapping double X's. "My guess is that you know more than you're telling us."

"I don't know any more than I'm telling you," Ralph answered, his voice unsteady. "I just met the same person at the same place outside of the museum every time they called me. He picked me up in some kind of a limo or a big taxi with a window between the driver and the back seat. Him and me would drive to a parking garage underneath a bank"—Archer winced again—"I think it was the Capital Bank of Texas—something like that. He always hustled me along so it was hard to see where I was going. Anyway we got in the elevator—it was a private elevator, I'm pretty sure—and he told me told to turn around so I couldn't see what button was being pushed. Then I had to put on a blindfold, and when the elevator stopped, he led me into a waiting room. He took the blindfold off there and told me to wait until someone called for me. That's it."

"If you ever start a sentence in the English language with 'him and me' again, I promise you I'll fry everyone of your parts that you consider private for abuse of the English language," Archer offered heatedly.

Sherwood brought the conversation back on course. "Who was he, Metzger, this man who picked you up every time?"

"His last name was Sparrow. I don't know how it's spelled. I heard someone say, "Good morning Mr. Sparrow" once in the garage when we were getting into the elevator. I thought it was a strange name."

"What did he look like?" Archer asked.

"Another sort of big guy but tall, maybe 6'3", and skinny. He wore a suit. He looked kind of like an undertaker."

"Did he say anything—anything at all", Archer asked.

"He never spoke except to give me directions. You know, like 'put on the blindfold', 'turn around', 'wait here', and so forth."

Sherwood, who had been sitting on a kitchen chair close to Ralph, spoke to Archer.

"Cut him loose. He's told us all he knows and all we need to know for now. And he's harmless." Then he turned to Ralph. "You're free. Go change your name and get a face-lift or something, if you think it would help. I know a good plastic surgeon. As a matter of fact I know a couple of bad ones, too."

"Let me try the clamps—just once. He knows more than he's saying," Archer said, and took another step in Metzger's direction.

"No, he doesn't. He's just a low level employee. He was paid, used and then dumped for not doing his job well. He's as useless to us now as he is to them. We have all the information we need. And you, Metzger, are lucky you're still alive."

"At least let me tingle him a little bit for using 'him and me,'" Archer implored.

"It won't improve his communication skills in the future, I can promise you. It's a waste of electricity."

Archer discarded the battery clamps looking disappointed and pretended to shut off the charger. "I could have lit him up until his ears glowed." He cut the duct tape, and a relieved Ralph rose hesitantly from the chair.

"Listen. Do you guys need any help? Anything, I'm good at lots of things, and I could be useful to you. You interested in some real estate? Maybe the three of us . . ."

Sherwood cut him off. "Go home, Ralph, and forget you ever saw us or talked with us. That's the smartest thing you could do. If you hang around us, you won't find yourself any safer—on the contrary. Now, disappear. And don't let any grass grow. Your Group Twenty will be wondering where you are." Sherwood opened the door and ushered him out.

Ralph started for the door doubtfully, looking more apprehensive than relieved.

As he was leaving, Archer simply couldn't help himself. "And, if things get rough, you might consider a sex change operation. With that and your new Irish identity, you might be able to find work with Mary O'Kay," he added, completely out of character. He was not one normally given to puns or levity. Ralph hustled through the door without acknowledging the comment.

Archer turned to his friend and spoke in a genuinely serious tone. "I'm not sure I'm picking up on all this. You seem to know a good deal more about this situation than I was led to understand. Perhaps you and I should talk about this at greater length."

"Sherwood nodded in assent. "There's more," he said quietly, "a whole lot more. And it gets better and better."

* * *

No one at the table knew Sanjay's full name. His reputation, however, was the stuff of legends. He was, in the simplest terms, alleged to be the quintessential assassin, discreet, proficient, and lethal. He entered the room almost silently and stood at the end of the table most distant from Bowen. Incongruously, he was dressed in the blue scrubs of a surgeon. Tawny and dark-skinned, he was a small, willowy man with blindingly white teeth who generally spoke only when addressed directly, and then only to answer questions in a soft whisper.

"Why am I here?" he asked simply.

"You're here because you're needed again," Bowen answered.

Sanjay waited, his face expressionless and impassive. He said nothing.

"We have two factors which are causing interference to our business—or, that could potentially cause interference. They need to go away."

"Then send them away," Sanjay answered in a slight Middle Eastern singsong. "You don't need me."

"They need to go away permanently—and quietly. As usual, there can be no association with us whatsoever. And, as usual, if you're caught, you will be expected to keep your relationship with this organization completely secret. We simply do not exist."

"I understand." Sanjay answered.

"Needless to say, the pay will be generous, as it always has been. We expect to pay for professionalism and anonymity. We also expect it to be an accident, as before. There can be no indication that it was anything except a tragic mishap. You're to make the decision as to how to carry it out. I would suggest that it not be an automobile accident again. You understand why—the last time that happened you were a little . . . Let's just say it didn't work out so well. Things seem to have been handled a bit carelessly," Bowen spoke evenly, cautiously. While he made his remarks with authority, they were tempered with a curious undertone of respect. Sanjay remained impassive.

"There are two of them this time," he continued. "It might even be best if a few other people went with them—an explosion, a fire, or some kind of natural disaster. That would make it more difficult for investigators to figure out a motive. It might be the cleanest way."

Again Sanjay said nothing. He stood silently while Bowen, growing a bit disconcerted, continued on.

"These two are around a whole lot of public places—bars, restaurants, a hotel, and so on." He paused, waiting for some kind of response. Then he said, "What do you think?"

"I will know how, you will not need to," Sanjay said evenly. "You will please pay me, and then they will go away. That is all you need to know."

Bowen nodded. "The usual amount?" he said.

"It will be double, for the two," Sanjay said. "Two is more difficult. Forty thousand dollars."

Bowen didn't blink. "We hired you because you have a reputation for being efficient, and because you keep your clients names and identities secret. We're willing to pay for that kind of service. But be sure it's professional this time. It must be an accident." He did his best to sound menacing, but something in his eyes failed to carry it off.

Sanjay smiled slightly at the word "service" but said nothing. An uncomfortably long silence followed.

"Their names are Sherwood Tualatin and Archer Brownlow—he's also called the Parson. They're not hard to find. If you want addresses . . .

"I have all I will need," Sanjay answered. "I will ask please to be paid. Then I will go."

"Shylock," Bowen said, his voice gaining in authority, "take Sanjay to the office and ask him to wait for you there. Then withdraw one half of the funds equally from three of our banks—be sure it's three. You should be able to get that done within the hour. And Sanjay, thank you. We expect to hear about the successful completion of your assignment soon. Then you will be paid the remainder of your fee. Please wait for Shylock outside. I want a word with him."

Sanjay rose and left, saying nothing.

Bowen turned to Nine and said, "Shylock. I've wanted to ask you this for a while. Why did you write that note that sounded like it was written by Paul Revere or someone, for God's sake? I mean the one you gave to Metzger to put under that meddlesome hotel worker's door."

Shylock looked at Bowen almost as if he were offended that the question even had to be posed.

"We have a history that reaches back to the Confederacy and before, One. We owe our existence and the work we're doing to the treasure that was entrusted to us and supports our organization now. It's that legacy that I believe deserves to be recognized, and the note was one way I chose to do that. I have others."

"Listen, Shylock," Bowen answered, "you're very good at what you do, but the language in that note was a little over the top. It also might lead someone to exactly where we don't want them to go—to the reason you just gave for writing it-to our organization. Now I've read "Cold Mountain" too, but no one speaks that way anymore. Our purpose was to frighten the man off, not to rewrite the Gettysburg Address. Next time let's keep the correspondence a little more current and a little more difficult to trace back to us."

Nine stared at Bowen for a moment, and then replied, "If that's what you wish," he said as he turned and walked away.

The meeting was adjourned, and Seventeen turned to the well-dressed man wearing the bow tie and a matching handkerchief in his jacket pocket still sitting at the table. "What the hell's with Sanjay and the scrubs, anyway? Does he think he's a doctor or something?"

Five answered with a slight smile but without turning his head. "Apparently he wears them all the time. He thinks of himself as a surgeon in the business of homicide, as I understand it."

* * *

Henry Louis and Sampson Weeks had spent the better part of three solid weeks in an effort to identify the body of the homicide victim. Initially the coroner had found little about the charred corpse that seemed helpful with the exception of one mark that she nearly overlooked during the preliminary examination. She called Weeks and Louis into the examination room in the early afternoon. Chavez and Lasansky were to join them in the lab within the hour.

"There's something here you should see. I almost missed it, this poor guy's such a mess. I've never seen one of these before, but maybe one of you has. Look," she said and gently raised the corpse's scorched arm high over its head. "What do you think?" she said, addressing both men.

The coroner's name was Kate Smith. Unlike her namesake, she was a wispy, waif-like woman with blonde hair, sharp features and piercing green eyes. Like most of the other doctors Louis knew these days, she seemed to be just under the legal drinking age, although hc knew she must be close to 35. She was attractive in a restless, high velocity sense, and while she moved swiftly and fitfully, there was obvious care and decisiveness in the movements of her hands and fingers.

Weeks, who had never been a fan of autopsies or corpses, was too far across the room to see anything, and he took pains to stay there. Louis bent closer and saw the faint traces of a tattoo. He asked for a magnifying glass.

"Those we have," Kate said and handed him a large stainless steel magnifier. Louis focused the glass and saw a tattoo of a small sword, less than three quarters of an inch long, with a blade from which flames seemed to be emanating. The blade wasn't straight, but irregular and undulating.

"Sam, come here and look at this." Weeks took a tentative step or two forward, said something about not having his glasses, and instantly retreated to the back of the room again. "You don't wear glasses, Sam," Louis said, smiling. Dr. Smith interrupted, pointing at the tiny tattoo. "Best I can tell it's supposed to be a sword or a knife or something." She waited.

"It's new to me," Louis said. "We'll do some research, ask around. Unless it's one of a kind, there must be some information out there about it. It's too unusual not to be mentioned somewhere by somebody in that business. We'll start with the local tattoo parlors. Then we'll try the same thing in Houston. That'll take some time, given the size of that city."

Three days earlier they had received a list of reported missing persons from the Texas Rangers. Dental records and fingerprints had confirmed the man's identity. Weeks commented that maybe Gil Grissom and CSI weren't so far off base after all. This had all happened in record time, not hours perhaps, but within a month.

The victim, they learned, was an investment banker from Houston named Brady Sullivan. His wife had reported him missing on a business trip several weeks earlier. Mr. Sullivan's career had been steady but unremarkable until shortly after September 11th, 2001, when his personal bank account and investment portfolio had inexplicably skyrocketed. In addition they knew that he was fifty-three years old, had been married for twenty-four years and had three children. Other than that, the man's life was an enigma. He was exceedingly private. What was known was that he attended the Baptist Church in the Houston suburb of Baytown, that he had few contacts outside of his business, and was thought of as a social recluse. He appeared to be a particularly devout member of his congregation, and was an "habitual tither", as Louis referred to those who happily surrendered one tenth of their earnings to the church.

"I think we can let the church of the hook on this one," Louis suggested. "Given Sullivan's income, they'd have to be nuts to ice him. It'd cost them almost seventy grand a year."

"I'll take that as sarcasm, Louis," his partner said. "But the police can't come up with anything that looks like a motive of any kind. And we sure don't have much to give them, either. The guy's a mystery man. His wife either knows nothing or won't give us anything. What's a guy from Houston doing in Midland, anyway? He had no reason to be here. His wife thought he was on a business trip to Dallas, and he ends up on our street char-broiled in the trunk of a car. It makes no sense at all."

"You two don't have much to work with," Kate offered quietly, "and I can't help you much. The only thing I can say for sure is that he was dead before the accident—unless you can do this to the back of your head yourself and then climb into the trunk of a car." She put her gloved hands on either side of the corpse's head and moved it gently to the left. "That's what killed him. Or at least it was a major contributor." She pointed at a spot on the back of Sullivan's head that had been spared from the fire and had been shaved.

"It's almost penetrated the skull," Louis said, looking at a wound almost an inch in diameter. Weeks began to show a bit more interest and actually moved several steps across the room. Then discretion took over and he retreated again.

"It's really a pretty serious dent," Smith said. "This could have been a hammer or some kind of interesting club like a golf club. Whatever it was, it came close to penetrating the skull and would likely have caused massive hemorrhaging."

"Well, we know three things," said Weeks, making for the door. "We know our dead guy is Brady Sullivan. We know he was murdered by someone who was inexperienced, sloppy or in a hurry, and we know the corpse has a strange tattoo. Do the first two remind anyone of anything?"

The door opened and Chavez entered with an older man. "This is Jim Lasansky," Chavez said, and the man crossed the room to shake hands with the two Crime Scene Investigators. He nodded politely to the coroner, acutely aware that her hands were occupied. "Nice to meet you all," he said softly, as if concerned that his normal speaking voice would disturb the presence on the table. "Sorry to interrupt. Please go on."

Louis resumed their previous conversation. "Do you mean sloppy homicides?" he asked. Kate Smith had already anticipated the question. "The others," she said quickly. "There have been two, a while ago. Both went unsolved. So you think there's a connection?"

"Could be," Weeks answered helpfully from across the room.

"Time to call in the Texas Rangers," said Louis, and then made the sound of a trumpet through his cupped hands.

"Are you enjoying yourself, Henry?" Weeks asked as the four men left the autopsy room and stood grouped in the corridor. He knew Louis hated his first name, and every now and again enjoyed firing off a well-aimed barb.

"It's a conundrum, Weeks, and that doesn't mean what you think it means." Louis knew that Weeks had a degree in Criminal Justice from Remington College in Fort Worth, but enjoyed giving the needle in return.

"Listen, I'm really not kidding, Weeks," he continued. "The Rangers have resources we can't even dream about. And they're good. And they specialize in cases that are going nowhere."

"Why don't you give us a chance?" Lasansky asked, emphasizing the word 'us'. "My partner isn't quite as optimistic as I am, but I'm sure we can make progress on this. The Rangers are busy spending a lot of time adjusting their Stetsons and polishing their boots and badges. They also have a pretty high opinion of themselves, not always deserved, I understand. No need to bring them in on this. We'll keep it on a front burner and keep you posted."

Lasansky was a burly man with sloping shoulders and a blond, thinning brush cut. His features were heavy and humorless. He wore a long sleeve shirt with a button-down collar and the top button loosened. His necktie was unknotted and hung loosely from his collar. The tie, Louis noted, was a combination of the most lurid colors he had ever seen on a single piece of fabric. It was a study in sheer tastelessness, he thought, though he considered himself far from a fashion plate.

As they left the building, Weeks turned to his partner and said, "I think she likes you, Henry."

"She likes bodies—dead ones, ones that aren't moving and can't talk back. That would seem to leave me out,"

"I'm not so sure" Sam responded.

"And don't call me Henry."

* * *

Back in Sherwood's apartment and following Dillinger's raspy and raucous welcome, both men settled into chairs opposite one another in the living room.

"You suggested at the motel that I knew more about Group Twenty than Metzger had told us. You remember?"

Archer sniffed his wine again suspiciously, said nothing and nodded.

"Well, I did know a few things about them. At least I knew they existed. Actually, they're relatively easy to find, if you know where to look. What I didn't know was some of the specifics that Metzger let us in on." He felt slightly uncomfortable ending the sentence with a preposition. Archer said nothing.

"Do you want something to eat?" Sherwood added quickly. "There's a lot to digest here, no pun intended."

"No thanks. Just open the shades and let some light in, please. Figuratively, I mean."

"These people—Group Twenty," he began. "We do know some things about them. We know that they guard their turf and their identity carefully, and that very few people really know or care about who they are or what they do. This appears to be crucial to their mission. We also know that they have certain well-defined objectives. It's apparent that should those objectives became known, it would threaten their entire organization. At the very least, if they were exposed they would have to restructure and reorganize, which would cost them time and money, to say nothing of the reputation they've worked so hard to build for well over one hundred years." He paused for his words to take effect. When Archer said nothing, he continued.

"The name Group Twenty has an interesting history, Arch. It's apparently derived from an old Charlie Chaplin Film, "The Great Dictator", that came out in 1940 just before the start of World War II. Chaplin plays the part of Adolph Hitler. It's a satire, and a pretty brilliant one in its own way. You'll have to watch it some time. In one scene, in a caricature of Hitler, Chaplin stands under a huge symbol of the Roman numeral XX, which is supposed to represent the NAZI swastika. He has the little mustache, the hair, the Nazi salute, the whole thing."[5] He paused and drew a pair of large XX's on the napkin in front of him, then continued.

"As you well know, my over-educated friend, X is the Roman numeral for 10, and double X stands for twenty, which has become the emblem of the Group."

"I am familiar with Roman numerals, Sherwood."

Sherwood smiled and continued. "Let me fill this out completely. The word 'Group' is taken from the German word 'Gruppe'. A 'Gruppe' was a small, elite military unit in the German Wehrmacht during the Second World War. So Group Twenty, loosely translated, is designed to be a clever emulation of a World War II Nazi military unit."

Archer interrupted him. "Hold on for a moment." He rose and went to Sherwood's desk. "May I?" he asked, and held up a pencil and a pad of paper. "I think it might be best if I took some notes."

"Be my guest," Sherwood answered. "Now, where were we?"

"We weren't anywhere. You were describing a group of Nazi imitators who like to watch Charlie Chaplin movies. I don't doubt your sincerity, Sherwood, but you must admit that this stretches the imagination a bit," he said dubiously. "You're suggesting that a group of twenty successful, grown men are playing Nazi? In beautiful, downtown Midland, Texas? Are these people white supremacists as well?"

"No. There's absolutely no evidence that I've found which would indicate that." He tipped the wine glass to his lips. The lamp behind him shone translucently through his large ears. "These guys don't appear to have any direct connections to white supremacists at all."

"The term suspension of disbelief comes to my mind here, S.T."

---

[5] See Appendix 5

"Be that as it may, it's all quite true, best I can tell. And there's more." Sherwood added. "The tattoo you asked about on Metzger's neck—the two overlapping X's." He pointed at the symbol he'd drawn on the napkin again. "Anyone connected with Group Twenty, even a temporary employee, is required to get that tattoo. I guess you could call it a form of indelible identification. It also distinguishes them from the senior members of the Group. There are about two dozen of those, and they are also tattooed to distinguish them from their subordinates.

"And that tattoo would be?" Archer asked, an undertone of doubt still in his voice.

"The flaming sword that Metzger described. It's the symbol of the inner circle, and they're the ones who make the decisions, or at least are empowered to carry the decisions out."

"What decisions, and why a flaming sword?" the Parson asked.

"One question at a time, Arch. The concept of the flaming sword is derived from another German word, Flammenschwert, which in English translates as "flame blade"[6]. The blade shape is undulating, or wave-shaped, and most often they were used as two-handed swords. They're also called flammard, in French. They're pretty familiar, and you've probably seen them in museums or collections that specialize in 16th century weapons. In the case of this tattoo, flames have been added around the blade of the sword. But that's not historically a part of the Flammenschwert. It's purely an innovation on the part of our Group Twenty."

"I'd prefer it if you didn't call them 'our' Group Twenty", Archer said. "So far I find I've developed no meaningful relationship with them whatsoever."

"I'll refrain in the future."

"Well, if accurate, all of this is fascinating," Archer said, "but where does it all lead?"

"It all leads quite simply to the fact that I know too much, and they'll now no doubt try to kill me, and most likely you as well."

A somewhat subdued Archer sat quietly while the further complexities of Group Twenty were explained to him in detail.

"Group Twenty heads up a large network of smaller units that are divided into three groups," Sherwood began. He took a legal pad from the table beside him and wrote three names in large, precise letters. Then he explained each of the names in turn.

---

[6] See Appendix 6

"Each one of these names is derived from Nazi units formed and deployed during World War II. SIPO stands for Sicherheitspolizei. It's a very small, elite security arm of the Group. Their responsibility is to ensure that the security of Group Twenty is not threatened. They have people in place in organizations across the country whose job it is simply to watch and listen. Should they hear of anything that hints of a threat to the Group, they report it to the KRIPO, the Kriminalpolizei. I don't think I need to translate the name. Anyway, if they receive news of a threat, the Kriminalpolizei sends an anonymous representative to a closed meeting of Group Twenty, reports the suspected violation, and waits for instructions as to how to respond. It has all characteristics of a paramilitary unit, but with skilled and effective leadership. There's nothing haphazard here. It's a well-oiled, well-run machine with a defined mission."

"What is this last one? Posse comitatus?" The Parson asked pointing at the last of the three names and suddenly quite serious.

"That's the bottom of the ladder. It's described as . . . Wait a minute." He rose and picked up a thick binder across the room. After thumbing through a number of pages, he read; 'a loosely organized, far right social movement that opposes the United States federal government and believes in localism.' It really should say it opposes the federal government as currently constituted, but Wikipedia is only as good as its sources," he added. "Actually, Posse charters were originally issued in 1969 in Portland, Oregon by a man named Henry Lamont Beach, a retired dry cleaner and one time member of the "Silver Shirts." Silver Shirts was another Nazi-affiliated organization that was established in America after Hitler took power in Germany. My, oh my, you know it's a wonderful country when dry cleaners and pest control people can rise to the top like foam on a beer." There was no amusement in his expression or voice.

"Anyway, the Silver Shirts eventually gave rise to both survivalism and the formation of paramilitary militias in this country. And right in the middle of this whole thing we have Texas. In 1997 the so-called 'Republic of Texas' published a manifesto declaring that the annexation of Texas as a state in 1845 was illegal. I repeat, in 1997 Texas was affirming its belief in its independence from the Union—once again, almost 150 years after the Civil War."

"That's a bit chilling, I will admit," Archer agreed. "Texas certainly seems to be dancing to its own music. But tell me, how does this Posse comitatus fit into the picture? It would seem to me to be a completely separate entity, if it's an entity at all. What is their agenda?"

"Their agenda, to use your term, is quite simply to do two things; to blow up things and to hurt people, maybe not in that order." Again there was no smile.

"For instance," the Parson pressed ahead.

"Well, you remember the Oklahoma city bombing in 1995. McVeigh, Nichols and the Fortier brothers were all said to be members of Posse comitatus. Eric Rudolf, who was responsible for the Atlanta Olympic bombing in 1997, apparently was as well. And there have been any number of other, unrelated things—police officers shot, small scale bombings, failed bombings, fires, and so on. It's impossible to know how many, but it's likely that the Posse played a role in a majority of them. No doubt some of them were also rogue incidents—loonies acting on their own in the interest of a better America."

"So these people run around blowing up people and things. To what end?" Archer asked. "What's their purpose?"

"Their purpose is to carry out Group Twenty's purpose—to disrupt the workings of our system and to create fear. In some ways you can compare it to the suicide bombings in Iraq, minus the suicide part. It's their way of making a statement, attracting recruits, and building an organization that will have the power to cause dysfunction at all levels of the federal government. Think al-Qaeda," Sherwood said soberly. "But most important, I believe, is that the Posse's ultimate purpose is to be available," he concluded.

"Available for exactly what?" Archer asked in a subdued voice.

"I'll get to that in a minute. But let's back up for a moment. Although Posse comitatus is technically at the bottom of the power hierarchy, they are also at the very heart of the movement," Sherwood explained. "As I understand it, Group Twenty exercises a vigilant level of relaxed control over the Posse, you might say, and I know that sounds like an oxymoron," he added, certain that Archer would pick up on it.

"They're apparently allowed to do pretty much whatever they want to do, as long as they understand the limits of their independence. They run around in camouflage outfits in the woods preparing for what they call the Big Event, whatever that is. There is no effort to bring them into the fold directly, but great pains are taken to send a signal to their representatives that they have influence on the goals and successes of Group Twenty. This is in fact something of a joke, but it does act to keep a pretty large, dangerous and potentially very useful group of subversives and malcontents off center stage for the time being, while at the same time having them available at a moments notice."

"I'll repeat", Archer asked. "Available for what?" This time it didn't sound like a question.

"Available to support a unified effort to take the reins of government from the hands of those currently holding power," Sherwood said simply. "Available to help change the very structure of the country when the time comes."

"That's either called an election or a revolution to my way of thinking." Archer's reply sounded humorous, but his demeanor was deadly serious.

"Not necessarily a revolution," Sherwood replied. "It could be called a number of things. Something fairly similar was called secession in the 1850's and 1860's. It can also be called the normal, natural transfer of political power, if it's worked carefully enough and through the right channels."

"What you're describing sounds a great deal like the Lernaean Hydra," Archer suggested, calling on his substantial and typically useless reserve of mythological knowledge. "It had half a dozen heads, and everyone of them breathed poison, as I remember. It was so lethal that even its footprints were poisonous. You'll have me believing in dragons before your done with this."

"I'll take your word for the Hydra, but poisonous footprints or not, Group Twenty and its tentacles make for an very dangerous adversary. It's streamlined, efficient, and consists of a significant number of very angry and very alienated citizens."

"Money," Archer said suddenly. "This sounds like a very expensive game. Where does the money come from to support all this activity? Texas has oil money and Ross Perot and the Dallas Cowboys and the Mavericks, but this game sounds bigger than that."

"This is no game, I can assure you, and chasing down the money is what I've been after all these years."

He rose and retrieved a wine bottle from the kitchen and filled two glasses. Archer was particularly pleased with the liquid reprieve given the direction of the conversation and despite the quality of the wine. He didn't even hazard a glance at the label this time.

"The money, where it went and how it was used are the reasons I've followed Jefferson Davis's route from Richmond south with so much interest," Sherwood said, then paused, stretching out his long, bony, bare forearms in front of him. Looking at them critically and then at Archer, he abruptly shifted the subject of the conversation to a lighter one.

"You know, speaking of tattoos, I've never quite understood them. You voluntarily pay to let some inked-up ruffian drive a needle under your skin for forty-five minutes. For that privilege you suffer both physical and financial pain. You end up with a strange design that you thought was incredibly meaningful at a young age, but which doesn't mean much of anything twenty-five years later. Then your skin and the tattoo decide to age at different rates. After thirty years you find yourself with a meaningless and basically unrecognizable blur of ink on your arm, and everybody, including you, wonders what it is and why you got it in the first place."

Archer couldn't stop himself from smiling. "We weren't speaking of tattoos, but I do have two suggestions, Sherwood. First, I don't think it would be prudent to bring the subject up in front of Uncle Desmond. Second, in your case, and with your wingspan, I suggest it would be ludicrous for you to cover that vast expanse with tattoos, if that's what you're considering. I would, however, encourage you to consider a single example of the art from your shoulder to your wrist. That would of course be Jeff Davis's journey from Richmond to Georgia, with all the stops in between. That way you'd have a built-in cartographer's dream right there with you all the time, and you wouldn't have to carry notes or draw maps from memory when you recount your quest—Don Quixote." He stopped, smiling at the image of Sherwood Tualatin, spindly arms and legs thrashing, caught up in the arms of a windmill.

"Uncle Desmond? Who is Uncle Desmond?" Sherwood interrupted his thoughts.

"Uncle Des is quite likely our deliverance, Sherwood. Just think 'deus ex machina.'"

* * *

The wine bottle empty, Sherwood made a large pot of coffee. He didn't normally drink coffee in the evening, but this was proving to be a long haul. He poured a cup for each of them and went into the annex, returning with a piece of white poster board approximately 8 by 12 inches. On it, Archer saw, was a larger and more legible map of most of the eastern half of the country, similar to the one Sherwood had roughly sketched at Harry's, but this one had the appearance of something professionally prepared.

The map extended from the far eastern tip of the Chesapeake Bay to the Gulf of Mexico. Sherwood explained that he had used MapQuest, and by inputting towns he knew Davis had traveled through along the route, MapQuest had plotted out the route. The map was conveniently marked by letters, from A to H, which indicated each of those towns.[7] He had glued the map to a piece of poster board to better preserve it. He also brought a notepad filled with notes and scribbling to accompany it.

He abruptly swept the small dining table clear and put the map down so that he and Archer could study it together. Then he extended his head over the map like a gooseneck lamp and turned to speak.

"I don't want to be patronizing, Arch, but humor me for a few minutes. I know we've talked about Davis's route from Richmond south in general terms, but there are some specifics that you need to know. Forgive me. This is going to sound a lot like a combination history and geography lesson. I'll try not to be overbearing."

"You're forgiven. You'd have been even more forgiven if you hadn't run out of that unpleasant wine of yours."

"I'll do better next time, both in terms of quantity and quality. Now, bear with me, please." Sherwood held the poster board map in front of Virgil. He moved his finger along a route that ran roughly from north to southwest as he spoke.

"I'm afraid a lot of this is going to be old hat, but bear with me. It's relevant to everything we've been talking about. Jeff Davis left Richmond on April 2nd, 1865, and headed generally southwest to Danville, Virginia. Shortly after he left a second train followed, and that was the train that carried the financial assets of the Confederacy. This is what's been called the 'treasure train,' rumored to be worth from five to seven million dollars at that time in paper currency, gold, silver coins and specie. Other estimates made at the time put the figure a great deal higher. I'll get into those later." He reached for another notebook and leafed through it until he found the page that was pertinent.

"A Confederate Naval officer whose name was Captain William Parker was in charge of the train and the assets. When he reached his destination, he was instructed to turn the assets over to John Reagan, president's Davis's Postmaster-General. That much is historical fact . . ."

---

[7] See Appendix 7

"Two questions," Archer interrupted. "Explain to me exactly what "specie" meant at the time, and tell me what this captain's destination was."

"I'll answer the second question first, but I'll have to jump ahead to do it. On May 2nd, Davis left Cokesbury, South Carolina and rode into Abbeville, a short distance away. Captain Parker was waiting for him there. Parker, according to the records kept at the time, turned the treasure he carried over to Postmaster General John Reagan." Turning from his notes, he looked at Archer. "My father insists that I'm supposed to be related in some way to Reagan, but let's not get into that now. In any event Reagan was the last man known to have been in possession of the assets of the Confederate treasury. Now to the first question, which is easier. Specie is what is commonly called hard money—coins, silver and gold bullion."

"Thank you. Now back to your geography lesson." Archer said.

"As an aside, Arch, and an important one, Parker proposed that he and three of his officers leave with Davis and escape to the west coast of Florida, where they might find a boat and sail to Cuba or the Bahamas. Davis refused, because he had long entertained the idea of going directly to Texas and continuing the conflict against the Union from there. It's important to remember that to Jeff Davis the war was not yet lost, even with Lee's surrender at Appomattox on April 9th. He fully intended to continue the conflict somehow, and that required an escape plan and plenty of money."

Taking a deep breath, Sherwood continued, moving his finger slowly along the line he had drawn. "Davis travelled in a southwesterly direction towards Greensboro, Salisbury and Charlotte, North Carolina. He continued into South Carolina through Union, Goldsboro, then Abbeville." He looked up at Archer. "That brings us back to May 2nd." He pointed to the map at a spot roughly situated between Greenville to the north and Augusta to the south. "There; Abbeville. After Abbeville, still heading to the southwest, Davis moved on to Warrenton, Georgia, travelling through Sandersville, Dublin and finally reaching Irwinville." Again his finger moved along the map until it finally rested on a spot just north of Tifton. "That brought him to a place that lies about 110 miles due north of Tallahassee, Florida. He as captured in Irwinville on May 10, 1865." He paused and waited.

"Then the obvious question arises," Archer said. "Where is the money?"

"Exactly. But let's back up again for just a second so that we can finish the story. On May 5th, Davis and the few men still travelling with him made camp near Sandersonville, Georgia. On that day he met with his wife, Varina, after the two had not seen one another for more than a month. Several days later, on May 7, Colonel Robert Minty, Union Commander of the Second Cavalry Division, was ordered to 'make immediate arrangements to prevent the escape of Jefferson Davis across the Ocmulgee and Flint Rivers, south of Macon.'" Sherwood paused and looked at his friend. "You see, they were restricting Davis's options to the east and west. As a result the only route left for him was almost due south." Another pause, this time for effect.

"Then On May 8th, Davis left his family and rode to Abbeville, where his family subsequently caught up with him. As it was late in the day, he decided to join up with Varina's wagon train and make camp near Irwinville. They camped in a grove of pine trees, but for some reason did not set up a defensive perimeter. On the next day, Davis decided to leave the camp, but not until late in the afternoon. No one seems to know why he waited until it was nearly dark, but in the meantime, and unknown to him, a mounted detachment of the Fourth Michigan Cavalry regiment was closing in on Irwinville and his encampment." Again he paused briefly, referred to his notepad again and looked at his friend.

"The rest is history, Arch. Davis was captured after a brief skirmish. He was wearing a simple raglan overcoat at the time, known as a "waterproof." He was spotted by a Union trooper who ordered him to halt and surrender. Davis briefly considered mounting his horse and fleeing—he was a superb horseman—but Varina rushed up beside him, and the opportunity was lost."

"I remember," said Archer smiling, "and he was wearing a dress."

"There was no dress involved, Arch, and you know it," Sherwood said instinctively responding to the jibe. "In any event, as you also know, on May 10, more than a hundred men and officers of the 4th Michigan Cavalry regiment led by Lt. Col. B.D. Pritchard captured the president of the Confederacy. There was no sign of the Confederate treasure."

"Not one in Davis's group was injured, if memory serves," Archer continued Sherwood's account for him. "But as I remember the Union troops suffered a number of casualties. They mistook one another for Southerners and opened fire—friendly fire, it's called now, although there seems very little friendly about it. Anyway, I am certainly familiar with most of this. And not to be impatient, but could you move on to something a bit less concerned with names, dates, towns, and counties? There is a point here, I imagine." There was more than a hint of impatience in the Parson's voice.

"There are a few more facts to go over before we're finished, and they're important ones. More coffee?" Sherwood asked.

Archer shook his head.

"Let me show you a couple of things." Sherwood returned to his notes. "On Wednesday, April 27, 1865, Secretary of War Stanton sent this telegraph to Union Major General George Thomas regarding the treasure that Davis—or Reagan—was supposed to be carrying. Here." Sherwood handed a typewritten sheet to Archer, who read aloud.

> *'The following is an extract from a telegram received this morning from General Halleck, at Richmond: 'The bankers have information to-day that Jeff. Davis' specie is moving south from Goldsborough in wagons as fast as possible. I suggest that commanders be telegraphed through General Thomas . . . to take measures to intercept the rebel chiefs, and their plunder. The specie is estimated at $6,000,000 to $13,000,000" (S)pare no exertion to stop Davis and his plunder. Push the enemy as hard as you can in every direction.'*

Archer stopped reading, handed the sheet of paper back to Sherwood. "That is certainly a substantial amount of money. A penny or two more than the five to seven million you mentioned earlier."

"There's more still," Sherwood said enthusiastically, and slid two additional sheets across the table. Again the Parson read:

> *'General Thomas forwarded Stanton's telegram to Major General George Stoneman, then dispatched a second more urgent telegram to Stoneman:*
> *'If you can possibly get three brigades of cavalry together, send them across the mountains into South Carolina to the westward of Charlotte and toward Anderson. They may possibly catch Jeff. Davis, or some of his treasure. They say he is making off with from $2,000,000 to $5,000,000 in gold. You can send Tillson to take Asheville, and I think the railroad will be safe during his absence. Give orders to your troops to take no orders except those from you, from me, and from General Grant.'*

"It looks like General Thomas has come up short between three and eight million dollars," Archer said with amusement.

"This is the last one, I promise." With the lamp situated as it was, Archer found himself again fascinated by the way the light shone through Sherwood's oversized left ear as he leaned over the table.

"One can hope," Archer answered dryly. Then he read:

> *'The existence of caches of hidden or lost Confederate gold has been the source of numerous Georgia legends. These legends are fueled by the fact that the state of Georgia was a hub of gold mining, minting, and trading and that, as Richmond, Virginia, fell to Union forces at the end of the Civil War (1861-1865), the bulk of the Confederate treasury was brought to Georgia, where much of it disappeared . . . other specie could be found in Civil War Georgia. Gold from civilians made Macon second only to Richmond as a Confederate depository.'*

As he finished he stood, walked to the kitchen and emptied his coffee cup in the sink. "Too much information, S.T. I'd really like to know where this is headed. It's past my bedtime."

"Mine as well," Sherwood answered, and began to read again from his notepad. "I've done a bit of research. This is hard to pin down exactly, for any number of reasons, but from what I can come up with one million in 1865 dollars could now be worth as much as sixty million, and that may be low-balling it. So let's say we play with both of the General's estimates and come up with an acceptable midpoint. I vote for a conservative, middle-of-the-road six million. How does that strike you?"

"Fair enough." Archer said, no longer looking so bored.

"That would bring the value of the Confederate treasury to well over five hundred million in today's dollars. But even more interesting is this question. What do you think specie—the gold or silver coins that were in the train—be worth to a collector today? "We're talking about coins struck in the south by the Confederacy during the war. I submit their value would be nearly incalculable."

"Six hundred million dollars would certainly pad one's checking account nicely, but it's hardly a great deal of money in terms of today's billionaires." Archer suggested. "Think of Bill Gates. His net worth is over sixty billion, one hears, and even his friend Paul Allen isn't exactly impoverished. I think he's in the ballpark of fourteen billion. As they say, that's a nice ballpark."

"You're in the wrong ballpark, Arch. That six million represented the Confederate Treasury. It was paying for a war—training, arms, ammunition, supplies, wagons, horses. Translate that into today's situation in Iraq or Afghanistan. How much do you think it costs to carry on a war today for a year in current dollars? That's the neighborhood that you should be playing in."

"I admit I didn't play in many ballparks as a youngster, but I think your analogy requires revision, or at least modification. The South didn't have to be concerned about aircraft and aircraft carriers, nuclear weaponry, tanks, drones, or any of those intriguing creations that we now seem to feel required to carry in our military arsenals. Even our foot soldiers are equipped with paraphernalia that would make a Civil War soldier look Paleolithic by comparison. Those are the contrivances that represent the enormity of the real cost of waging war today."

"I take your point. Modern equipment is expensive. But, in comparative terms, the costs are in many ways equivalent. The manufacture and maintenance of equipment—rifles, artillery pieces, horses, food, ammunition and the rest of it, were extraordinarily costly to both the Union and the South, and the correlation between that and the cost of equipment in modern warfare is an absolutely plausible one. Perhaps not exact, but comparable." Despite his best efforts, Sherwood sensed he had been subtly outmaneuvered.

"That would be an interesting discussion I'd gladly leave for another time, Sherwood, but it's beyond the scope of our subject for the moment. Wherever all this has led us, I think we've pursued it far enough." Archer was a uniquely skilled debater, and his smile was a reflection of the fact that he felt he had scored sufficiently well to be able to retire from the arena gracefully. "I would, however, be genuinely interested in briefly pursuing the question of the hypothetical value of Confederate coins and specie today, should either one still exist. One coin, for example a five dollar gold piece of Confederate manufacture. Where would you put its value? You have a great deal of familiarity with artifacts of that period." The words sounded very much like an attempt to salve a challenger's self-esteem after a thorough drubbing. Aware of his friend's unintentional tendency to sometimes appear condescending, Sherwood expected this was the case.

"I'm not an expert here, Arch. I'm not sure anyone is. But one five dollar gold piece from the treasury of the Confederate States of America, providing it had appropriate provenance, might bring several thousand dollars or more from the right collector. Several coins, or, for the sake of argument, a million dollars worth of coins—well, you do the math. Of course you would have to offer them cautiously, and over a period of time," he paused. "And be very sure of your buyer. But collectors are a deranged group, I can assure you of that from personal experience. Many of those who can afford these things can be downright greedy. And Confederate specie would bring in the heavy hitters. They tend to operate on a "must have" basis, and then the sky's the limit. That's the kind of thing that drives auctions as well."

"Interesting, interesting." Archer was working numbers through his head. "But one must assume that the gold and silver, wherever it ended up, was sold or melted down and the money spent decades ago. There can be little doubt that it's gone now—the cash drawer is empty."

"Unless, my erudite friend, the funds were invested wisely initially. Then only the interest need be spent and the corpus would remain protected. If the investments mirrored the growth and returns of the stock market over a hundred and fifty year period, you're talking about an enormous amount of income generated—not to mention the borrowing power of the corpus if it remains in tact. And imagine if Group Twenty had in its ranks past and present a competent fundraiser or two at any point in time. What if individuals or groups interested in the future of the south were approached to support the cause over the years? Think about Texas money alone—oil, venture capital, on and on. Imagine what those coffers could look like now, as the result of one hundred and fifty years of effective fundraising."

Archer stood, yawning. "That's an interesting concept that we can delve into at a time when coffee replaces wine as the stimulant of choice. But for now, time for all good men to go to bed." He stood and turned to his lanky friend. Sherwood rose awkwardly and stretched, his long arms and bony knees incongruously highlighted by his shorts and short-sleeved shirt.

"Speaking of wine and coffee, what a combination," Archer continued. "I'm caught in the middle of a running battle for supremacy between the two of them right now. I certainly hope the caffeine doesn't get the upper hand. In any event I'll let my bed make that decision."

"I'll go down in the elevator with you."

Archer looked Sherwood up and down with a critical eye. "It's cold out. You might try a pair of long pants and a jacket for a change," he suggested, and pushed the down button for the elevator.

"It's balmy," Sherwood replied, which ended the matter.

They reached the bottom floor, and as the elevator door began to open, something clattered through small the gap in the door and bounced noisily off the back wall. Then there was a soft 'pop', a small puff of smoke, and both men turned and looked at each other.

* * *

"I tell you, I seen the whole thing." The boy who spoke sat in front of Weeks, Louis and Lasansky in the corner of a small office in the Midland Police Department. He looked uncomfortable and was slumped deep in his chair. The boy seemed to want to disappear. Sixteen or seventeen years old, he was sallow-complected and victimized by a virulent case of acne. His baseball cap was worn with the visor turned sideways, a mannerism that always confused Louis. He was baffled that anyone could regard it, or by the same token pants dangling precariously below the pelvis, as either engaging or appealing. He was no prude. In his younger days he had experimented briefly but hazardously with motorcycles, raced an old sports car unproductively, and come as close as he dared to emulating James Dean in "Rebel Without a Cause." The word cool in his world was leather jackets, blue jeans, engineer boots, wide belts, and an arrogant swagger, all habits that had been inherited from his older brother. But this new look, which he supposed was designed to meet the modern standard of cool, amused him. It was disarranged, muddled and untidy, like a partially made bed, but at the same time it was intentional. To complete the effect, the boy was nurturing a ragged patch of facial hair that also failed to work in his favor. It was at moments like these that Louis was very glad not to have teenage male children.

"Son," Weeks said, and the boy slumped even deeper into the chair. "We need more than a glimpse from around the corner of a dumpster. You must have been thirty yards away and it was real early in the morning, not even real light yet."

The young man tried an unsuccessful scowl in response. "I tell you, man, I seen it and I can even identify the dude. There's like a streetlight near where he stopped the car. He looked all around before he got out, and that's when I got like a real good look. He was a little guy, short, kind of skinny. He had on, you know, like doctor's clothes. Then he opened the trunk and like poured some stuff in it out of a can. Then he tossed a match in and slammed the trunk and ran like hell. There was like a whoosh sound and then boom—it like just exploded."

He paused, and Lasansky said, "Go ahead. What happened next?

"Anyway, he got out of there real fast, running. I was like watching the car and the fire so I lost sight of him.

"What about the can he had?" Weeks asked. "Did he throw it away? Did he run with it?"

"I dunno," the boy answered, pulling at his scraggy van Dyke, "but I'm pretty sure I seen headlights down the road a minute later and heard a car start up—from where he was like running to."

"This guy—what did he look like?" Lasansky asked, his voice as soft and gentle as if he were at a wake.

"Like I said, a little, skinny guy. He had kind of dark skin and like a curved, pointy nose."

"Dark skin," Weeks said. "Dark like mine?"

"Jeez, no, not as . . ." The boy stopped, realizing that he was on treacherous ground. "No, sir," he added quickly.

"Dark like what? This table, coffee, honey, molasses, tea?" Sam asked, although he doubted that the boy had any knowledge of the kind of tea he meant.

"Like honey, more or less, sir," said the boy, suddenly very polite. "But look," he added, and pulled out a battered cell phone, "I got a picture of him."

Weeks took the cell phone and looked at the photo. It was a blurry shot of a figure that appeared to be standing next to a small, non-descript automobile. The figure was leaning into the driver's side door and seemed to reaching inside. Weeks could make out no skin color or features from the picture.

"Why'd you take a picture?" Lasansky asked, leaning forward. The sound of his voice made Louis realize that he was turning up the pressure. No longer gentle, it had a harsh edge and was intensified by his posture.

"I take a lot of pictures at night, man. That's when interesting stuff happens, you know," the boy said relaxing a little.

"How far away were you? This makes it look like you were pretty close."

"There's a dumpster in the corner of the parking lot," the boy answered, clearly relaxing. "I was sitting behind it when the guy drove in, so I was like pretty close."

"Sitting behind a dumpster in an empty parking lot at almost six in the morning? What we're you doing, reading the 'The Odyssey' by flashlight?" Weeks asked, a knowing smile on his face.

"I was just smoking . . ." the boy paused, reddened perceptibly, then continued. "Like I just wanted a cigarette," he answered defensively, sensing he was digging himself into a hole.

"One of those funny cigarettes you roll yourself?" Louis asked, his voice indicated that he was enjoying this turn of events. "Early morning is as nice a time as any for a little weed."

"No, man," the boy answered, clearly disconcerted. "No, man. I don't smoke that shi . . . stuff. Just like an ordinary cigarette," he offered lamely.

Weeks paused, remembering that the boy was volunteering and not under investigation. "We appreciate your coming in, son, but we'll have to keep this for a while." He held up the cell phone. "We may be able to enhance the photo and make out some details."

"Hey, wait a minute . . . sir." Again the word 'sir' was added after an awkward pause. "What am I gonna do without my phone? How are my friends like gonna get ahold of me? Let me just email the picture to you."

"Try a pay phone or a land line," Weeks said, not trying to be too unkind.

"We'll keep the phone for a few days, download the picture, and you'll get it back before you even miss it," Louis added.

"A week or so?" the boy lamented, sounding as if he'd been sentenced to an extended prison sentence. "C'mon dude," he added, palms out imploringly.

Louis could, to a large extent, put aside his normal distaste for the boy's dress and mannerisms. He reminded himself that he was prehistoric as far as his sense of propriety was concerned, and also that the boy was volunteering to identify a murderer. If only these kids could learn to dress and speak like rational human beings. He sighed audibly and let his thoughts return to the problem at hand. "I'll tell you what," he said. "You drop the 'dude' stuff and I'll do my best to speed it up. I'm a Crime Scene Investigator, and not a dude to you or anyone else. I'll go along with man, but dude's out."

The boy cringed and looked at his feet, not knowing how to answer. Louis softened. "It'll do you a world of good, son," he said, his tone almost kindly. "Maybe you can read a book or something while you're waiting for your phone."

"Man, like maybe a week?" the boy repeated as if in acute physical pain.

Weeks smiled. "I guess we can't call you," he said, looking at the cell phone, "but why don't you drop by on Thursday afternoon? We'll do our best to have it finished up by then."

"You can't do it now?' the boy persevered.

"Thursday afternoon," Weeks said more firmly. "We're not a photo lab. We'll see you then." He rose, opened the door and escorted the boy out. He turned to his partner and said, "I don't think we'll get anything from this photo. Dark skin and a pointy nose?" His tone was incredulous. "There's no way you can make out any of that from the picture."

"He may have had a good, long look, Sam," Louis said. "And that cell phone—it's pretty well beat-up, and they don't take very good pictures anyway. A little guy with sort of dark skin and a pointy nose," he said shaking his head. "Good luck. Incidentally, Chavez says Hudson's all for involving the Texas Rangers. I think the Chief feels the department is overwhelmed when they have a traffic stop and a cat in a tree on the same day." He looked at Lasansky. "And to add to the situation, Chavez called and there's a second body. It was found in another jurisdiction, but Chavez thinks it's connected to our case here."

"So Midland's not involved?" Weeks asked.

"So far they're not, and there hasn't been a whole lot of volunteering, either."

Lasansky interrupted, and the hard edge was back in his voice. He leaned forward aggressively. "Chavez isn't here, and he's not always the best source of information. We know about the second case, and we're following up on it. And let's not turn this into a pissing contest, Louis. Not a good idea with me, I promise." Louis glared at him in response.

"Do they have any information about the victim?" Weeks interjected, trying to alleviate the growing tension between the two men.

There was a long, uncomfortable pause. Then Louis responded. "Just a body, and apparently enough was done to it to make identification tough. Anyway, I think I'll get in touch with the Rangers about our Houston guy and see if they can get any information on him. They tend to be all over murder cases that are just too tough for the local authorities to handle." He looked pointedly at Lasansky. "It would seem pretty much everything is too tough for the good old Midland P.D. these days, and there's bound to be another cat in a tree soon to add to their troubles."

"You're not going to quit, are you?" Lasansky said, this time both the voice and the posture had grown ominous.

Weeks stood up quickly, his size enough to discourage the situation from growing more hostile. "Enough, please," he said, his physical presence dominating the room. "This is getting pretty childish. We're all on the same team, unless I missed a briefing or something. Now declare peace, or at least a temporary cease-fire. The case is more important than marking territory."

Both men looked ashamed, but neither responded. Finally Weeks broke the silence.

"Back to the matter at hand, there are lots of reasons our guy may interest the Rangers," he continued, "and solving the case is, after all, the issue here. We've got an identified victim and we know that whoever did this was pretty sloppy about it—either an amateur or someone in a hurry. You might call it a classic case of underkill," he said, pleased with the word he'd just coined. "They might find it pretty easy to step in and get it solved quickly. They're sure not against taking credit whenever they can get it." He looked at Lasansky. "When they're not adjusting their ten gallon hats and polishing their badges, I mean." The effort to lighten the mood fell flat.

"You want the Rangers, you go ahead and get the Rangers. And despite the fact that you two think we're a bunch of incompetents here, we've got a lot of years of experience aimed at solving this case." Lasansky paused. "And we'll get it solved, that I promise you." He abruptly left the room.

An accusatory silence surged in behind him. Weeks broke it and said, "What the hell have you got against those guys, anyway, Louis? They do their job, at least they try, and if they're understaffed, it's not their fault. Why can't you give them a break?"

"O.K., Sam, listen. They foul up crime scenes, they overlook evidence and witnesses, they pursue false leads and end up accusing the wrong person, and that's just when they're warming up. If you and I could get into the field once in a while, the way C.S.I. guys do all the time on TV, we could tie things up in half the time it takes them. And in the process, we'd preserve the evidence and get the right man."

"You mean 'person.' I understand the frustration, Henry," Weeks said, "but it's not going to help the case if we're playing on different teams here. Try working with them. You might even end up liking it."

Louis looked at him sourly, and then softened and changed the subject. "My money's still on the wife," he said, changing the subject completely. "If the Rangers take it on, I'll tell them they should go there first. Either he or she was having an affair, or there's a million dollar insurance policy on his life, or she just plain didn't like him. That's my bet."

"That doesn't surprise me, given the way you feel about women. Man, Trudy really messed you up, didn't she?"

"It's common sense, Sam. It's always the wife—or the husband. Don't you ever watch any of those true crime programs? This one's a slam-dunk, mark my words. And let's leave Trudy out of it."

* * *

Bowen stood at the table trying to decide whether or not to sit down. It was to be a short meeting, and the pain involved in bending his leg often sucked the breath from his lungs. He hated the knowledge that it showed on his face, and he hated the grunts that escaped from his lungs when he attempted to rise or sit. His voice and his features simply joined forces to betray him.

The pain had kept him company since his time in the service in 1972. He never discouraged the speculation that it was the result of a combat wound. When asked, he refused to discuss his injury, a response taken as stoicism by his friends and associates. In truth, he had been a supply sergeant in North Carolina during the war, and had never left the country. He had, in fact, been one of the best personally supplied supply sergeants in the United States Army. Also, he had neither volunteered to join the infantry nor to go to Vietnam.

The injury was the result of an evening of senseless over-indulgence at the end of his third year of service. He had managed to better his previous record of nine boilermakers, or what he and his buddies called beer and a bump, in Fayetteville one night. On the way back to the barracks his stomach mutinied, and he exited the car almost before the Specialist driving managed to pull over. Stumbling into a field, his sonar inoperative, he failed to notice in his sozzled state that he had tottered into an old artillery impact zone. The ground suddenly disappeared and he abruptly dropped more than four feet into a shell crater. More accurately, he stepped, confidently pickled, into a four-foot void, landing with his left leg straight in front of him, secure in the belief that it was on course to find firm and level purchase. The fall drove his femur into and beyond the hip socket, dislocating and shattering it and breaking his pelvis. It also compromised his knee, but that damage was relatively minor compared to his ruined hip.

In retrospect it seemed to Bowen that he was instantly sober when he heard the sharp crack of his thigh bone and felt hot pain radiate from his knee to his lower back. Somehow the sound was the worst. Punctuating his words between howls of pain, he begged his friends not to touch him, to let the medics handle it. But they insisted on pulling him out, and he passed out before they got him to the rim of the shell crater.

He spent four months in the hospital at Fort Bragg, and was released with what amounted to a fused hip, a pronounced limp, chronic pain and a medical discharge. When his discharge finally came through, Bowen hobbled into civilian life looking for all the world like a wounded veteran. When asked he would artfully and simply answer, "I was in the service during Vietnam," and that seemed to resolve the matter.

He put his hand on the back of the chair and tested his leg and hip. He decided to stand. "We have a problem," he intoned in a voice void of emotion. "It seems that yet another of our employees has given us cause for concern. Sanjay not only has failed to locate and deal with Mr. Metzger, but his third attempt to deal competently with a task he was entrusted with . . ." He let his voice trail off briefly. "He has put our mission at risk. He will, I'm afraid, have to be dealt with." He paused again, not expecting any interruptions, but the tall, well-dressed man wearing a bow tie spoke without being recognized.

"Just what did Sanjay do to indicate that he needs to be dealt with?"

Bowen's face grew red and he responded with ill-disguised fury. "What he did, Five, is he threw a goddamned hand grenade at them, if you can believe it. And not only that, it was a goddamned dud, a practice grenade they give troops in training. It even had a goddamned cork in it. And you know what those things do?" He almost seemed to be directing all of his anger and frustration at the bowtie and mustache. "They blow the cork out with a little 'pop', that's what they do. It must have scared the crap out of those two guys, don't you think?" He calmed himself with effort, but then added with profound sarcasm.

"Sanjay apparently decided that a hand grenade exploding between two citizens as they were standing in the elevator of their apartment building would be seen as an accident. I can see the newspaper headlines now; 'Two Men Killed by Hand Grenade in Apartment Elevator: Police suspect suicide or accident.' He gathered his breath and composure. "It would appear that Mr. Sanjay's resume, like Metzger's, was exaggerated," he continued, and swept the table with his eyes. "Nor was it properly researched and examined for accuracy. Both processes, if you can call them that, are now being scrutinized."

The bowtie spoke again, unapologetic. "Sanjay was under my direction. It was my presumption that he was legitimate and competent. We've always felt that SIPO was very thorough. What exactly went wrong?"

"In the simplest of terms, Sanjay is a con man in scrubs. He simply talked his way past our interviewers and convinced them of his professionalism. When that was presented to SIPO, they simply bought it. A clear lack of due diligence."

"So underneath that quiet exterior lurks the soul of a great performer," Five said with a touch of admiration in his voice. "The man should be on television. I expect he'd do very well. Might even get his own show."

"This is not a matter deserving of humor, Five," Bowen said sharply. "In any event the issue is this. We've been relying on rank amateurs who presented themselves as consummate professionals. And we bought it, twice. That stops now. We will regain our footing and re-examine our vetting procedures. Anything else does a disservice to our organization and its legacy. Does that answer your question?" This time he looked directly at the handlebar mustache for response.

"It does indeed," came the reply, and the table was silent.

"This time we will not rely on outsiders. Sanjay will be dealt with internally. You all know the drill." He turned and spoke to the mustache. "Five will pass out the slips." There was a palpable sense of unease around the table. Well-dressed men with expensive wing-tip shoes and $300 dollar neckties fidgeted nervously with note pads and water glasses.

The mustache and bowtie passed out folded slips of paper, then waited while each member of the group stood, came forward and selected one. When they were seated, Bowen said evenly, "Open them, please." He was the only one excluded from the process.

Papers rustled softly. Finally, a slender, mild-appearing man in his late forties said, "the black spot!" and paled visibly. The man whose nickname was Shylock had drawn the unlucky slip.

"Please, One, this is not what I do," he said weakly.

"You'll do what is in the best interests of the Group. If you need help, you'll get it from members of the Posse. But you will be in charge of carrying out the assignment." His statement allowed no room for discussion.

As the men left the room, Five took a moment to pull Bowen aside. "A black spot, J.D., really. Right out of Treasure Island. Can't we come up with something a bit more original in the future?"

* * *

The two men returned to Sherwood's apartment having been sufficiently stimulated by the appearance of the hand grenade to continue their previous conversation. Sherwood sat idly rolling the spent grenade back and forth across his dining room table, making enough noise to cause Torpid to briefly raise his head and re-position himself on the couch.

"All right," Archer began with more than a hint of skepticism in his voice. "Let me see if I've got this straight. This Unit Twenty heads up a loosely organized organization—talk about a borderline oxymoron—of paramilitary malcontents, secessionists, revisionists and revolutionaries. How am I doing so far?" Sherwood started to respond.

"Just a minute. Let me finish. These are all people who despise the federal government for a variety of reasons, as I understand it. In any case this Group Twenty for some reason hires Ralph Metzger, a complete incompetent who shares none of their beliefs. They proceed to tattoo him and send him out to terrorize you, and therefore, of necessity, me. Metzger's combined native intelligence and creativity are inadequate to the task, which results in his dismissal. Then, inexplicably, a practice hand grenade follows us into the elevator of your building, causing nothing but a small puff of smoke and an inquisitive look. These don't seem to me, at least, to be the exploits of a formidable enemy. I'm finding difficulty taking them seriously, Sherwood."

"Sarcasm was never your strong suit, Arch."

"Probably not." Archer said, and then asked the question that had been on his mind since their hotel room conversation with Ralph Metzger.

"When we were talking with Metzger," he waved his hands around menacingly as if he still had his 12-volt battery clamps in between his thumb and fingers, "it was apparent that you already had a great deal of previous information about Group Twenty. Am I right about that?"

Sherwood turned and looked directly at him but said nothing.

Archer continued. "Just where did you come across all of this information—Group Twenty, the tattoos, the Posse whatever-it-is? All of that obviously wasn't news to you at the motel."

"A friend's wife," Sherwood began, looking down at his hands. "Well," he backed up, "I can't really call him a friend—he was a classmate." Archer waited.

"I'll explain. He and I met at a reunion a three or four years ago—maybe more like four. His name was Grady Sullivan and he was from Houston. He'd moved there after college and I guess he did pretty well financially. He'd gotten married, raised a family and was living the good life. We sat next to each other at a reunion dinner and went through the standard reunion stuff. You know, girls, old friends, girls, fraternities, professors, girls, majors, and so on. Pretty predictable stuff, really. Eventually he told me that he'd majored in history and had started a thesis during his senior year about the plight of the Seminole Indians in the 19th century. I guess he found out a few other people had plowed that ground before him, so he changed his subject late in the game to what he called the post-war accomplishments of Jefferson Davis. I guess he found some new territory there, even though Davis has been the subject of numerous biographies."

"I can see where this is going," Archer said.

"It was really pretty interesting. I learned a lot from him. Davis was an admirable man and a real southern gentleman, and his life didn't stop when the war ended. He even encouraged reconciliation in the 1880's, and prior to that he urged the south to accept the Union and become a part of it. In the meantime . . ."

"Sherwood," Archer interrupted, "I'm familiar with Davis's exploits after the war."

"Anyway, I listened to him for a while, and then told him that I had a specific interest in Davis's flight and his capture in Georgia. As you can imagine things moved along pretty quickly after that. We got on well and decided to get together after the reunion dinner for a couple of drinks at my place. I showed him my collection and talked about my interest in Davis's route south. Then I explained my theory that Davis was heading to St. Marks to be picked up on a ship and taken to Texas. When I brought up Texas and the Confederate treasure train, he got very interested, but at the same time kind of guarded. He wanted to know how I came to that conclusion—what kind of proof I had. I told him I didn't have proof as such, but if you look at the route and read all the related historical material, the whole thing falls into place pretty neatly. He didn't disagree with me, which surprised me, I guess, but he got very quiet.

Anyway we went on for quite a while after that—lots of conversation and lots to drink, but he seemed to want to avoid anything about Davis's flight and the treasure. When he finally left my place he seemed pretty nervous. He looked around as if he thought he was being followed, and he seemed to be in a big hurry to get out of there fast. It was obvious he was really spooked." Sherwood paused, rubbed his neck and stretched out his long arms.

"You still haven't told me how you learned about Group Twenty and the rest of it." Archer finally added impatiently. "And what about your friend. Where is he now?" he asked.

"First question; he finally opened up about Group Twenty and the fact that he was a member the second or third time we had lunch together. Second question; he's dead," Sherwood answered, clipping the word short.

"I am sorry," Archer said apologetically. "If I'd known I might have muzzled my sarcasm a bit."

"You didn't know. And as I said, he wasn't really a friend, more of an acquaintance—and a brief one at that."

"How did you learn about his death?" Archer asked.

"His wife. Apparently he'd talked to her about me and our meetings, and she called me pretty soon after his body was identified."

"How did he die?" the Parson asked.

"It seems he was murdered. The specifics are pretty unpleasant, apparently, and knowing your sensitivity, we might leave it there. Anyway, she wanted to see me right away. She said it was very important, a matter of life and death, so I flew to Houston and met with her about a week after her husband was found."

"Why in God's name didn't she go to the police?"

"Her husband had warned her that both she and their children would be killed if any word of the activities of Group Twenty got out and could be traced back to them. She was scared, and wanted help from someone she could trust. She seemed to think that someone was me."

"With good reason," his friend added quietly. Again Sherwood paused, endlessly, it seemed to Archer. "And what did she have that was so important?" he asked finally asked.

"She said she had found some files in a safe he kept in his office at their home, but she didn't have the combination. She finally had to have the lock drilled to get it open."

Archer was finding his friend's long silences unnerving. "The files, Sherwood, please. I really don't care if she had to have the safe dynamited."

"They contained the notes and material that probably got him killed, or at least were at the basis for why he was killed."

"Do you mean the details about Unit Twenty, the KRIPO and the Posse business?" Archer asked.

"I do."

"And you think that's why they were harassing you?"

"I think they were trying to send me a warning. They must have suspected I knew something and thought that they could scare me off. And by now I'm sure they know we caught up with Ralph, and if they know him at all, they'll know he spilled his guts and their secret society isn't so secret anymore."

"Whoa, my friend. How did they find out about you in the first place?"

"Ears, Arch. They have ears everywhere." Archer found himself involuntarily looking at Sherwood's ears. "I'm sure they watch their own members like hawks, and they must have seen me and Sullivan at lunch. If they did any research into what I'm interested in, and put two and two together . . ." He shrugged.

"So, you think perhaps they may send someone after you now, because they think this Brady Sullivan passed you classified, internal information about their organization. And if he didn't, then Metzger surely did. Am I accurate?" Again it was put as more of a statement than a question.

"If I were in their shoes that's what I'd think. And if I were in their shoes, I'd go about cleaning up what I thought might be any possible loose ends. And I imagine I represent a major league loose end. So do you, incidentally."

"Then I suggest we need help," Archer submitted.

Sherwood leaned forward and looked at him intently. He'd anticipated this. "We have nothing to give the police at all. There's no evidence. Linda Sullivan burned every one of the files. She's terrified, and not just for her own life. She's anxious to protect her husband's reputation, and there are children involved. All we have to give the police is guesswork and supposition with a little hearsay thrown in," he concluded unenthusiastically.

"I don't mean the police," his friend said, "I mean uncle Desmond," he said with a tight, deliberate smile.

Their conversation was shattered by a series of loud, rapid explosions from outside, and both men moved quickly to the window at the back of the room facing the parking lot.

"What in God's name was that?" Archer said.

"I'll tell you what it wasn't. It wasn't a backfire."

Sanjay was standing silent and motionless on the street below, carefully shaded from the streetlight, watching the window of the third floor apartment with great patience and concentration. He could see outlined on the wall the shadows of the two men as they moved about the room. Apparently satisfied, he walked around the building to the parking lot, pausing briefly, a small shadow in the late evening darkness. He was carrying a five-gallon can of gasoline. Well behind him, unnoticed, a large black Hummer moving at idle speed kept pace with him, its lights extinguished. The four men inside sat quietly with shotguns in their laps, not speaking. Suddenly the driver accelerated gradually and turned into a side drive adjacent to the parking lot.

"He's coming out the other side of the building," he whispered nervously above the low growl of the engine. "Lock and load, people. We can catch him on the far side of the lot."

* * *

Louis and Weeks sat in a small office adjacent to the autopsy lab and waited for Kate Smith.

"I think she's taken a shine to you, Henry," Weeks said mischievously. "It's pretty obvious from the way she looks at you and hesitates when she talks to you. No question she's got a thing for you."

"Listen, Weeks," Louis said, "she doesn't look at me any differently than she does at you," he paused, "except maybe, well, you know."

"Aha, I see", Sam answered, "the race thing again. I knew it. The minute I hit a sore spot, it's the race thing every time, know what I'm saying?" he said grinning. The two were just getting up to speed when Kate Smith opened the door. Both stood.

"How is it going with the Sullivan case?" she asked.

"We've run ourselves clean out of evidence and suspects, and Chavez and Lasansky aren't even as far along as we are," Weeks answered. "The guy's wife has an airtight alibi, Sullivan apparently didn't have a girlfriend, wasn't on drugs, he's straight, no singles bars—clean as a whistle. Everybody seems to like him—or used to, anyway," he corrected his tenses. "We're chasing the only lead we have now—that tattoo. So far, nothing."

"So it isn't a cold case yet?" she asked.

Weeks answered her. "These things don't officially become cold cases for a long time, but it sure has all the earmarks of becoming one. The good old MPD finally tossed it like a hot potato to the Texas Rangers as soon as they realized it wasn't going to unravel quickly. The Rangers will work it, but there's nothing to go on. It's one of those murders with a clean victim, a spotless family, no suspects and virtually no clues. In these things you look for a nice, neat angry wife, or one who has a boyfriend, or the guy's got a girlfriend, someone's gay or there's a pissed-off employee around somewhere, anything like that. Relatives make good suspects too. But this one has none of those things. Just a dead guy who's got no reason to be dead. We can't even get off of square one. The Rangers will play with it for a while, but it'll die out in a couple of months."

"Well, the reason I called you in here is in the lab. It's pretty ugly. Come in and see what you think," Kate said, and gestured toward the autopsy laboratory. "Just arrived fresh today," she said as if advertising Pacific salmon in a seafood market.

"You go ahead, Louis," Weeks said. "I've got to go to the can."

"I think you both ought to see this," Kate said, and motioned them insistently into the lab.

The body on the table was still fully clothed, though the clothing was filthy and tattered. "I think he was a doctor," Smith said, pulling gently at a sleeve of the scrubs the corpse was wearing. "For the moment that seems to be all we have. Whoever did this didn't leave much to identify," she added. "No face to speak of. See?" She pointed at what remained of the body's face.

Weeks paled from umber to a moderate yellow ocher. He turned away quickly and stood with his back to the table, pretending to take notes on a small pad. "Why don't we just wait for the DNA and fingerprints," he asked his notepad hopefully.

Louis had walked within four feet of the body before he stopped and looked away. "Jesus," he said softly, "that's not nice."

"Looks like a shotgun," Kate explained. "Once in the shoulder, which wouldn't have been fatal, but then the face . . ." She pointed again at the ruined face. "It looks as if he took at least three or four from a large gauge shotgun at close range. We found dozens of pellets and there's residue in his hair and on the neck of his scrubs," she said, peering more closely at the body.

"Why weren't we called to the scene?" Weeks asked from a comfortable distance. "Where'd they find him?"

"They said the body was in a dumpster. There was no crime scene. Someone just dumped him in there with the trash and the rats," Kate said, increasing Weeks's level of discomfort.

"Man, that's a mess." Louis said. "Somebody wanted to make real sure." He moved closer to the body. "He wasn't a white guy—look at the hair and skin. Maybe Mexican, or Puerto Rican. What do you think, Sam?" Sam had already quietly left the lab. He found himself talking to Kate.

"How does Sam do his job with the way he is about bodies?" Kate asked.

"It's not bodies, just dead bodies." Louis answered without humor. "Sam's good. He's really good with crime scenes and forensic evidence. I'd be lost without him. He just doesn't like to get up close and personal with this kind of thing."

"I'll take that as an endorsement of sorts," Kate said turning again to the body. "Well, any ideas?"

"Black hair and dark skin." Louis was thinking aloud. "That may take us somewhere. The Mexican gangs have been at each other real hard lately."

"He could be Mexican, or he could be Indian or Pakistani, or Algerian, for that matter," she said, confusing the issue without meaning to. "Unfortunately he wore false teeth, and they weren't found with the body. Some poor policeman had to empty the dumpster, but they found nothing. In any event, no dental impressions here for sure."

"Dammit. They should have called us to the scene," Louis said heatedly. "It's protocol, and they could have missed something. You just don't haul a body out of a dumpster, throw it into an ambulance and truck it to autopsy. We'll have to start three steps behind." Then he brightened. "If he's Mexican or Hispanic the gang thing could be a good lead. Any tattoos?"

"Nothing I've seen yet. So far he's clean as a whistle, in that regard anyway," Kate responded without humor.

"Shit," he spat out disgustedly before he stopped himself. "Apologies," he added with exaggerated formality. "Any photographs of the scene? The dumpster itself? Anything to jump start this thing?" Louis added.

"Not that I know of," Kate answered, turning her attention to the body on the table. "The police are overwhelmed—spinning their wheels. This is the second one in two months, and the first one's still unsolved. They need some help over there."

"They need talent more than help. Let me know when you've finished the autopsy, Kate. Who knows, you might find some incredible clue, like a butterfly stuffed in his throat, you know? Like in 'Silence of the Lambs,'" he said smiling.

"That was a tobacco moth cocoon, and you of all people should know that," she teased him genially. "But you may be right. You never know. I'll be in touch."

"Do that." Louis said, smiling at her over his shoulder as he went to retrieve Sampson.

* * *

The Parson's car was a sleek, metallic silver BMW 650 coupe, and the trip to Gainesville would take less than two hours. The car floated powerfully and nearly silently at over 90 miles an hour, the only sound was a CD of a Beethoven triple concerto that Archer had playing on the car stereo. After a perfunctory comment about his friend's taste in music, and asking if Beethoven came before or after Elvis Presley, Sherwood settled his long limbs into the soft leather of the seat. "Nice ride," he said, "how much?"

"Just about enough to buy a small condominium," Archer answered. "And if you weren't a good friend, I'd tell you it's none of your business."

"You're right—it isn't. "But didn't you have a real nice little sports car not so long ago? A red one?"

"I did indeed, past tense."

"Well?" Sherwood persevered.

"Well, it was a Porsche Carrera. It was as fine a piece of German automotive machinery as can be found, in my opinion. Fast as a cheetah, agile as a gazelle. I just decided it wasn't suitable, that's all."

"Not suitable? The finest piece of German automotive machinery not suitable? That doesn't sound like you, Arch."

"The truth be told, I came to a realization—perhaps more of an epiphany. On thinking about it, I realized that there are only three kinds of people who own ostentatious and expensive two-seater sports cars. First, the pampered college student whose overly solicitous parents were browbeaten into buying it for him—or her. Second, the wife who discovered her husband was having an affair and suddenly received one as a gift, and finally, the egotistical, testosterone-charged male who is suffering a mid-life crisis. I decided that I didn't qualify for either of my first two definitions, and therefore just might qualify for the third. As you know, I hold the whole notion of mid-life crises in the greatest of contempt, and therefore I decided to distance myself from both the appearance and the reality of that affliction as soon as possible. You are riding in the result."

"Super result," Sherwood said as he digested his friend's unusual view of mid-life crises for a moment, and decided that there were more than a few traces of validity hidden in his assessment. He resolved to change the subject in that it was effectively closed.

"Uncle Desmond—tell me about uncle Desmond, Arch."

"Uncle Desmond lives just outside of Gainesville," Archer answered superfluously. That was, after all, where they were headed.

"And that's all?" Sherwood asked.

"Uncle Desmond is a bit over 40, he spent twelve years in the Marine Corps, and he's now part owner of a motorcycle sales and repair shop in Gainesville proper."

"I never did see much proper in Gainesville," Sherwood said. Archer didn't respond to his attempt at humor. "But tell me, why are we in such a hurry to lay our problems on uncle Desmond's doorstep?"

"Uncle Des is what you might call a problem—solver. He's lived a bit of a different life from the rest of us in the family. He was in line to inherit a very comfortable income when he reached the age of twenty-one, but he chose, for reasons known best to him, to enlist in the Marine Corps instead.

"Not what you'd call a good career move," Sherwood said, eyebrows raised. "And it led him to a life in a motorcycle repair shop?"

"His choice. He enlisted, stayed in for twelve years or thereabouts and did quite well, as I understand it. He was some kind of a Sergeant—I'm not sure which one—there are so many of them—but he had a great deal of responsibility, and appeared to love his job."

"Why did he leave?" asked Sherwood, watching the speedometer nervously as it settled at ninety-five.

"As I understand it, he'd been drinking a bit and got into an argument with another kind of Sergeant who, it seems, had significantly more authority than uncle Des. In any event, rather than lose the argument, uncle Des struck the man, quite hard apparently, and knocked him down. That was Desmond's idea of winning an argument. It still is, actually."

"That kind of thing will get you arrested," Sherwood observed.

"It seems it will also get you expelled from the Marine Corps, although I think they have another word for it," Archer responded. "He did spend a little time in jail before they sent him home. He's always said the best marines are in the brig."

"And that's what uncle Desmond has to recommend him—discharged from the Marine Corps and now owner of a motorcycle repair shop?" Sherwood asked incredulously.

"Part owner," Archer corrected. "And you might not want to approach uncle Des with that attitude," he advised solemnly. "I expect he might not take it at all well. As a matter of fact, I can assure you he would not take it well."

"My thoughts will remain my own," Sherwood responded, something about loose lips sinking ships coming to mind.

They pulled into the "Orange and Blue Motorcycle Shop" in the late afternoon, just as the sun was losing its ability to paralyze the citizens of Gainesville with its intensity. "I can't say as I care a whole lot for the name of the place," Sherwood commented.

"Simple public relations, S.T. Desmond says it draws the college students, and since they are more impressionable than the general public—except for the voting public, I should say—they're more easily swayed when it comes to buying a machine that carries two people at best and has the reputation of being the leading cause of amputation in the country."

"That's a bit cynical, wouldn't you say, Arch?"

"Practical, uncle Desmond would say. Let's go on in," and he opened the car door to the late afternoon heat shimmering off the black asphalt.

"I've never noticed before, Arch, but you never seem to sweat," Sherwood observed as he tried to pull his shirt free from his sweaty back.

"It's a family trait. I understand my namesake, the Parson himself, first perfected it on the pulpit when he felt he was treading on problematic turf. He could pull it off in full clerical regalia, as well. It was said of him that he was a good preacher but a better politician, because he had the ability to espouse causes to which he wasn't entirely committed. But wait until you see Desmond if you think I have that issue under control."

The Orange and Blue Motorcycle Shop was a squat, one story building in a small strip mall on a side street just south of downtown Gainesville. The showroom was both spacious and spotless, with half a dozen shiny new motorcycles carefully arranged around the room. Sherwood noticed that not a drop of oil was to be seen on the gray painted floor beneath the motorcycles. Someone took great pride in the cleanliness and appearance of the showroom.

They walked past a bulky salesman towards a door with a sign that read "Employees Only" leading into the shop itself. Sherwood reached out and grasped Archer, who was walking briskly towards the door. "A short visit after a long trip and too much coffee," he explained, and turned to an adjacent door marked "Men's Room".

"Don't be too long," Archer said frowning as he waited for Sherwood in front of the shop door.

Prepared for the worst, Sherwood took a deep breath before entering the men's room, hoping it would last him through the upcoming interlude. He opened the door and was surprised at how sanitary the condition of the bathroom appeared. He cautiously exhaled and breathed in again, picking up nothing but what he speculated to be a hint of jasmine in the air. A small white machine fixed to the wall hissed quietly and dispensed quiet puffs of fragrance into the room. On the front was a label that read "Lily of the Valley."

When he was finished and was washing his hands, he noticed a sign skillfully hand-painted and fastened just above the faucets. "All Customers Must Wash Hands Before Entering Showroom." He pondered the humor briefly before he joined Archer outside the door.

"Have you ever noticed the sign above the sink in the men's room?" he asked his friend.

"Bathroom humor, uncle Des calls it. Irony might be a better word. He makes an avocation of it," Archer explained, leading the way to the shop door.

The shop stood in stark contrast with the tidy organization of the showroom on the other side of the door. The steady, hollow hammering of huge twin cam engines echoed in the room, punctuated by the metallic clanking of tools dropped or discarded on the concrete floor. The odor of exhaust was pervasive. Desmond Brownlow was on one knee beside a huge, garishly painted Harley Davidson, its engine pulsing, as he deftly adjusted something that seemed to be connected to the bowels of the ignition system. He was a large man, shovel-jawed, with massive hands and fingers shaped like small spatulas, but his fingers functioned with precision and dexterity in the tangle of wires he worked through. The sides of his head were shaved to the skin, and the top showed a close-cropped dusting of what appeared to be light brown hair, so short it was difficult to discern the color. He was surrounded by four men, all large, all overweight, all tattooed, all with shoulder-length hair or ponytails.

Sherwood noticed that uncle Des had only a single tattoo on his bicep, a scowling bulldog with USMC in large block print letters below it. The bulldog flinched visibly and changed expression when uncle Des moved his arm and the muscles under the skin flexed. Sherwood felt at once intimidated and entirely out of place. He watched as Archer strolled in with unflinching confidence, his posture erect, impervious to the oppressive level of noise and pure testosterone in the shop. He decided that Desmond and John Wayne would have made equally impressive posters, Desmond having the edge in carriage and physique, Wayne leading in the laid-back-no-problem category. Watching Archer, he marveled that the same lineage could produce such dissimilar specimens.

Heads and ponytails turned, and Archer waited. The man working on the Harley left his work reluctantly and turned. "Parson," he bellowed, rising and rubbing his blackened hands against the sides of equally grimy blue jeans.

"Uncle Des," Archer shouted above the clamor. "How are you?"

"Never better, Parson, never better." He vigorously shook his nephew's hand and the bulldog temporarily seemed to lose its identity completely. "You know what they say—dirty hands, clean living, just like cold nose, warm heart—something like that." His face broke into a broad grin. "What finally brings you to the home of the Gators?" He signaled to the men standing behind him to stop working and kill the sounds of the engines. The shop gradually quieted.

"Personal family matters, uncle Des. We'd like to talk. This is my friend Sherwood," Archer with a gesture towards Sherwood.

Desmond thrust forward a huge hand and delivered a lengthy, agonizing handshake.

"Next time try squeezing," Desmond said and looked Sherwood over from head to toe. "You sure could stand to put on a few pounds. And what the hell kind of name is Sherlock, anyway?" he added abruptly. "They name you after that detective? I don't get it why people can't name their kids Joe, or Fred, or Sam or something. Now it's all Sumner or Logan or Dawson or some other damned weird damn thing. They're all last names, or towns or airports. Just think about Bristol Palin—that's the name of a town in Connecticut or Rhode Island. It's beyond me." He obviously wasn't worried about confusing the two states, given the fact that both would fit handily into Palm Beach County. He looked at Sherwood again and shook his head, adding. "And I thought Desmond was bad. Well, it's not your fault. Nice to meet you—and I like your outfit." Before leaving Tallahassee Sherwood had changed from his work uniform into a pair of frayed khaki shorts and a black T-shirt with "Hooters Event Staff" emblazoned on the back. Archer had quietly discouraged him from wearing his aging but revered "Choke at Doak" shirt.

Desmond turned to his nephew. For once Archer was without a necktie, but the top button of his Brooks Brother's shirt was fastened "Why don't we go into my office? It's damn near the end of the day, and it's quieter in there."

"It might be better if we went somewhere else, somewhere completely private. We'd like to avoid distractions and interruptions as much as possible, uncle Des."

"Well, we could go to my place, but it's a hike." He turned to the bulkiest of the bulky creatures standing behind him. "Raunchy, can we borrow your digs for a couple of hours? Will it take more than that, Archie?"

"A couple of hours should be fine," Archer answered. Raunchy' place, Sherwood thought to himself. This should be an interesting couple of hours.

"Help yourself, Sarge," answered the man called Raunchy. "I'll kill some time at The Gullible Grape. They're having a wine tasting tonight. The little woman made me swear off the suds," he said, rubbing his distended belly with a wide grin. "She didn't say nothin' about wine, though." He was a huge man with the guileless face of a happy child and an expanding paunch that pushed its way past the open front of a tattered leather vest. A large Confederate flag was sewn on the back of the vest. Raunchy's left arm bore a long, jagged scar from just above the wrist to the bicep, which had the effect of twisting the forearm inward at the elbow. He used the arm somewhat awkwardly, but displayed neither pain nor restriction as a result.

"Will she be home tonight?" Desmond asked.

"She plays bridge every Thursday afternoon. I think today is duplicate. It's supposed to be afternoon, but she's never home until after 9:00." Raunchy was smiling good-naturedly. "Thursday nights she leaves two cans of Dinty Moore stew and a can opener on the counter. That's my Thursday night dinner. That and two Dos Equis. Otherwise she's a gourmet cook."

The words 'gourmet cook' caused Sherwood to look at Archer doubtfully.

"You might put a shirt on underneath your vest before you go to The Gullible Grape, Raunch," Desmond continued. "All that nasty hair and stuff hanging over your belt might not go over so well at a wine-tasting. I've got one in my office. It's not clean, but it'd be a whole lot better than what you're wearing now." He said this with obvious affection, then turned to Archer and Sherwood.

"Raunch's place is right around the corner. It's walking distance and it's private. He's got it done up real nice. You'll like it," he said confidently.

Then he looked at Sherwood again. "Play a little basketball in school did we, Sherlock?" he asked.

"No. I'm afraid I'm not very good at jumping." He let Desmond's confusion regarding his name pass, unsure if it was accidental of not.

"I can see that," Desmond replied. "I'd guess football wasn't your game." This was not posed as a question.

"I spent most of my time studying, but I did a little acting in college," Sherwood added, hoping to gain some traction.

"Whoa," Desmond said and took two steps back. "Let's not go there, big fella. You know I don't believe everything I hear, but let's you and me not plan any camping trips together. I didn't see it, but I sure heard a whole bunch about 'Brokeback Mountain'." He said this without a hint of malice, and smiled amiably at Sherwood. Archer quietly closed his eyes.

"Hey, I'm just riding you, Sherlock. If I don't like someone, I don't ride 'em. That's when you gotta worry. When I'm not riding you." He looked back at his nephew. "O.K., troops," He added cheerfully. "We're off to Raunch's place."

'Raunch's place,' Sherwood thought to himself. Not a bad name for a pool hall.

* * *

Raunchy's apartment was on the second floor of a shabby three-story building that appeared from the street to have developed a moderate list to starboard.

"We call it the Tiltin' Hilton," Raunchy had warned them with a grin as they were leaving the shop. "It's just an optical illusion, though. You put a level on the staircase and the bubble ends up smack in the center. I've even put my bowling ball on the hall floor, and it didn't roll an inch."

Climbing the stairs, Sherwood dreaded what awaited them at the top. Desmond turned the key in the lock, opened the door and led the way into the apartment. It was surprisingly neat and well cared for. There was a worn but freshly vacuumed mocha colored rug on the floor, and while the furniture wasn't new, it was nicely ordered, with lace antimacassars covering the upper backs of the chairs. Sherwood tried in vain to link the images of Raunchy and antimacassars. He decided Mrs. Raunchy must be a real compensating force in the marriage. His curiosity finally got the best of him.

"What's your friend Raunchy like? He certainly seems like an interesting person," Sherwood asked a bit nervously.

"Raunch is a very interesting fella," Desmond answered easily, emphasizing the word 'is'. He was in the Seals for nine years—you know, Navy Seals? He was real good at it and had a terrific career ahead of him. I think he got to Petty Officer 2nd or 3rd Class, or something like that. Never could figure those ratings out. And what the hell sense does it make to call a senior non-commissioned officer 'Petty' anyway?" he added irritably.

"What happened to his career?" Sherwood returned to the subject, his confidence escalating a bit.

"Motorcycles," Desmond answered. "He was just too damned into motorcycles, especially hogs. He opted out of the Seals to sort of devote his life to Harleys. He lives and breathes the things." Desmond turned, eyes narrowed, and directed a penetrating stare at Sherwood. "You're having a hard time picturing Raunch as a Seal, aren't you? Well, he was, and a goddamn good one. His arm was messed up in Afghanistan somehow. He doesn't like to talk about it. For sure he's let himself go a bit in the last couple of years, he'd be the first to admit it. I guess one reason has to do with enjoying the freedom of biking a little too much. Beer may play a role too, but the main reason is his wife's a hell of a cook." This was offered a something of a challenge, and Desmond's look had graduated from penetrating to piercing. "You ever get the invite, just try her cooking. You'll see. One of her meals and you'll ask if they'll take borders in here."

Sherwood felt his confidence slipping again, and tried to redirect the conversation he'd started. "Do you have a lot of military veterans in your club?" Here he was on entirely unfamiliar turf, but it had the desired effect. Desmond relaxed visibly.

"We have Raunch, a few Marines and a couple of army guys. Most of us are Iraq veterans, but we got some Afghanistan guys who are interested. We welcome pretty much all former military types, except Air Force guys, of course.

"And we're careful about officers, as you can imagine."

Sherwood decided not to pursue the final comments.

"Sometime ask me about Air Force guys, when you have a spare couple of days. And please don't tell me your dear old dad was in the Air Force." Desmond turned and headed directly to the refrigerator. He opened it, sorted through some containers of milk and orange juice and asked if anyone would like a beer. Sherwood accepted in an effort to demonstrate camaraderie, Archer refused. Desmond twisted off the tops of two bottles of Bud Light, sat down and turned to his nephew.

"What's up, nephew? Why the mystery?"

* * *

Bowen and Five waited impatiently at the long table, sipping bottled water and not speaking. Glowering, Bowen turned to the other man and said.

"What the hell was he thinking, Five? Anybody talks and there's a clear trail that leads right back to our front door."

"You'll have to ask him." Five looked at his watch. "He's late, and you don't have to call me Five when we're alone, Bowen. You know my name."

"It's habit, Five, and discipline. If anybody's name is used in the wrong company, we've got a possible leak. We've had enough of those as it is. We don't need any more."

The door opened Shylock entered the room.

"Gentlemen." He nodded as he greeted the men hesitantly. "How are you?" He started to pull out a chair and sit opposite them at the table.

"Don't bother," Bowen said curtly. "This won't take long, and I'd rather you were standing."

Shylock understood the tone of the voice. "What's the matter, One?

I did what you asked me to do. He's dead." He waited with a nervous grin on his face. "As a matter of fact, he's really dead."

"How many people did you involve in this, anyway?" Bowen asked.

"Only four," he answered. "I wanted to make sure. I watched the whole thing from my car to be sure it was done right."

"Who were they?" Bowen's voice hardened.

"You know, the Posse. I got four good ones who don't seem to mind messy work. I watched the whole thing from my car to be sure." Shylock was taking obvious pride in the outcome of his enterprise.

"You involved four strangers from the Posse and you watched from your car?" Bowen was incredulous. "Four people, any one of whom could talk to four other people over a few beers, and those four could . . . do I need to go on?" His eyes had narrowed and the pupils took on the color of coal. "And, just to round things out nicely, you watched from your car, with your own tags on it, and no doubt pulled out of that lot in a hurry—with your lights on—after all the noise from the shooting. How am I doing so far?" His voice was heavy with sarcasm.

Shylock seemed to deflate, his shoulders sagged, and his eyes fixed on the floor at his feet.

"No one will talk, One. I warned them. And they're all Posse. They can be trusted. They . . ."

"Anyone can talk," Bowen interrupted. "I could, you could, they could and they probably will. It's called human nature. It's just a question of how much and to whom. It's called bragging." This had become a lecture between a teacher with the limited patience and a student of limited ability.

"Now, just tell me that you didn't give them your name, or make any connection with Group Twenty."

Shylock brightened. "I used an alias, One. And all I told them was that I was on my own, and that Sanjay was a lawyer working for the government and trying to uncover incriminating information about the Posse. I didn't even use Sanjay's name."

"Sanjay a lawyer—in scrubs? Do you think they bought it?" Bowen asked, his anger moderating somewhat.

"That group isn't made up of the swiftest of intellectuals, One. A couple of them actually asked if Sanjay was 'like an ACLU guy or something.' I had to enlighten them a little about the ACLU." Shylock seemed to be gathering confidence. "That was a real uphill battle." He ventured a hopeful smile as he spoke.

"Then we have to count on stupidity and lack of curiosity, and I don't care for either," Bowen said after taking a deep breath and stretching his leg out under the table with noticeable difficulty. "O.K. I know this isn't exactly your line of work—the kind of thing you were trained for. But you have to think about every detail, even the most minute and unlikely occurrences, and figure that any one of them could, and probably even will happen."

"I'm COO of a plastics company, One. This wasn't exactly what they taught me in business school in the '70's." This was said respectfully, and followed by a look towards Five for support.

"Well, they may be teaching it there now," Bowen said dourly. "Let's call it a lesson learned, and buckle down tight and hope none of this finds its way back to Group Twenty. As you know we have the lives and futures of very important people at stake here. They depend on our confidentiality and professionalism. If we go down, they go down and the whole structure collapses with us. You know what that means."

Shylock paused before answering. "Perhaps I better go back to the man who recommended those four and tell him to keep his eyes and ears open."

"Leave it alone, Shylock," Bowen answered without hesitating. "The more attention we bring to the situation, the worse. But if we do get wind of someone talking, it will mean some pretty messy housekeeping, and that will have to stay in-house. No more outside contractors. Now go on home and don't worry until you have something to worry about." He paused and looked at Shylock for a moment with is eyes narrowed. "Or unless you hear from me."

When the door had closed behind the man, Bowen turned to Five.

"You didn't have much to say, Stillman."

"You didn't leave much for me to say," Stillman replied and followed Shylock out the door.

* * *

Archer spoke first. "We think some people may be trying to kill us."

Desmond waited a moment and then said, "You never were much for long explanations, nephew. Anything more, or do we just run with that?"

"It might be best if I let Sherwood explain. He is, I suppose you might say, at the heart of the problem."

"Speak up, heart of the problem," Desmond said, turning to Sherwood.

"Well," Sherwood began. "It's a long story. It might be better if I started off with a map.

"I don't mind long stories, Sherlock, as long as they don't last beyond supper—and dinner is at 1800 hours." This was a friendly rejoinder, but Sherwood made a point of looking at his watch.

"Incidentally," Desmond continued. "Has anyone ever told you that Sherlock is a strange name?"

Something having to do with a large, burly marine named Desmond flashed briefly through Sherwood's mind, but he decided not to pursue it.

"Actually, it's Sherwood, and I didn't have a whole lot to say in the decision," Sherwood said, wincing inwardly at his own audacity. Deciding that the best course of action would be to scamper along to his subject, he quickly posed a question. "Would you have a piece of paper?" He realized he had adopted a somewhat deferential tone.

"That might be out of Raunchy's area of interests, like the opera, but I'll look," Desmond replied and walked into an adjacent room. Sherwood noticed that the Marine had to turn slightly sideways as he passed through the narrow doorway in order to accommodate the width of his shoulders. At least he didn't have to duck, he thought to himself.

A few moments later Desmond came back waving a single piece of paper. "Did either of you know that there's a blank page in "Hustler" at the end of the personals section?" he said, and handed the paper to Sherwood.

Sherwood didn't know whether to laugh, nod sagely or ignore the statement. He chose the last.

He took the sheet of paper and drew a now-familiar map of the area from Richmond, Virginia to Irwinville, Georgia. Desmond was peering languidly over his shoulder as the route through both North and South Carolina was drawn.

"Camp Lejeune," Desmond said almost reverently, pointing at a spot midway down the state on to the coast. "Spent more than four years there." Then he looked at Sherwood. "You wouldn't have been a Lieutenant in the Marine Corps, by any chance? That map looks real familiar."

"I was never in the service," Sherwood answered, not sure whether or not the comment was made in jest. Then he turned back to his drawing and began by addressing Desmond directly.

"I've been interested in the fall of the Confederacy for years. I became particularly interested in Jefferson Davis's flight from Richmond to Georgia when the capital of the Confederacy collapsed."

Desmond interrupted; "Let's not call it a flight. I like the sound of 'journey' a whole lot more."

Sherwood corrected himself. "Agreed. His journey took him from Richmond roughly down this route." Again, as in his apartment with Archer, he moved his finger slowly down the pencil line he'd drawn from Richmond south. This time he avoided mentioning specific addresses and towns along Davis's route. Desmond watched with undisguised interest. "Missed Parris Island, huh," he commented quietly. "Can't blame him for that."

Sherwood continued, purposefully truncating the specifics of Davis's route for the sake of brevity. "He had the whole Confederate treasury—millions of dollars in gold and coins—in what's been called a treasure train which followed him along the route. When he reached this point," Sherwood pointed the pencil at the general location of Irwinville, "he was captured by Union forces."

"Not a good day for the south. If he'd gotten away it would have been a different story," Desmond stated firmly.

"Anyway, his treasure train has never been accounted for—at least not accurately. There's been a lot of guesswork—that he used some of it to pay off his troops, that he lost it to bandits or marauders, or he had it sent elsewhere. Lots of speculations, no really solid historical explanation."

"However, Sherwood has uncovered a good deal of information that provides some nearly incontrovertible evidence," Archer interjected, adding a distinctly scholarly tone to the discussion.

"Well, let's say lots of things point in a certain direction," Sherwood said modestly.

"How much money and what direction?" Desmond asked abruptly. "It's getting mighty close to supper time."

"In today's dollars, as a guess, maybe as much as six hundred million."

"Holy shit!" He looked immediately at Archer. "Sorry nephew. I know how you feel about that kind of language.

"Perhaps better to say that I know how my aunt felt about it, Desmond." Archer responded gravely.

"Jesus, dear old mom," Desmond reflected solemnly. "She was a hot ticket until the Baptists got a hold of her. Then it was praying half the day, church four times a week, praise this and halleluiah that, no more swearing and worst of all, no more drinking. It completely screwed up her sense of humor to say nothing about her personality. You can only imagine what not drinking can do to a person." He shook his head sadly and continued.

"She was a real hoot before they got a hold of her. I could tell you some stories . . . Anyway, we wore out the knees of our trousers when we were growing up. We weren't quite sure why we were doing it, but that's what we did." He looked suddenly thoughtful. "It sure kicked the shit out of my plans for the future." He looked at his nephew. "Sorry, Parson."

Sherwood was trying to determine if Desmond was being serious or not. "What plans, Desmond?" he asked.

"Bugs," Desmond replied simply. "I liked bugs a lot when I was a kid. You know, entomology, or etymology, I forget which one now. It's been a long time. Whichever one's the study of bugs. I loved bugs. I messed around with 'em every chance I had." Sherwood realized Desmond was being serious.

"Why did you give it up?" his nephew asked quietly.

"Mother decided I was going to be a preacher. Sixteen years old, and she had me destined to become a goddamned Baptist preacher. Can you imagine? And she wasn't kidding. I remember when I was fourteen the preacher stood up in the pulpit—a tall, lanky, scrawny kind of a guy." He glanced at Sherwood quickly. "No offense, high pockets," he said and continued. "Anyway, the guy pointed his long, bony finger at us and said in this booming voice; "Some of you will go to heaven, and some of you won't go to heaven." As he spoke Desmond swept his finger across the room.

"And when he said the last part—some of you won't—he was pointing his goddamn finger straight at me, like the Grim-frigging Reaper. I'm here to tell you I goddamn near slid under my seat to get away from that finger." He stopped for a moment and took a deep breath, lost in the past.

"Well, when I thought it over, I got mad—mad at him, mad at the Baptist Church, and mad at my mother for making me sit through that kind of . . ." Again he paused and glanced at Archer, ". . . crap. The guy didn't know me from Adam. He didn't really know anything about any of us in that church, and he didn't have any right to say that." Desmond was clearly still deeply affected almost thirty years the event.

"Anyway, all I was doing in high school was trying to get drunk and get laid, and I only had luck with one of those. That's when I made my decision."

"What decision?" Sherwood asked. He immediately sensed the answer to his question.

"Do you know how good the Marine Corps looks to a kid if his only other choice is becoming a Baptist preacher?" he asked leaning forward. "I took off like a big bird and enlisted the day after my eighteenth birthday. Never looked back."

There was an awkward pause until Desmond's mood brightened and he broke the silence. "Anyway, back to the subject. Six hundred million is a whole bunch of change in any language." He looked at both men sitting across from him. "And now I'll bet comes the part where you tell me what you think happened to it, right?"

"Forge ahead, Sherwood," Archer encouraged.

"This may take a while," Sherwood said, looking nervously at his watch. As close as he was sitting, he was becoming acutely aware of pure physical power in Desmond's arms and shoulders. He felt acutely discomfited. "Would you like to eat first?" he asked cautiously.

Desmond rose and walked to the refrigerator. "No, you go on," he said, opening two more beers. "This is getting good. Water, nephew?"

Sherwood used his map and notebook as one would teaching aids and continued, quickly becoming consumed with his material. He lapsed unconsciously into the hypnotic, singsong tone and of a lecturer at a history symposium.

"Jefferson Davis's escape plan was to eventually get to Texas by ship and to re-establish the Confederacy there. I've read a number of communications that suggested that, once there, he planned to rekindle the fires and encourage Texas to continue the struggle against the Union. It had been arranged for him to join Confederate General Edmund Kirby Smith there, and then reclaim possession of the Confederate treasury. He had been advised not to travel with the treasure, in order to prevent the capture of both at the same time." He quickened his pace.

"Shortly before his capture, if you believe the historical records and correspondence, he arranged to entrust the treasury to John Reagan, who was what today is called the Post Master General of the Confederacy. Reagan was a Texan. The plan was to have a Confederate Colonel named John Taylor Wood take the treasure to Cuba and then to Texas and await Davis's arrival there. That much is history." He looked up and tried to gauge the interest of his audience. "Ironically, Davis was captured but Wood, in the confusion of the moment, escaped and fled to Cuba on June 2nd, 1865." He turned to Archer. "You may already know this, but Wood had served as an officer in the Confederate Navy, and had commanded the CSS Tallahassee during the war in battles off the east coast. Talk about coincidences."

"Davis and the money," Desmond brought him firmly back to the subject.

"Sorry. Now I'm in the area of conjecture."

"I'd rather be in the area of food," Desmond suggested.

Not to be taken off his game, Sherwood continued. "Colonel Wood arrived in Cuba with, I believe, the entire Confederate treasury but without knowing for sure that Davis had been captured." Unable to stop himself, he turned again to his friend. "Davis had his personal belongings shipped to Cedar Key, but they were first hidden on the plantation of Senator David Yulee on the Homosassa River. 'Yulee's Gold', you remember?"

"I'm getting hunger pangs again, Sherlock. Do you mind?" said Desmond.

"Sorry," Sherwood said again, not bothering to correct the mistake, and took up the thread of his story again. "By prior arrangement Wood met James Webb Throckmorton in Cuba. Throckmorton had served in the

6th Texas Cavalry during the war, but was discharged because of a kidney problem. Now a civilian, Throckmorton took possession of the treasure in the early summer of 1865. This is important. He went on to serve as Governor of Texas from 1866 until 1867, when Union General Philip Sheridan dismissed him because of his Confederate sympathies and his connections with the Ku Klux Klan. Nevertheless he was elected to the Texas congress and served from 1875 until 1879, and again from 1883 until 1889."

"I'd be exaggerating if I said I'm fascinated," Desmond mumbled, frowning slightly.

"The reason this is important is that in order achieve that kind of political success, Throckmorton must have controlled a great deal of money at the time, and therefore wielded considerable influence. It's been suggested by others better versed than I in the history of that time that he controlled the Confederate treasury and safeguarded it until his death in 1894. I repeat, this is conjecture, but it has historical underpinnings."

"Listen." Desmond said, leaning forward in his chair, his beer can dangerously close to empty. "Nephew here said you were in trouble—someone was trying to kill you. If you get to the point, I'll sit for a little longer, but I didn't come for a history lesson. It's damn near 7:30 and my stomach is getting very unhappy with both of us."

"Just one more thing," Sherwood added, turning back to the map on the table in front of him. "Davis was captured about 110 miles to the northeast of Tallahassee. If you follow his route from Richmond south, it forms a nearly direct line to Tallahassee. Look at the map!" His enthusiasm was beginning to get the best of him. He paused for a moment and gathered himself. Then he looked nervously at Desmond again and continued.

"The town of St. Marks is approximately 20 miles from Tallahassee. If you continue his route in the same direction, it would take you right through Tallahassee and in the general direction of the St. Marks River. Tallahassee was controlled by the Confederacy at the time. The St. Marks or the Apalachicola Rivers were the most obvious destinations for someone looking for a ship to escape to Texas, or anywhere else, for that matter, and they were friendly ports. Davis knew he was being pursued, and that Union troops were pretty close behind him. There are some who think he might have been heading to Apalachicola, but that's almost certainly not the case. Apalachicola was simply too busy, Union shipping was arriving and leaving on a regular basis, and like every other major port in the south, it was alive with Yankee spies at that time. Also, it was the obvious choice, which is exactly why a man as savvy as Davis wouldn't have chosen it."

Sherwood took a deep breath, realizing that he might have conveyed too much information too quickly. He decided to limit his scope.

"Anyway, if I were he, my choice would have been the St. Marks River, no question about it. It was a very quiet spot, and it had no permanent docks to accommodate shipping in 1865. The only way to reach a ship, or for a ship to reach St. Marks, was to board or disembark at the lighthouse near the mouth of the river. There was deep water in the river three miles inland of the lighthouse, and Confederate shipping had access to that deep water."

Archer interrupted. "The Union had blockaded the mouth of the river and prevented Confederate traffic, Sherwood. There was no possibility Davis could have escaped from St. Marks."

Sherwood looked at his friend with a startled expression on his face. "Arch—the battle of Natural Bridge. The dates, remember?"

"Oh Christ," Desmond groaned, rolling his eyes. "Here we go again."

Archer thought for a brief moment. "Spring, 1865, wasn't it? Uncle Des, this is important."

Desmond obviously wasn't convinced.

"March 6th, actually," Sherwood responded, trying but not succeeding to avoid being pedantic. Realizing that he had capitalized the conversation for far too long, he looked at his friend in near desperation.

Archer, his historical memory energized and realizing Sherwood needed support, picked up the story immediately.

"The Union had blockaded the St. Marks River in March of 1865, if memory serves." It always did. "Their intention was to take the capital of the state of Florida, and begin a land march from the south to join forces with friendly troops in Georgia. They were opposed at Natural Bridge by a very small group of Confederate troops composed mainly of volunteer blacks and students from what was then Florida Military and Collegiate Institute. They defeated the Union forces at the battle of Natural Bridge more than a month before Davis's capture in south Georgia. Can you see the connection, Uncle Des?"

"Whether I see it or not, you both might as well go on," Desmond responded glumly. "Dinner's a lost cause, and breakfast isn't all that far away at this point anyway." He was rummaging through the refrigerator again. "Raunch must have more beer in here somewhere." He turned to

Archer, ignoring Sherwood entirely. "However, maybe before reveille I would like to know why someone is trying to kill you two."

Sherwood directed a hesitant look at his friend. "Politics may be involved here, Desmond. I don't want to step on any toes." Particularly yours, he almost added.

"Politics and self-help books piss me off," Desmond said abruptly and somewhat off the subject. A bit flummoxed, Sherwood looked at Archer.

"For heaven's sake, he's not going to bite, Sherwood, of that I can assure you," Archer said in an encouraging tone. "Desmond may be a bit on the conservative side, but he is also a patriot." He looked at his uncle with a touch of uncertainty, then nodded to Sherwood. "Go ahead. Carry on."

"You are sure about the biting thing, nephew?" Desmond turned to Sherwood. "I may be a conservative patriot, but I'm also a hungry conservative patriot," he cautioned.

Sherwood took a deep breath. "There is a group—they call themselves Group Twenty. They've been directly or indirectly in control of the Confederate treasury since the late 19th century. They operated under a different name until about 1950 or so." He realized he was losing Desmond fast. "They're the one's who are trying to kill us."

* * *

Sampson Weeks sat across from Henry Louis, his feet up on the desk that separated them. He cradled a cup of cold coffee in his hands.

"You're smirking," Louis said. "What the hell are you smirking about? You look like a Cheshire cat—an all black one, that is."

"How are things going with Katie?" Weeks asked, his grin widening.

"It's Kate, and things aren't going."

Chavez and Lasansky, who had just entered the room, were standing near the door. Apparently the rift between the Crime Scene Investigator and the detective was on the back burner for the moment.

"That's not what I hear," Weeks responded, rocking back precariously in his chair. "I hear you and she are getting it on, full speed ahead from a dead stop just a few weeks ago. What an operator," he said, shaking his head and still smiling broadly.

Louis sat up straighter in his chair and looked at Weeks, then at Chavez, and then concentrated on the ceiling above the desk. "Cobwebs," he said. "We got cobwebs."

"Come on, Henry, tell us. We're grown-ups. We can take it." Weeks was now thoroughly enjoying himself.

Chavez stepped forward, began to smile and joined the banter between the two friends. "Just give us the rough outlines, Louis, and we can fill in the rest," he suggested. "We don't need all the gory details."

"There are no gory details," Louis answered, fidgeting in his chair. "We've gone out a couple of times, that's it. There's nothing to tell."

"A couple of times," Weeks hooted. "Whoa! We've had some unofficial surveillance on you and, according to our reliable sources," he winked at Chavez, "you two have been burning up the town." He paused, relishing Louis's discomfort. "And this one calls himself a committed bachelor, monk's robes, sack cloth, ashes and all." He turned back to his partner. "Some monk, from what I hear. You be getting quite de rep in de 'hood, my man," he said, trying his hand at a dialect as foreign to him as Cantonese.

"Listen," Louis interrupted, trying desperately to reroute the conversation. "We've got important stuff to deal with here. I'd like to hear what Chavez has to say about the suspect he's come up with in these two homicides. You think you've found the guy?"

"I don't have a doubt in the world," Chavez answered immediately. "We've as much gotten a confession from him. If he's innocent, I'm Kobe Bryant. No offense, Weeks.

"None taken. Tell us about this fella who's guilty before he's charged and indicted." Weeks was obviously reluctant to move away from the subject of Louis's personal life.

"He's certifiable—that's the only drawback. He could try an insanity plea, and after 20 minutes with him, you'd probably buy it."

"What makes you so sure he's the guy?" Louis asked.

"He's a nutcase, completely over the edge. He's a young guy, maybe twenty-five or so. I heard he was one of those occupiers who's pissed off at Wall Street or something. We had an informer tell us about him, and we caught him in the park outside the Midland Bank. He was sleeping in a packing box, for God's sake. What does that tell you? Anyway, I take him for some kind of Nazi skinhead or something. Whatever, he hates Muslims, and we've heard he's decided to take out as many of them as he can. And, we got half a dozen witness will testify that he was planning some kind of one man assault on the Arab population of Midland. After that he was planning to recruit some friends and branch out across the country. We've got one witness who swears the guy confessed to him while they were both occupying the square in front of city hall."

"But that guy Sullivan was no Muslim. He didn't even look Irish," Weeks said.

"Mistaken identity, pure and simple. He'd followed some Muslim guy into the bank building and waited for him until after dark. When he saw Sullivan leave the building he figured it was the Arab. Like I said, it's dark and he's not picky. That's it."

"C'mon, Chavez. Sullivan was much bigger than the guy on Kate's table, and he had white hair and a crew cut. It's not even close," Louis said.

"Like I said, it was dark, and the guy's a nutcase. In any event that's the way the chief wants it. And I don't think he wanted to call in the Rangers—too embarrassing, he said. He tried CAPERS, but that didn't lead anywhere . . ."

"What's CAPERS?" Weeks asked.

"It stands for Crimes Against Persons Unit. They sent in two clowns from Austin, but they got nowhere." After a moment he continued. "Anyway, we've got a good suspect here, we've been told to drop the investigation, and that's the word from the top," Chavez responded

"Sounds like the Hudson's a little over-anxious to put this one in the win column. Case closed nice and neat, even if the wrong guy's in jail," Weeks said sarcastically.

"You don't know that," Chavez responded defensively. "You meet this guy and you'll see what I mean. He hates Arabs, says we should nuke everything east of France. I didn't ask him about Africa," he added thoughtfully.

"Chavez, you don't even know if the guy on the table's a Muslim. And even if he is, he could be third generation American," Louis added. "You've got circumstantial evidence and hearsay, that's all. It'll never even get to the Assistant D.A.'s desk."

"Talk to the Chief," Chavez answered and paused at the door. "Listen, you guys are pretty good. Enjoyed working with you, but I don't follow up on cases when I've been told by the man that they're over. You understand, don't you?" and he closed the door behind him.

Weeks slowly shook his head in disbelief.

* * *

With Archer's assistance Sherwood repeated what the two had discussed about Group Twenty. Archer was able to fill in details that Sherwood was either overlooking or had forgotten in his haste to keep Desmond's attention. But despite the pace of his delivery, Desmond finally interrupted him.

"What, in 6,000 words or less, are these cowboys up to?" He asked, his words icy with impatience.

Sherwood took a deep breath. "The want to disrupt the current government of the United States. They do everything they can to create anger, disorder and discontent. They have created groups of separatists, dissidents, sovereigns . . ."

"Stop all engines," Desmond interrupted. "Sovereigns?"

"Sovereigns are people who refuse to pay taxes. Group Twenty has also underwritten militia groups, the bombing of clinics, the shooting of police officers, sit-ins, strikes, you name it. In a word, they run a network of homegrown terrorists.

Desmond looked incredulous. Sherwood stopped and waited, hoping for support. Archer obliged.

"Uncle Des, we believe these people have lived and thrived off of the invested proceeds from the original Confederate treasury. They are a powerful, Texas-based organization that has coast-to-coast tentacles and national aspirations. If they can create enough disarray and havoc in the country, they plan to capitalize on the confusion and assume the reins of power in the country. And, they've already made significant progress towards their goal."

"What power are you talking about, nephew? I'm a little at sea here," Desmond said, involved in spite of his appetite.

Archer nodded at Sherwood, who braced himself for the worst. As he began he knew he was walking a thin political line.

"We have to start with Governor Throckmorton in the late 1860's. He had absolutely nothing going for him at the end of the Civil War. He didn't come from money, he had very little political influence and even fewer friends who could help him politically. Yet he became Governor of Texas against all odds—and after that served in Congress for four years.

"We believe he simply bought the job, uncle Des," the Parson added. "At the end of the war Texas was in a real pickle." Desmond raised his eyebrows and smiled at the word.

"There are a whole lot of better words that come to mind than pickle, Archie."

"The last battle of the Civil War was fought in Texas in May of 1865, well after Lee's surrender at Appomattox," Archer continued. "The troops and the populace simply had a no-surrender mentality. When they finally understood that it was over, morale was so low that troops mutinied and supply depots were plundered. Thousands of dollars in gold was stolen from the state treasury in Austin, and at the time of Davis's capture more than half of the original Confederate force in Texas had deserted and turned to banditry and lawlessness."

Again Desmond smiled at his nephew's exposition. "You sound like a textbook, nephew."

"I suppose I do. But what Sherwood is inferring is that the only way a person like Throckmorton could rise to the governorship in that kind of chaos is with enormous financial backing—in other words, we have good reason to believe that he had access to the Confederate treasure, or at least its proceeds." Archer sat back and waited for Sherwood to take the reins from him.

"From here on there's a bit more intelligent guesswork involved. Arch calls it calculated reasoning." Sherwood smiled uneasily. There was something about Desmond that continued to unnerve to him. He wasn't sure if it was the tattoo, the physique or perhaps the atmosphere of Raunchy's apartment. In for a penny, in for a pound, he thought to himself and plunged on.

"We have reason to believe that Throckmorton was the first of a long line of politicians to benefit from the treasure. We also believe that the money was intended to support only politicians with Confederate sympathies, and that this is still continuing today.

"Nothing wrong with Confederate sympathies. You might say I lean in that direction myself," Desmond said, looking defensive, bored and hungry at the same time.

"It's more than that, uncle Des," Archer added. "We're convinced that the money is being controlled by senior operatives to fund and direct an organization that is at its heart fundamentally anti-government."

"Anti-federal government," Sherwood added quickly, emphasizing the word federal. "These are the people who are nominally in control of Group Twenty, and Group Twenty controls a network of domestic terror groups."

Desmond lost his bored and hungry expression. The defensive one remained. He looked directly at Sherwood. "Two questions; who the hell is "they," and what the hell do these terror groups do that's so anti-government?" He snapped the questions out with irritation.

Sherwood looked to ~~Virgil~~ ARCHER for help. Once again he wasn't disappointed.

"They, uncle," Archer said soothingly, "are the persons who have control over both the treasure proceeds and Group Twenty. They are the ultimate power brokers. We'll make some educated guesses about their identity later, when we have more information."

"Obviously I'm waiting."

Archer continued. "You asked two questions. The answer to your second one is that they propagate suspicion of the government. Their goal is to foster unrest and anger, and to use that anger to their advantage. These are people who in their hearts still believe in the cause and the destiny of the Confederacy, and their intention is to someday re-establish something very much like it in this country."

"Nothing wrong with the Confederacy that I can see," Desmond responded with the trace of a smile. Then he became serious. "But you're talking treason, am I right? If that's the case, it stops being funny. But I sure hope you've got more than just a bunch of wild guesses and maybe's to back this whole thing up."

Sherwood found himself quite comfortable letting his friend complete the picture.

"We have a lot more," Archer was serious and unsmiling when he spoke, "and we are indeed talking sedition. We have bombings, murders, plots, assassination attempts and," he took a deep breath, "we're quite sure they're the ones who are trying to kill us."

Desmond sat back in his chair. "Sedition?"

"Insurrection, but treason will serve just as well. These are traitorous acts against the republic, and their organization is ultimately responsible for those acts," Archer said decisively.

"Overthrow the republic. Well, we can't have that, now, can we?" Desmond responded thoughtfully. "But in the meantime, why don't we go to my place. I want to hear a little more about this, and at least I know there's something to eat there."

* * *

"This witness," Bowen began, looking through Shylock, "are you sure he's reliable, and he has no idea who we are?"

"Yes to the first, no to the second," Shylock answered. "He's been handsomely paid and he's Posse. He doesn't know who we are or where his orders came from. I arranged for a middle-man to deal with him." He paused looking straight into Bowen's eyes. "A reliable middle-man."

"He'd better be, and a silent one as well." Bowen cautioned. "There have been too many screw-ups already. We've managed to hire two completely incompetent, bungling idiots who were advertised as skilled assassins. Now we have to backtrack and try to cover up their ineptitude. That's not our trademark, Shylock. I suggest for starters you revisit our networking and information-gathering methods from top to bottom."

"We'll take care of that, I assure you," Shylock responded.

"Metzger," he said reminding himself of a loose end. "Has he been dealt with? He knows just enough to make trouble, and he has a big mouth."

"We're in the process of taking care of him. For the moment we've lost him, but I've authorized two people from KRIPO to pick up his trail. If they can't find him, he's either already dead or homeless in Guadalajara."

Bowen nodded and returned to the subject. "The witness—tell me more about him."

"There's really no need," Shylock answered in a tone that bordered on the patronizing.

"There's a need. Take my word for it."

"He's trustworthy, committed, and willing to go to jail for perjury if necessary. He's been led to believe that his testimony will prevent a cause that he is deeply committed to from being exposed. He hates the federal government, and in the past he's shown himself willing to give up his life for what he believes in. He's unmarried and has no children—and no relatives in the area that we could locate." Shylock added as an afterthought.

"Have your middle man arrange a meeting. Tell him you just have a couple of questions to go over with this person before the whole thing is finalized. Then have him bring the witness to the First Capital Bank of Texas. I'll have a conference room prepared. You'll ask him several questions we'll decide upon beforehand, and I'll monitor from an adjoining room. After that we'll decide just how committed and trustworthy the man is. In the meantime check more deeply into any family he has—anywhere. It would be convenient if we could use them as a threat, if they exist and if it becomes necessary."

Bowen rose slowly from his chair wincing, and left the room.

* * *

The three men had driven to Desmond's house in Virgil's two-door BMW coupe, Sherwood's lanky frame squeezed excruciatingly into the diminutive back seat. When they reached the house, he unfolded himself with difficulty, and they walked together down the short pathway to Desmond's front door.

The house was a small, single story framed building with an oversized front porch that dwarfed the entire front of the structure. Sherwood noticed a collection of lawn chairs and a few small end tables scattered on the porch. He looked for beer bottles or ashtrays, but there were none. There was clutter but not disarray, and he guessed that the motorcycle club employees were frequent but fastidious visitors to the porch. Desmond led the way and opened the door.

"You don't lock it?" Sherwood marveled.

"No need," Desmond said. "People know who lives here, and there's not a whole lot here to lure a respectable thief away from the more profitable neighborhoods."

They entered the house and were greeted by a massive, ponderous bulldog. Desmond squatted down and leaned close to the dog taking the immense head in his hands. He spoke to the dog quietly, as if he were greeting a respected colleague.

"Ermey[8], old man. How are you? Sorry I didn't get back at lunchtime. I had visitors." He turned and looked at Sherwood and Archer, then back to the dog. "It won't happen again, old friend." Then he rose and led the dog to the back yard, speaking softly to him along the way. This was a side of Desmond that Sherwood hadn't anticipated.

The three men stood obediently on the back porch while Ermey took care of business in a spectacular fashion. Sherwood wondered briefly how a deposit of such immensity would be disposed of. The backyard was newly mowed and spotless, save for the steaming mound the dog had left in his wake. Desmond roused him from his reflections by calling Ermey into the house. All three followed the dog into the living room.

Sherwood attempted to break the ice. "Seems like a nice, gentle dog."

"He'll tear you another . . . navel if he doesn't like you. Apparently he likes you." Desmond's arm swept the living room with an inclusive gesture. "Take a seat, and I'll see what there is to eat."

"Ermey?" Sherwood whispered quizzically to Archer. "Why Ermey?"

---

[8] See Appendix 8

"I'm not sure. I asked him once, but it's escaped me. All I remember is that Ermey is a name of some importance to him, but I've forgotten why. Ask him yourself. Remember, he doesn't bite." Archer smiled at his unintended double-entendre.

Desmond returned shortly with a tray of crackers, cheese, a quart of milk and three glasses. "We'll start with this. By then Claire will be home and we'll get some real chow." He put the tray on the table between them.

"How is Claire?" Archer asked.

"Fine. She's working the afternoon shift at the hospital, and chow's always late when she's on that shift." He glanced at his watch. "She'll be here in less than an hour." He looked at Sherwood. "You'll like her." It was almost a challenge.

Sherwood felt a slight surge of elation at even being included by the big marine. Encouraged, he asked, "What does Ermey mean?"

Desmond looked at him appalled. "You don't know who Gunnery Sergeant Ronald Lee Ermey is?" He turned to his nephew. "For Christ's sake, does your friend live under a rock?"

Archer didn't answer, and Sherwood felt marginalized again.

"Next you'll tell me you've never seen Full Metal Jacket," he went on, giving Sherwood more than enough time to answer. Sherwood's silence was his only answer.

"Jesus," Desmond muttered, staring at him and shaking his head in disbelief.

"Desmond, Sherwood is an amateur historian. He is extraordinarily knowledgeable about certain aspects of the Civil War, and that leaves him little time to pursue other interests, much less movies. I'm sure you understand."

Looking somewhat mollified, Desmond said, "O.K. History lesson time. Your first assignment is to watch this—on your own time." He walked to the television set and retrieved a DVD, which he brusquely handed to Sherwood. "When you've done that, we'll talk about it and you'll know why my dog's name is Ermey. For the moment, I'll give you a lead-in. Gunnery Sergeant Ermey is a contemporary legend in the Marine Corps. The movie's just a movie. Gunny Ermey's the real thing." Then he turned back to the dog and patted him robustly on his haunches. The sound of the thumps was alarming, but the dog didn't wince, instead he burrowed even closer to his master's leg. "We'll educate him, Gunny. Don't you worry your head about it."

Sherwood was equally puzzled by Desmond's use of the word 'Gunny', but decided to let it rest. Desmond continued. "Now, finish up with what you've got about this twenty group so we can figure out a way to prevent any more of this kind of crap from happening."

Sherwood resisted the temptation to explain to Desmond that wasn't quite that easy. Instead, in a very edited version, he gave him the abridged rendition of all that he and Archer had learned about Group Twenty, Metzger, the Posse, Brady Sullivan and Sparrow. While he talked, Desmond ate huge handfuls of crackers and cheese and drowned them with noisy gulps milk as he listened. At the mention of the name Sparrow, he interrupted.

"Sparrow," he said, spraying the coffee table with cracker crumbs. "How many Sparrows do you think there are in Midland, Texas?"

"I have no idea," Archer replied in surprise.

"Well, let's see something" He said stood and wiped his hands on his jeans. He crossed the room again and retrieved a large phone book from under the kitchen counter. Leafing through it, he repeated "Sparrow, Sparrow," to himself until he found the page he was looking for.

"I can tell you how many there are in Gainesville," he said looking up from the phone book. "Exactly seven, and three of them are women. Now I don't know how big Midland is, but my bet is it's not a shitload bigger than Gainesville."

The front door opened as Desmond closed the phone book and he looked up as Claire entered the house. Although Sherwood hadn't consciously formed an image of Desmond's wife, somehow she seemed shorter and a bit more substantial than he'd expected. Without knowing it, he had conjured up the image a tall, willowy, formidable woman with broad shoulders at Desmond's side. This Claire, while not exactly the opposite of his imagined Claire, differed markedly. She had short, dark brown hair that emphasized her high cheekbones and well-defined features. Sherwood might have described it as a pleasant, open face, even handsome in the approbative sense of the term, but he understood that a great many women might not regard the word as complimentary.

She pulled an over-sized Harley-Davidson windbreaker from her shoulders and threw it over a kitchen chair. "Thought it might rain," she said, smiling at the visitors, then turned to Desmond's nephew.

"Archie! I'm so glad you could come. And who might we have here?" She said crossing the room and kissing her husband lightly on the cheek.

"This is Sherlock, and he'll tell you his last name. I can't deal with it." Desmond answered.

"It's actually Sherwood, and the last name's Tualatin," Sherwood answered automatically, pronouncing it painstakingly. "Sherwood Tualatin."

"Is that an Indian name?" She asked immediately.

"From what I understand," Sherwood answered, unsure of his footing.

"Great," she said, with an even wider smile. "My maiden name was Shingoitewa. You think you've got a mouthful, try that one on. My ancestors way back were Hopi Indians from Arizona. Desmond doesn't even pretend to be able to pronounce it, let alone remember it." She winked at her husband and crossed the room and shook Sherwood's hand warmly. "Where are your people from?"

Sherwood wondered how to answer her question and stumbled a bit. "I guess from Oregon, the Portland area," he said, hoping that would suffice. It didn't.

"Is that the name of your ancestor's tribe?" Claire preserved.

Sherwood reached back to the research he had done on his family name as a youth.

"The Tualatin Indians are also called the Atfalati Indians. Other than my family being from the Portland area, I'm afraid I don't know much more about it." He didn't feel that this constituted either the right surroundings or the right audience to go into his real lineage and his father's checkered flight from Texas.

"Well, you don't look Indian," she said pausing, then smiled broadly, "but it's very nice to meet you. You will stay for supper." The affirmative aspect of the verb was emphasized. A family trait, Sherwood surmised.

"That would be very nice," he answered, still trying to determine whether not looking like an Indian was a compliment.

She turned to the kitchen. "Archie, you come help me in the kitchen. We have some catching up to do, and Desmond can entertain your indian friend."

Sherwood winced slightly at the word, but smiled back at her. Desmond took Sherwood's upper arm securely in his huge hand and led him back to the living room. Sherwood reverted immediately, feeling once again like a six-year old being taking to the bedroom for a lecture. Though taller, his long and relatively underdeveloped arm reminded him of a parboiled strand of spaghetti in Desmond's grasp. He passively allowed himself to be steered. Desmond guided him gently but persuasively to the couch, turned him around, raised his eyes to Sherwood's and said, "Sit!" Sherwood sat.

"That," said Desmond, settling into a chair and out of earshot of the kitchen, "is one patient woman. And wait until you see what she comes up with for supper. A magician in the kitchen, and that's not the only place she works her magic." He grinned and winked.

Sherwood once again didn't know whether to smile, laugh or let it pass, so once again he opted for silence and smiled imperceptibly.

Desmond broke the silence and leaned forward. "Now, while we're waiting, finish what you were saying about all those crazies. It's got me interested. And everyone thinks bikers are a weird group."

"That's about it, Desmond," he said, hoping he hadn't disappointed the man. "You've heard about all we know." The Parson joined them from the kitchen.

Desmond addressed them both. "I've seen a lot of things, and been through a lot of things, but I want to know where do they grow these people? Is it the climate, the food, some kind of pollution thing? Global warming, maybe? It's a bunch of certifiable psychos. They must have some good recruiters at the funny farm."

"You'd be surprised, uncle Des," Archer interjected soberly. "They're not alone. The world is full of discouraged, lonely people looking for something to believe in—a life ring, you could say. People who are in desperate need of a cause, a messiah, a belief system, anything they can be a part of. And angry people, too," he added as an afterthought. "Think of Jonestown, the Manson family or even Heaven's Gate. Those people were so committed to a messianic leader's beliefs that the majority of them would readily die or kill for him." No one spoke for a moment and Archer felt compelled to fill the void.

"I read something recently in the local paper that seems to me to be worth worrying about. Let me see if I can recall it correctly. In March of this year, three men were arrested by the F.B.I. attempting to purchase hand grenades and silencers in Fairbanks, Alaska. They were members of a group that called themselves the Alaska Peacemaker Militia. The group's leader, a man named Cox, was the home-schooled son of a Baptist minister. A second man joined the group after the Internal Revenue Service tried to chase him down for failing to pay his taxes for several years. Instead of working out a plan to settle his debt, he decided instead to become a sergeant in Cox's militia and prepare for war against the government. The third person was a Mormon, a family man and a churchgoer, and he helped formulate the militia's 2-4-1 plan. When violence occurred, the militia was to take out two government officials or agents for every one militia man lost."

"Wouldn't you know there'd be a Baptist somewhere in the goddamned woodpile," Desmond mumbled.

Archer reached deeper into his astonishing archives of his memory. "I also remember hearing about two brothers, both Mormons, who were sentenced to death for murdering five innocent people in San Francisco. A man named Helzer, who was a stockbroker turned messiah, convinced his brother that he spoke for God. The two men enticed a young woman, whose name I forget, to join them in their crusade as well. She was just another lonely person trying to find her way and seeking some kind of spirituality. They called themselves 'The Children of Thunder,' and Helzer named his religious program 'Transform America.' It resulted in eight ruined lives."

Given the breadth and depth of his friend's prodigious memory, Sherlock was mildly surprised that Archer had forgotten the name of the young woman involved in the organization.

After a pause Archer continued. "Helzer might bring to mind the agenda of the Branch Davidians, or Charles Manson with a religious twist." He spoke the last words with a trace of bitterness. "Those would be what you call your crazies, Desmond. Compared to that crowd, Group Twenty and the Posse look positively rational."

"Who the hell are the Branch Floridians?" Desmond asked, genuinely confused.

Sherwood started to laugh at what he thought was a joke, but caught himself.

"It's the Branch Davidians," Archer stepped in quickly. "I'm afraid I ran that together too quickly. The Branch Davidian's was the group in Waco that was basically wiped out when the government tried to dislodge them from their compound. Remember David Koresch?"

"And the fire, sure I remember, it was all over the television." Desmond thought for a moment. "Probably Baptists involved in that one, too," he muttered under his breath.

His nephew continued. "What's hard to overlook is the fact that Texas seems to be at the center of things here, a breeding ground of sorts, if you will. It's a bee hive of anti-government activity, and Group Twenty is its queen bee," he added, pleased with the metaphor. He reached into his pocket, evidently well prepared for this moment.

"Oh, and there's more. Let me read you something I just found in the New York Times book review last week." He removed a tattered page that had been torn from the Times Book Review section and unfolded it. "I'll just read part of a review of a book by Gail Collins, an Op-Ed columnist for the Times." He began to read.

'With its zest for guns, military adventures, right-wing dogma, regressive taxes, deregulation and privatization . . . Texas is an ideological oil slick . . . '

Desmond started to say that he wasn't a big fan of the Times in the first place, but Archer interrupted him. "There's something else in the review that's even more compelling." He continued to read.

' . . . At a 2009 Tea Party rally at which the fabulously coifed Perry'—"That would be the Governor," he added superfluously—'invoked Sam Houston's famous warning against Texas' *submission to any oppression*, and threatened secession as a possible response to President Obama's stimulus package.'" Archer folded the page carefully and returned it to his pocket with an air of satisfaction. "There you have three very significant words used by a current Texas politician, gentlemen—'submission, oppression, secession.' Does that remind you of anything the Confederacy stood for—or against?" He looked at both men keenly.

"To me that means we go to Texas," Desmond announced, his tone effectively ending any possibility of disagreement. "If that's where the trouble is, then that's where we confront the trouble." This left no room for debate. The matter was closed.

Sherwood was baffled. "What are we going to do in Texas?"

Desmond leaned forward and answered, formulating his plan as he spoke. "We're going to Texas to discourage people, my friend. To create the pucker factor, you might say. Discouraging can be fun, and I've had lots of practice. But first of all," he said, turning to Archer, "you lose that Ferrari or whatever it is. We'll find you something to rent that will fit your new image better, like a Hummer." Then he addressed them both.

"Next we'll get Shank and Dakota. Shank's a little guy with a big talent and Dakota's a huge Indian guy—American-type Indian." He looked at Claire, then at Sherwood, aware that he might be on thin ice. "Looks like we're pretty well-stocked with Indians on this mission," he said smiling thinly at Claire. His smile wasn't returned.

"Anyway," he continued, "Dakota's size is his strong point. He's really intimidating. Actually, he's a pussycat, but he's a terrific actor. He looks like Arnold what's-his-name, the Nazi weight-lifter guy out in California, but real ugly, acne scars, nasty beard, the whole package. And Shank has a specialty—his knife. He's a true professional with that thing. He believes you can get more information from someone with a sharp blade and a few words than with any other weapon, and it seems to work for him, every time. He thinks guns are for people with no skill or imagination. You've really got to see him work. It's a treat. He's an artist." He looked at Claire again, "We invite him over every Thanksgiving to carve the turkey, don't we hon?" He grinned more convincingly this time. Again it wasn't returned.

Archer interrupted, mystified. "What are we going to do with a couple of men on motorcycles against dozens of them, Des? At best it would be a hopeless gesture, and at worst . . ."

"You don't understand, nephew. First of all, not motorcycles—Harleys, hogs—and not a couple of men, but maybe a hundred or more."

Sherwood sat back in his chair, fearful of what he might hear next.

"I belong to a motorcycle club here in town. We call ourselves The Gators. You can probably guess why." He digressed briefly. "Actually, we got in some trouble with that a couple of years ago. Our logo was a gator's head with a foot sticking out of its mouth. The good old U of F called and complained. Rather than fight the thing, we got rid of the foot. That seemed to keep them off our backs."

Archer steered him back on course. "You said maybe a hundred Harleys?"

"Motorcycle gangs, when they're not trying to kill each other over women or turf disputes, have a lot in common. We're really are a pretty tight community. So, with a little luck and some phone calls, I'm pretty sure we could get a whole bunch of bikers to join us. It would be a break in the routine for them, and I bet they'd see it as a real lark. They like a challenge, you know, just like anyone else."

"Where are all these people?" Archer asked, instinctively avoiding appending the preposition 'from' to the end of the sentence. Sherwood had decided that listening quietly was his best course of action.

"They're from all over. California mostly, but Pennsylvania, Arizona, even Texas. A lot of them aren't all that far away. Hell, gas won't even be a problem for most of them," he added enthusiastically.

"Who are they, Desmond?" Sherwood ventured cautiously.

"Hell's Angels, The Highwaymen, the Warlocks, the Pagans, you name it. There are lots of them. And we stay in touch."

Sherwood looked at Virgil despairingly.

"Uncle Des," Archer said carefully. "How do you get these people involved. What reason would a motorcycle gang have to support the government? Most of the ones you named are considered borderline outlaw groups."

Desmond's eyes narrowed, but then a grin broke through. "There are some bad apples, I grant you. But for the most part they're pretty good people, and maybe you just don't understand what they're all about. They don't want to overthrow the government, or anything else, for that matter. They absolutely love the status quo. Just as long as they can deal some drugs, molest a few women, maybe have an occasional gang war now and then, they're happy folks. Believe me, you can count on them to do everything they can to keep things chuggin' along just they way they are." Desmond was smiling broadly now.

Archer seemed to be taken a bit off balance.

"What would your plan be once we got to Texas?" he asked quietly.

"Let's refer to it as a mission, not a plan. Plans are for officers. We're on an information-gathering mission." His voice lowered and he was all business. "We are going to find out who's in charge of this rinky-dink outfit, and we're going to soil some skivvies in the process. We will appear in force. We will have a company-sized unit of the nastiest looking bikers I can chase down. We hold them in reserve, just kind of idling on the perimeter, if you take my meaning. Anything goes wrong, we call them in as our back-up. And when we do call them in, after they've been hanging around and getting bored for a while, they'll be spoiling for some fun."

"What are we doing while they're in reserve?" Archer asked, trying not to sound dubious.

"We visit your Mister Sparrow. First we interrogate him, Guantanamo-style. Then we discourage him. I think we can influence him and maybe a few other people around him to rethink their tactics, no problem." He emphasized the word influence, but its meaning was clear in any case.

"Both Shank and Dakota are terrific influencers, you know. Take my word for it. And they're also real experts at discouraging people. Knowing the way they act together, we'll end up with a bunch of very disinterested, discouraged, unmotivated maggots when the day's done." He looked at his nephew and Sherwood and added with unmistakable pride "You know, it's kind of nice to be able to help your nephew and his friend and your country all at the same time. And we are going to be helping the country in the bargain, aren't we, Parson?"

"Indeed we will, Desmond, if it works," Archer answered doubtfully, adding, "and if we don't get ourselves killed in the process."

Desmond ignored his last remark. "After we eat you two go home and pack. I'll call and we'll meet up somewhere in the western part of the state, maybe Pensacola. I'll have some friends with me." He smiled again. "I'll call Bubba and tell him I may be gone for a while. And don't forget to get rid of that foreign sports car and rent a Hummer. If you can't find one of those, at least rent the biggest SUV you can find. That sports car will draw a crowd, and the only crowd we want around us will be riding Harleys."

"Bubba. You really know a Bubba?" Archer asked in disbelief.

"Sure I do. He's my shop foreman. He runs the place when I'm away." Desmond answered.

"Bubba." Archer shook his head, caught up in a bit of private humor.

"Well, that's not his real name, just a nickname." Desmond explained. His real name is Otis Trask. Seems his family has a whole bunch of money. They're in real estate somewhere. Bubba decided on a different route, just like Raunch, and I guess it thoroughly pissed his old man off. It didn't stop Bubba's inheritance, though. He was my main backer when I was trying to get the business off the ground. Without Bubba, I'd still be changing spark plugs and tuning exhausts."

Archer's became suddenly serious. "Des, we don't even know where in Midland to go,"

"I'm afraid we do." Sherwood interjected gloomily. "The First Capital Bank of Texas, downtown. That's where they meet once a month."

"And just where did we come across this bit of information?" Archer asked in a tone that was uncharacteristically caustic.

"Brady Sullivan's wife told me, Arch. I guess I forgot to pass it along."

"And we'll no doubt plan our arrival for the exact day of the meeting?" Archer said, the caustic tone turning sarcastic. Desmond listened, quietly enjoying the interchange between the two friends.

"Brady told his wife that the leader of Group Twenty was a board member of the bank. Apparently a very wealthy board member as well. His name is Bowen, he's in the oil business, he's influential and he's socially connected. Brady indicated that he wouldn't be hard to find."

"What about Sparrow?" Archer asked, clearly annoyed at being left out of the information loop.

"Sparrow's a whole lot easier," Desmond's smile broadened. "We knock on every door that has a Sparrow behind it."

Archer looked at Sherwood and relented. "All right. We'll Google the board members of the First Capital Bank and see if we can find this missing link Bowen. I do not, however, see how finding him will help our cause in the least. I have my doubts that someone such as you've just described will be very easily 'influenced.'" He directed his last words at Desmond.

"We don't go for any missing link, as you call him, we go for the weakest link," Desmond corrected him firmly. "Once we find Sparrow, we've got our foot in the door. And we'll make him one discouraged shit bird. Now, if the discussion's over, we can stop diddy-boppin' around. It's about three hours later than I like to eat."

When they joined Claire for dinner it was 9:30 at night. All three were famished.

* * *

Kate was standing by the coffee maker in the kitchen in her bathrobe and slippers. "How do you like your coffee, sir?" she asked smiling across the room.

"Black, and the stronger the better. It's a sign of a good cup of coffee if the spoon stands straight up in it without help," Louis answered returning her smile, then yawning.

"As you wish, Herr Investigator," she said, pouring two cups of coffee. "Can you linger for a while? It is Saturday, after all."

"I can't, Kate. I have a meeting with Chavez, Lasansky and the CAPERS unit at 10:00 this morning. They're going to fill me in on their progress. Rain check?"

"Should I keep the coffee warm?" she asked mischievously.

"It'll be a long day. You know the Midland P.D. and CAPERS. Nothing gets done efficiently or quickly. The Chief may be there too, which will add hours to the process. I'll be lucky if I'm out by dinner.

"That's O.K.," Kate responded, "I handle rejection well."

Louis crossed the kitchen, wrapped his arms around her and lifted her cautiously off the floor. "This is not rejection, sweet Kate, but it may put me in the hospital if I try it too often." He set her gently back on her feet. "It's an old football injury, you understand."

"You told me you never played football in your life," she chided.

"When middle age approaches, the memory suffers. In truth I was a terror on the football field."

"During the game or afterwards, with the cheerleaders? Your reputation is your undoing, Henry."

"Please call me Louis. It's much more macho and it suits me better."

"As you wish, Herr Henry Louis. And I'd like to say once again, it's very nice to get together with you without a dead body between us."

"My great pleasure", Louis said, and executed a deep and painful bow. He straightened with difficulty, smiled, and said, "I really have to go, Kate. Time's a-wasting."

With hands on hips, Kate wiggled her hips elegantly. "Come back and see me sometime, stranger."

* * *

As they drove home, Sherwood bombarded his pensive friend with questions. It was apparent that the tables had turned.

"Arch, you're not really thinking of going through with this, are you? It's suicide. Let's call your uncle and tell him we can't make it—we've got an important appointment or something—maybe a dentist's appointment. For God's sake, you and I and three men on motorcycles are going to terrorize Group Twenty? And this is going to trickle all the way down through the other groups—the Posse, the separatists, the militias? There's simply no way, Arch. Please, just get a hold of Desmond and call it off. We'd really be better off calling the police and telling them what we know and letting them handle it. Anyway what we're doing is probably against the law. Arch, are you even listening to me?" His run of questions had left him temporarily breathless.

Archer had been driving and listening in silence for nearly twenty minutes. He appeared deep in thought, brows knit, silently and persistently chewing on his lower lip. Sherwood had never seen that peculiarity before in his friend. Archer finally turned and looked at him for a long moment, obviously still not concentrating on what Sherwood had said.

"First of all I'd prefer it you to keep your eyes on the road. Second, I'd appreciate it if you'd listen to what I'm saying, or at least indicate that you'd heard it," Sherwood said clearly agitated.

"I heard everything you were saying, Sherwood. But I'm not sure I agree with parts of it. Most of it, to be perfectly honest." He began speaking very slowly and thoughtfully.

"For one thing, as you so accurately pointed out previously, we don't have a thing to give the police, except Metzger. And wherever Metzger is right now, if he's still alive, he'll either do everything he can to stay out of this or he'll lie to anyone about everything simply to stay alive. The last thing I would do if I were he would be to unburden myself to the police with details about a very powerful organization that is predisposed to killing people it doesn't approve of."

When Archer paused, Sherwood thought to himself that at least he didn't say 'of whom it didn't approve'. There were times when Archer's adherence to English grammar and syntax was ponderous, and although charming in an old-school way, it could slow his conversation to a tedious crawl.

Archer continued at the same pace. "We could tell them that someone tried to run us over, but if we describe the truck, they'll trace it to Ralph in no time and we'll have effectively written his obituary. We could also tell them that someone rolled a hand grenade—a dud—into our elevator, and they'd tell us it was a practical joke, which it very well might have been. Who knows? We could tell them about Group Twenty, and even if they believed us, we have no proof of their illegal activities whatsoever. Finally, we have nothing that would establish a connection between us and Group Twenty, and even it we did, we have no way of proving they were trying to harm us. I'm sorry, Sherwood, but we have nothing to give to the police, the FBI or anyone else. What we do have, like it or not, is Desmond Brownlow and associates."

"That sounds like a law firm," Sherwood mumbled. And while he recognized both the logic and the pragmatism behind Archer's words, the feeling of being without options was alien to him. He continued to feverishly search his mind for alternatives, but after a few minutes, had found none. The only solution seemed to be a forty-year-old Marine and a band of bikers, and that thought made him feel queasy. He had achieved moderate success in his life by zealously safeguarding his alternatives. He believed in never fully closing doors, and in always keeping a vigilant eye open for escape routes. The practice had served him well, and now he was on unfamiliar ground. Now doors were closed and Desmond Brownlow appeared to be the only viable escape route.

Archer quickly and accurately interpreted Sherwood's silence. "Please hear me out, Sherwood. I'm not willing to admit that Desmond is our last and only solution. To the contrary, I'm suggesting that he's our best solution. I grant you that the situation will be an uncommonly difficult one, but it will, without doubt, be one over which the three of us will be able to prevail."

Sherwood was momentarily lost in a thought, wishing that his friend would revert to an amplitude of common English usage. He was tempted to plead with him to tumble into an orgy of slang, or at least dangle a modifier or two. He'd even settle for a simple lack of agreement between subject and verb, which he knew was wishful thinking. 'Deal with the ideas, not with the way they're expressed,' he told himself, and immediately realized that he had successfully turned the entire grammar system of the English language on its ear.

"What do you suggest, Arch?" he conceded, fearing the worst.

"Exactly what you would surmise. We put ourselves in Desmond's strong and capable hands and allow ourselves to be directed by his resourcefulness and his experience. He has an ample supply of each, I assure you. You won't be disappointed."

"And what do you think we're going to prove with our little expedition?" Sherwood asked hesitantly, almost as if he really didn't want an answer.

"I'm not sure what we'll prove," Archer answered quietly, "but with a bit of luck we just may be able to prevent ourselves from being killed."

Sherwood sighed and after a moment raised his hand holding an imaginary glass in a toast. "Here's to uncle Des and his plan. May it prosper and nurture all those who participate in it."

Archer turned to him with a smile. "That, my friend, has the very familiar tone and character of a toast at a bachelor party, of which I've heard a great many."

"We may have need of more than an imaginary toast before this little venture is finished," Sherwood said bleakly, and turned his attention to the flat, vacant landscape on either side of the highway.

* * *

They had agreed to meet at a Piggly Wiggly parking lot on the outskirts of Pensacola near the intersection of Pensacola Boulevard and the Interstate at ten the next morning. Archer had wrestled the huge Lincoln Navigator over the highway for nearly two hours, radically oversteering while he mumbled pejorative comments about the size and clumsiness of American automobiles. While Sherwood remembered not a single incident when his friend had resorted to blasphemy in the past, he wished fervently that he could piece together the muffled syllables that Archer was quietly sputtering and make some sense of them. He was confident that he would discover a few creative expletives buried among the more decorous mumblings.

Archer pulled the Navigator in a corner space at the back of the market, threw the shift into park too quickly and the car jerked to a neck-snapping stop. He had loosened his necktie, and dark circles of perspiration had soaked through under the arms of his white shirt. He attributed his condition to the pure, mechanical obstinacy of his rented vehicle, and had orally composed several hate letters to Alan Mulally, president of the Ford Motor Company, during the drive. The content of his letters would, he assured Sherwood repeatedly, propel Mulally ignominiously from office, or at the very least besmirch the reputation of both the man and the marque.

Archer drew in a very deep breath and, staring out the window, said, "Group Twenty will be a breath of fresh air after being behind the wheel of this beast for two days. This has been an experience that could well be included among one of the circles in Dante's 'Inferno'. You've no doubt read it. Perhaps, 'Abandon hope, all ye who enter here,' would be an appropriate label to affix to the door of this monstrosity." Archer was seldom given to hyperbole.

"Relax, Arch," Sherwood said comfortingly, understanding his friend's antipathy to being behind the wheel of anything made beyond the borders of Italy or Germany. "I'll drive the next shift. And you'll get used to it eventually, believe me."

"I have absolutely no desire to get used to the act of imprecisely aiming this piece of iron down a roadway and hoping for the best. You don't drive this insensitive machine, you point it and correct its blunders as it wanders off course. It's neither nimble nor sure-footed, S.T., it simply plods. And it entirely lacks any scintilla of precision." He said this with finality of a physician diagnosing a terminal illness. Sherwood realized further attempts to placate his friend would be futile, and decided it would be best to sit quietly until Archer subsided and regained his emotional footing.

Less than twenty minutes later the first of the motorcycles appeared around the corner of the store, accompanied by the thudding, throaty rumble of unmuffled twin-cam, four cylinder engines. They came in pairs, led by a distinctively painted orange and blue Harley Davidson whose rider was instantly recognizable as Desmond. He was wearing a standard military issue lightweight combat helmet decorated with the motto "SEMPER FI" painted in alternating colors of orange and blue on the front. Behind him came a collection of the most unusual human beings that Archer had ever seen, on motorcycles or off.

"This is our reserve regiment?" the Parson asked a speechless Sherwood, his voice and face betraying a combination of astonishment and concern?

"If nothing else, they qualify as the ghastliest collection of creatures I've ever seen outside the confines of a Walmart Superstore."

Riveted by the sight, Sherwood was momentarily unable to respond as he watched the motorcycles, led by Desmond, slowly turn and arrange themselves in an orderly semi-circle around the Navigator. Their movements seemed choreographed, and one after the other they came to a stop, engines pounding thunderously. Sherwood counted more than thirty of them.

For several moments the machines and their riders were nearly motionless. Sherwood marveled at the leather vests covered with patches, the tattoos, the ponytails and the obligatory headbands. Except for Desmond, only a handful of other helmets was to be seen. He watched, sure that he could feel the rumble of the engines in the roots of his teeth. Then Desmond powered off his Harley, dismounted, and moved to a position at the center of the semi-circle and in front of the Archer's rented Navigator. Acting as on an unspoken command, every other machine shut down almost simultaneously.

"Nice wheels, nephew." He said with a straight face, glancing at the Navigator. Once again Sherwood was left to wonder if the comment was made seriously or in jest. Then Desmond made a sweeping gesture with his hand, indicating the men and bikes assembled in front of them.

"A few good men. There'll be more joining us as we get closer to Midland, but right now we're trying to keep the numbers down. Two hundred motorcycles riding into a town like Midland at the same time is going to put the whole state on edge, and you know how Texas is. It's on edge already, and they're liable to charbroil you if they think you've stolen a couple of hubcaps." He paused and leaned forward through the window into the car. "They still have Old Sparky in Texas, don't they?"

"Lethal injection since 1978 I think, Des," Archer answered without changing expression.

"Count on the Parson to keep your facts straight," Desmond said cheerily. He turned and looked at his entourage. "I think this is all of us. Do you want to meet a few of them?"

Sherwood decided to test his voice. "Thanks, but I think we're all set, Desmond. We can meet them later, in Midland, maybe."

"Your decision," Desmond answered. "Well, we best saddle up. I figure we've got a good fifteen or sixteen hours to go. Some of the guys are going to run straight through, but most of us will hole up somewhere on the other side of Dallas. You two suit yourselves. We'll keep in touch by cell phone."

Desmond turned and started back to his motorcycle. Archer stopped him. He let his eyes sweep over the riders.

"Where are all of you going to stay when you get to Midland? It might be difficult for more than 30 motorcycle riders to make a clandestine arrival in the city without stirring up some interest on the part of the authorities."

"Bikers, Parson, bikers," Desmond corrected him patiently. "And don't worry one little bit about it. These guys are creative when it comes to keeping a low profile—or not, for that matter. The plan is to split the troops up between a bunch of motels in the area around the city. That way the law will be slow to react in case they're sensitive about a few dozen motorcycles suddenly appearing in one area—not that they'll have anything to react to anyway—until it's too late."

The last was said with a wide grin that highlighted a good deal of respectable dental work, despite the reputation of Navy dentists to the contrary. "You all enjoy the trip, drive safe, and we'll see you in Midland." With that he put his helmet back on, adjusted his goggles and returned to his motorcycle. As if on cue, every other Harley fired up sequentially, and the air was again filled with fumes and the jarring rumble of motorcycle engines.

* * *

Bowen had called an emergency meeting at the First Capital Bank at 8:30 on Tuesday morning. No one had been given a reason, except to be told the meeting was urgent and mandatory. As they filed into the paneled room each man watched Bowen, trying to read from his face or posture some indication of the reason for their meeting. They could read nothing. Bowen remained impassive, leaning slightly to one side in deference to his injured leg.

"Please sit, gentlemen." He spoke the words evenly and calmly. Chairs on casters rolled silently over the huge oriental rug. Each man sat forward stiffly, several fingered their note pads or picked up pencils. There was a palpable air of tension and anticipation in the room. Eyes flicked from left to right. One chair was empty; one man was missing.

"We seem to have a situation on our hands that requires our immediate attention. We have visitors to our fine city—unusual visitors—and they have been in contact with one of our number." He paused for some time, causing the level of tension among the men around the table to intensify.

"Mr. Sparrow—I feel free to use his name for reasons you'll soon understand—has been approached and apparently taken prisoner by these visitors." For the first time the group could hear an undertone of disquiet that Bowen was working very hard to camouflage. He continued, controlling his voice with effort.

"We've learned this through various unimpeachable sources. You're familiar with each of them. As of this moment we have no idea who is behind this, or what their motive might be."

A short, doughy man at the end of the table raised his hand.

"I'll take questions in a moment, Three. For the time being, please just listen, and when you've heard me out, I'll be glad to address your questions." The big man again shifted his weight uncomfortably.

"I believe we must, for the moment, assume the worst. And that would be that someone is trying to get information about our organization, and that their intentions run contrary to our interests. We may also be dealing with a blackmailing situation. My suggestion is that we do nothing for the moment, and that we wait to hear from the kidnappers. I'm quite sure there will be demands of some sort. When we hear them, then, and then only, will we formulate our response. Now, questions?"

The man referred to as Three raised his hand and spoke simultaneously. "Do we know who these people are?"

"They appear to be led by the very same person that we first attempted to frighten, and then sent Sanjay to eradicate—the tall, strange looking man who was in contact with our late colleague, Sullivan. Now, however, he seems to have joined forces with some kind of motorcycle group. What purpose this improbable group hopes to serve is unknown as well as of questionable importance to us at the moment. We've been in similar situations before, and we'll learn more shortly, no doubt."

Three persisted. "Why not contact the Posse and let them . . ."

"That would take too long, and there appear to be far too many of these people as well. In any event a reaction like that would likely draw more attention to us than we need or is necessary. The Posse has a tendency to be headstrong and reckless. An O.K. corral shootout in the streets of Midland is the last kind of advertising we need. I'm sure you of all people can understand that." His tone had suddenly become brusque. It was apparent that he was under strain.

"Now, I expect that there are no further questions. I will let you know what we find out from our sources, and as soon as we know what Sparrow's kidnappers want, we will meet again here and discuss it. Until then, please remain available and don't discuss this subject with anyone."

He looked around the table slowly. "If I hear no objection, the meeting is adjourned."

There was no objection.

* * *

The Victorian Inn on West Wall Street in Midland had rooms that started at $55 a night, an overly-optimistic two-star rating and reviews that would discourage the homeless. The walls of the room were painted institutional yellow and stained suspicious colors in suspicious places. Sherwood had once heard that a good many hotel bedspreads are cleaned only once a year. He would have bet his last pair of white socks that this one hadn't been out of the room in a lot longer than that. He was careful to avoid even sitting on it.

Curtis Sparrow had not been difficult to track down. Of the ten Sparrows in the telephone book, two were widows, three were single women, one was deceased, one an eighty-three year-old retired telephone repairman, one a roustabout on an oil rig, and the fourth an unemployed construction worker. Now, dressed in a dark pinstriped suit, the last of the Sparrows was sitting, glum and dejected, in a straight-back chair in the corner of the room. He was doing his best to let as little of his trousers as possible come into contact with the stained and faded cushioned seat of the chair beneath him. His tie had been loosened, and his face was damp with sweat. Above him loomed Dakota, an almost paternal smile creasing his coarse features. Shank, short, wiry and malevolent looking, was painstakingly cleaning his fingernails with the tip of his knife blade. Occasionally he would inspect his findings and carefully wipe the residue off on the leg of his trousers. He appeared to be consumed with his work, and took no interest in anyone else in the room.

Leaning against the wall across the room, Archer was doing his best to look nonchalant. He was dressed uncomfortably and improbably in torn blue jeans, a tattered shirt with a coiled rattlesnake embroidered on the front pocket, and a cowboy hat with an imitation snakeskin band. Polished penny loafers undid the effect, and were the only giveaway of a previous identity.

Sherwood also wore blue jeans, second-hand combat boots, and an ill-fitting leather vest with ragged leather tassels covering a faded grey T-shirt.

Desmond had bought all of the clothing at a consignment shop adjacent to the Desert Springs Medical Center on East Flamingo Road. It hadn't been possible to find a shirt with sleeves long enough to accommodate Sherwood's generous wingspan, nor a pair of size six men's cowboy boots that would fit Archer's feet. It was also decided, after trying several on, that a cowboy hat simply exaggerated the size of Sherwood's ears as well the astonishing distance between his shoulders and his chin, making him look more like an elongated puppet than a forbidding adversary. Instead, he agreed to sport a three-day growth on his face and hoped the effect would detract from his stork-like physique.

Desmond had positioned a chair directly in front of Sparrow's and was leaning slightly backwards, tapping a pencil against the heel of his boot. He wore blue jeans and a plain, blue denim long sleeve shirt that covered his Marine Corps tattoo. His eyes were narrowed and focused on Sparrow's. Other than the pencil tapping on the booth heel, the room was silent.

If Sparrow had at one time entertained thoughts of putting up any form of resistance, it was evident from his expression and posture that they had been abandoned some time ago. Desmond, who had served two tours as a drill instructor at Parris Island, recognized from experience the unmistakable signs of surrender in the man's carriage and features.

"Two possibilities, Curtis. First, we could make this easy, or second—well, you don't want to know the second." He leaned forward, sounding almost solicitous. "But to make it simple for you, tell us everything about you, your people and what you're up to, or the rest of us will leave the room and come back after Shank and Dakota have had some time to talk things over with you in private. The first way's is the easy one for all of us, and the second's pretty messy." He looked around the hotel room. "Although they might not notice it in here for quite a while."

"What do you want to know?" Sparrow asked in a whisper.

"We're not going to do this again, Curtis my friend. Once more, all together—everything! Everything you know, we want to know." Desmond's voice had risen stridently. Sparrow winced.

"No names, please. You don't understand. If they ever found out, they'd start with my family."

"Curtis, I'm trying to be patient. We have more than thirty friends out there now, and there are more on the way. Most of them are a lot like my two acquaintances here," he motioned towards Shank and Dakota, "but not as nice. We already have your family, Curtis. We know where they live, where your children go to school, where your wife works out, everything.

So they are ours whenever we choose. Now, whose hands would you rather put the future of your family in—ours or your friends in that group of yours?"

"Can you give me anonymity?" Sparrow pleaded.

Desmond sighed. "Curtis. We didn't force you to enlist in this little organization of yours, now did we? We're not the government, and we don't run our own witness protection program. I think you already know the answer to that question. But I'll tell you what we can do. You get in touch with the top gun at your Group Twenty. Tell him all about us, and be sure to tell him there are thirty more of us out there just waiting for an excuse. Then say you didn't give us any information that we didn't already have, no names, no . . ."

"But I don't know the names." Sparrow offered apologetically.

"Just like when you were in school, Curtis, you don't speak unless you're called upon. You want to say something, be nice and raise your hand, and if your timing's good, you'll be the first to know about it. Are you with me so far?"

Sparrow nodded dumbly.

"You tell your boss that we have some very important intelligence to pass along to him, and him only. You tell him that if he doesn't get back to us before O-dark-thirty, the shit will really hit the fan. And not just for you and him, Curtis—for your whole jerk-off crew. Are you with me there, Curtis?"

Looking at the floor, Sparrow nodded again, and then murmured, "What does O-dark-thirty mean?"

"You just tell him before tomorrow morning. We'll be awake. And give me your cell phone. Tell Bowen to call me on this phone, and advise him not to be late. It might be the most important phone call he'll make in his lifetime—and yours, for that matter."

"What happens to me?" Sparrow said, looking first at Desmond, then at Shank and Dakota.

"You, my friend, are on your own unless, of course, we don't hear from your boss. In that case we'll send our one-man flesh-eating disease after you." He nodded at Shank, who stopped working on his nails and responded with a malicious grin.

Sparrow's face was glazed with sweat and apprehension. Desmond rose and stood above him.

"Now be gone, earthbound Sparrow. We hope we never see you again—and you might just hope the same. But remember, we will find you if we need to." A faint smile didn't disguise the implicit threat behind Desmond's words.

Hesitantly Sparrow rose to his feet and paused at the door, his hand on the doorknob. He looked as if he wanted to say something important.

"You know," Shank said to no one in particular. "Texas sucks. All people do here is get born again and kill each other."

Whatever was on Sparrow's mind abandoned him, and he scurried through the door, closing it carefully behind him.

* * *

The meeting took place in a small conference room adjacent to the chief's office in the Midland Police Department. Chavez, Lasansky and a slender, over-dressed man in a brown suit and cowboy boots sat at a round table in the center of the drab space. A large color photograph in a gold frame of the chief of police in full dress was the only decoration on any of the walls.

Louis knocked and walked in, followed by Weeks. Louis looked tired, and Weeks looked buoyant. Their ride to the station had amounted to an interrogation session, Weeks asking the questions and Louis doggedly shaking his head and refusing to answer them.

"C'mon, Henry, I'm your partner. I won't tell a soul. What's she like in bed? When's the wedding, anyway? Will I have to rent a tux, or is it going to be casual? How about a destination wedding? I hear Bermuda's supposed to be real nice this time of year. Expensive, though. What are my chances of being best man?" Weeks threw one after another at him, grinning and thoroughly enjoying himself. Louis didn't respond but drove silently, his fingers clenched around the faux leather of the steering wheel.

Chavez rose and introduced Louis and Weeks to the brown suit, a man from CAPERS named Vitelli. They shook hands and as they sat down, Weeks whispered to Louis, "Think I'd look good in something like that at the wedding?" he said, glancing down at the cowboy boots.

Chavez opened the session by first announcing that the Chief would be unable to attend because of a ribbon-cutting ceremony at a supermarket opening on East Michigan Avenue. Louis fired a withering look at him.

"He said he was invited personally by the mayor. Politics, you know," Chavez said shrugging. Then he picked up a large stack of papers in front of him, slid them over to Lasansky and declared abruptly that the case was over.

"We're done, gentlemen. We have our suspect, we have a witness, and we have Barber, the assistant D.A., on board. The next step is the grand jury. Barber says it's a slam-dunk. The chief asked me to thank you both and CAPERS as well, but it's in the system now and on its way. We can all go home and sleep well tonight."

"What exactly does your suspect look like?" Weeks asked suspiciously.

"He's a tall guy, long, kind of ratty brown hair and a beard. Why?" Lasansky asked.

"White guy?" Weeks prompted.

"Yeah. Why."

"Well, we've got a witness—an eye-witness that is—who described a little guy with a pointy nose, dark skin dressed in doctor's scrubs. It sure doesn't sound like the same guy your D.A. is about to bring in front of a grand jury."

"Maybe you didn't hear me, Sam. We're done. It's in the system, the case is closed. Now I know it won't bring the dead guy back, but at least it'll give the family some closure."

Louis exploded. "Closure? Closure's pure horse shit. It's a goddamn noun, Chavez, and it means 'termination'—that's all. You say it like it means that now everything's neat and tidy, hunky-dory, and the family's happy again. The guy's still dead, the wife's still a widow, the children don't have a father, and that's your kind of closure? I think I hear the unmistakable sound of someone washing his hands. Closure's what people who aren't involved say to make themselves feel better. It's like saying a guy who's dead is in a better place now. Pure, unadulterated bullshit." Louis, still beet red, had finally wound himself down.

Chavez sighed and looked at Lasansky and Vitelli. Both seemed surprised by Louis's outburst. It was Vitelli who finally spoke for all three.

"Leave it alone, fellas. The Chief says leave it alone, the D. A.'s happy and the mayor's happy. Even the Rangers have pulled out. It's done, and anyone who stirs up trouble will find himself in front of the Mayor's desk."

"Oh, I see," said Weeks. "Better to fry an innocent homeless guy than make the mayor unhappy. Justice, Midland-style," he added derisively.

"Listen, Weeks," Vitelli interrupted. "I heard about your eye-witness. He's a kid with a 9th grade education who does a whole lot of weed and probably other stuff, too. Any decent defense lawyer would peel him like a grape. This one is wrapped and ready for delivery. And you're probably right. We'll fry the guy. The accused's a loony who lives on the street and threatens people, and you know what? No one will miss him." He sat back in his chair with a self-satisfied half-smile on his face.

Weeks rose from his chair. "So CAPERS has signed on, too. It's not Midland justice, it's Texas justice—no surprises there." He turned to Louis and said, "Come on, Louis. Let's get out of here." As they reached the door he turned back to the three men at the table.

"You guys should have someone check out this room. It smells a lot like something died in here. Sleep well, everyone." He slammed the door with such force that the three men inside felt a burst of pressure in their ears and the photograph of Chief Hudson on the wall was knocked askew.

* * *

The phone rang four times before it was answered. It was almost four-thirty in the morning, and in their small motel room Archer, Sherwood, Shank and Dakota watched in silence as Desmond pick up the receiver. "We know who you are," he said, his voice a hoarse whisper.

Bowen waited for a moment at the other end of the line, and then said. "What do you want?"

"First of all, be polite. Say something like 'hello,' or 'good evening,'" Desmond replied sounding almost affable.

Bowen ignored him. "And I know who you are, and what you do. That makes it a draw, doesn't it?" There was little concern in his voice.

"I don't do draws, and you do not know me, you do not know what I do, and you most certainly do not know what I'm capable of doing." Desmond emphasized the word 'not' each time he spoke it. His tone remained a flat whisper, and the words were chilling, even to his nephew.

There had been some discussion among the men in the hotel room as to who should answer the expected phone call. Archer was dismissed out of hand. The thinking was that his scholarly tone and his reluctance—Sherwood used the word 'inability'—to desecrate the English language would undo any suggestion of menace in an exchange on the telephone.

Archer strongly supported Sherwood, but Desmond had misgivings. Sensing them, Sherwood readily withdrew from consideration. Dakota was briefly considered, but deemed verbally undernourished, a term that Archer put forward well out of Dakota's hearing. Shank was outspokenly unresponsive, and sat silently picking imaginary pieces of lint from his grimy blue jeans.

It was ultimately agreed that Desmond, with his drill instructor's voice and vocabulary, would be the obvious choice. It was apparent from the expression on his face that the decision agreed with him. Sherwood turned to Archer and quietly asked, "Arch, why the whisper?"

"Don't you ever watch detective shows on television—'Person of Interest' for example? The hero always seems to talk in a whisper, as if his mouth is two inches from his listener's ear. It's clearly an affectation, but Des thought it sounded mysterious and menacing, and that it might be an effective device to use with Bowen over the phone."

Sherwood searched his memory and nodded. Unbidden, CSI Miami had come to mind, and others flooded in behind it. Unnatural and artificial though it might be, whispering certainly was in widespread use in television detective shows.

"I'll ask you once more. What do you want?" This time Bowen's voice lacked some of the assurance of his initial responses.

"We'll get to that. You were in the military." This was a guess, but an educated one. Desmond assumed a military background from Sparrow's description of the man's comportment and his injured leg. As did others, he incorrectly assumed it was a combat injury.

"That has nothing to do with anything." Bowen's voice was confident.

"Air Force?" Desmond quietly persisted. "I bet you were a Wild Blue Yonder guy."

"I was in the army, if it's of any consequence to our discussion. What do you want?" His voice rose aggressively.

"Army." Desmond's tone was caustic. "I'll bet you were an officer. Probably a REMF, too. Now that's a combination for you."

"This conversation is leading us nowhere. As much as I've enjoyed our little talk, I'm hanging up now." Bowen hoped his words conveyed more assurance than he felt.

"You do that." Desmond's response was immediate. "You do that and a tsunami of shit like you've never seen before is going to wash over you and your pathetic little cesspool of section 8's."

Sherwood found himself astonished by Desmond's spontaneous and fluent use of aphorisms and metaphors. He wondered if they were the result of his years in the Marine Corps, or simply products of a fertile imagination.

Desmond continued without pausing for breath. "Now strap this to your face, box-kicker. Your man Sparrow has flown the coop. We're done with him. He was a carrier pigeon, a path to your door, nothing more. We already had all the gouge on you we needed. For one, we know you iced one of your own people. We also know what your organization does for fun and profit and what your plans are. We know you like to do naughty things to nice people, people who haven't done anything to you. We know you hire worthless dirtbags to do your work for you. More than that, pissant, we know all about you, your family, your mistress, and your habits, good, bad and ugly." Archer flinched slightly each time Desmond fired off one of his well-chosen epithets.

Desmond paused, letting his words sink in. His mention of a mistress was simply an informed guess. He knew what tended to happen once men attained power and influence, from John F. Kennedy to Bill Clinton, from Jimmy Swaggert to Jim and Tammy Bakker. Power and money invariably drew flocks of admiring young women, and powerful men had powerful egos—egos that were easily flattered. Not that he wasn't a touch envious himself, he admitted, but at the same time he recognized it as an Achilles heel for those in positions of power. The silence on the other end of the phone confirmed the fact that he was on target.

"Now, keeping that all that in mind, pog—and I know that ain't easy for you—this is what you're going to do. You will call your pathetic little collection of maggots together and announce your resignation from whatever position it is you hold there. You will resign as of today. You will explain that your Group Twenty has been discovered—uncovered may be a better word, like a rat's nest—and compromised. You will tell them that we know that you killed a nice fella with a nice wife, nice children and a nice dog, and that we will expose every aspect of your dirty little plan if you don't follow our directions to the letter."

"And just who should I say this unidentified 'we' is?" Bowen was making a show of ratcheting up his courage.

"'We' are your worst nightmare," Desmond continued. "We are the ones who have infiltrated your organization, and we are the ones who can send every one of you to jail for a very, very long time. We also are the ones who have documented every syllable of what I am now telling you, and have sent that documentation to a law firm in the capital city of Florida. If anything happens to us, they'll be on you quicker than you can zip up your fly in the men's room at a gay bar."

This time it was Sherwood who winced at the imagery.

"We are also the ones who have instructed that law firm to send a copy of those documents to the F.B.I. in case they don't hear from us soon,"

Desmond continued. "This is an interstate matter, Jocko, and that means the F.B.I. automatically becomes a player."

Archer had assured Desmond that, even if it had been true that they had left documentation in Florida, it would be impossible to verify the fact, given the overabundance of lawyers and law firms in Tallahassee. Planting the seed of infiltration and betrayal had also been Sherwood's idea. He understood that any organization that was searching its own ranks for traitors was an organization that had been effectively neutered.

"You're lying." Bowen countered weakly.

"No such luck, Jocko. Try the name Sullivan on for size. He's the one who opened up your little can of worms for us before you had him charbroiled in the trunk of a car. Oh, and be sure to say hello to Shylock for us." Sherwood had made note of the name mentioned by Metzger in the motel, and passed it along to Desmond while they waited for the phone call.

The amount of information Desmond had gleaned from Sherwood and Archer was proving extremely valuable. They had spent several hours together in the grimy hotel room exchanging ideas about their aims and strategies. There had even been a brief discussion about the use of specific vocabulary and types of threats that Desmond might employ. In the end it was decided that he would essentially employ the "Full Metal Jacket" model and run with the ball without coaching.

"What should I call you?" Bowen asked, sounding rattled.

"I already told you—call me your worst nightmare." Desmond was now clearly enjoying himself.

"Your name doesn't really matter. But whatever it is, you're pounding sand. I've never heard of anyone named Sullivan or Shylock. I don't know anything about someone killed in a trunk, and I've never heard of this Group Twenty you're talking about."

He paused long enough to see if his denials had taken root.

"Well, now, Mr. Bowen. Never heard of anyone called Sullivan?" By using Bowen's name, Desmond was making it clear just how much information he had about Group Twenty. "Must be you're a Baptist, 'cause for sure you never met a Catholic in your life. A whole mess of them are named Sullivan, you know. Incidentally, I never told you. I plain don't like Baptists."

"You may think you're safe with your group of motorcycle friends out there, but if I were you I'd be very careful. We have a long reach." The threat was monosyllabic and ominous, but also suggested Bowen's first admission of the Group's existence.

"I couldn't be more relaxed if I were having tea with the first lady, Mr. Bowen," Desmond said, employing his Marine Corps 'never let 'em see you sweat' persona. "And my motorcycle friends aren't all that easy to scare. As a matter of fact, they thrive on threats like flies on shit, but I'm sure a man of your experience knows that."

The five men in the room waited, but there was no sound from the other end of the line.

"Fair enough." Desmond answered, his voice once again changing from folksy to ominous. "If you'd rather listen, I'll fill in the silent parts." The next part of the dialogue had been anticipated and rehearsed. He launched into his lines enthusiastically.

"First, you know now that you have a mole in your little group, which is another way that we came up with all the information we have. You can look for him 'til the cows come home, Jocko, and even if you find him, it's too late. We know all of you—names, faces, addresses, families. But my guess is you'll never find the guy. He's good, I assure you."

They had discussed using this additional ruse, and Archer had stood firmly against it. They had no mole, they knew no other names except Shylock's, but were gambling that Bowen was in a sufficient state of turmoil that skepticism wouldn't be his first reaction. Archer felt that it not only wouldn't work, but should Bowen see through it, the rest of their plan would unravel. Desmond had pulled rank, explaining patiently that his vote was worth at least three of anyone else's, and the matter was settled. Archer acquiesced reluctantly, and Sherwood nodded gravely, aware that he had become more a spectator than a participant.

Desmond resumed his conversation with Bowen in his deep whisper. "Now hear this, Jocko. I will say it once, and only once, and you will keep your mouth shut until I'm finished. Are you with me so far?" He paused for an answer he knew wasn't coming, then, undeterred by the silence, shifted into third gear.

"You have repeatedly tried to intimidate or injure two very good friends of mine." Sherwood felt flattered to be included as one of Desmond's friends. "That will stop. You will also terminate any efforts to dishonor the government of this country." The rehearsal had called for the word 'destabilize', but in his exuberance Desmond had inserted 'dishonor' instead. Archer regarded Desmond's choice a favorable slip of the tongue.

"By that I mean, you will disband your little band of rich, misguided friends and tell them their services are no longer needed. Suggest they fill their spare time doing other things, like volunteering at a hospital or watching reruns of 'I Love Lucy' or something, because there will be no more meetings, no more bombs, no more killings, no more trouble. Remember that we have eyes on you and your family. We will know when, where and if you stray off the straight and narrow. And if you do, Jocko, you'd better give your soul to God, 'cause your ass belongs to me."

Nothing in Desmond's voice betrayed the fact that much of what he had said was pure deception, and that the five men in the room had no possible way to monitor the future activities of Group Twenty.

Still there was no answer at the other end of the line, and for a long moment the men thought the connection had failed. Then Bowen spoke again, his voice firm and steady.

"I don't believe a word you've just said. And if you have nothing more to add, I think our conversation is over."

"You don't believe a word I just said?" Desmond's laugh was genuine. "That's something else. You know what it's like? It's like saying you live in San Francisco and you're not gay. Of course you believe me, because everything I've said is true. It's time to get serious, Jocko. I really hoped we could avoid this, but I guess it's time for a little show of force. Call your Group Twenty maggots together and tell them to watch the local news—it's on at six-thirty, I'd guess. At least that's what time the news is on in most civilized parts of the country. And while you're watching it, remember two things. First, what you'll see is just the tip of the iceberg, and we can arrange a meeting with the iceberg itself at your convenience. Every one of those gentlemen you'll see tonight is a friend of ours, and every one of them is your worst enemy. They don't like change, Jocko, particularly not the kind of change you're talking about. You remember your worst nightmare? Well, it'll be on the news tonight." He paused, and Sherwood wondered if he'd forgotten the second part of his threat. But after a moment he picked up where he had left off, his horse whisper turning even colder.

"Second, and this is the most important thing I have to say to you. If you do not carry through with even the smallest part of my instructions, we will find your family first. By 'we' I mean tonight's news. Do we understand each other? Your family first, then you. And then we'll turn our attention to your little group, maybe after we mess up your mistress a bit. Be sure you pass that along to the fellas when you get them together."

He listened and waited for a response. Satisfied that the connection hadn't been broken and his listener was still there, he abandoned his whisper and said cheerfully. "Goodbye now, Jocko. Enjoy your evening, and we'll see you on the news." Then he snapped the phone shut and cut the connection.

* * *

It was an orderly parade. They rode in pairs, the men on the first two Harleys carrying huge American flags that whipped lazily behind them as they circled the block. The procession moved slowly and methodically, well within the speed limit, and by the time the last riders had disappeared around the corner, the lead pair had again appeared. They were circling the block on which predominant structure was the First Capital Bank of Texas.

Television crews and commentators had crowded the sidewalk across the street from the bank. The thunder of engines threated to drown out the vacuous observations of the commentators, who were wildly speculating on this sudden invasion of what one of them called "a gang of decidedly brutal, menacing creatures." The police had been called, and five of Midland's patrol vehicles responded, instantly wheeling away from donut shops and the tranquility of constructions sites, sirens wailing, squealing to a stop at a respectful distance from the parade of bikers. Lights flashing on their vehicles, the officers were clearly at a loss as to what role they would play in this unexpected incursion.

The Harleys circled noisily for more than 20 minutes. A news helicopter appeared overhead, the commentator on board desperately competing with the double obstacle of the 'whup-whup-whup' of the rotors and the more distant rumble of the motorcycle engines. His listeners could barely make out his frenzied squawks when he estimated the size of the pack to be at least two hundred, then made an archaic reference to "The Wild One", a 1953 movie starring Marlon Brando.

The procession stopped as calmly and compliantly as it had started. Moving with stage-managed precision, pair by pair the bikers pulled into diagonal parking slots in front of the bank. They gathered at the first of the five broad steps that led to the entrance of the bank, most carrying paper bags and drink cartons, and sat down side by side. Carefully laying out the colorful paper bags in their laps, all take-out orders from MacDonald's, Hardee's and What-A-Burger, the bikers sat on the steps and chatted affably with one another while they opened their dinners and began to eat. The commentators were struck dumb but, as always, managed to jabber their way through their own confusion.

"Whatever these men are planning to do, it seems they intend to have dinner before they do it," shouted the airborne commentator from his perch circling above.

"The bank could very well be in jeopardy," crowed his female partner. "And after the bank, who knows? That's the meanest looking group of people I've ever laid eyes on, and there must be more than three hundred of them. What's your take on this, Jay?"

"As you know I'm never one to speculate or jump to conclusions," Jay responded gravely, "but as I see it this kind of evil could indeed threaten the entire city of Midland and our way of life in the bargain. These groups are notorious for being lawless and extremely volatile. They are also armed, Mandy, as everyone knows. Any provocation and this could develop into something that could make Watts look like a campfire. I have no idea why the police haven't intervened as yet—before the situation gets completely out of hand."

Mandy finally, and for the first time in her career as a commentator, seemed at a loss for words. She was far better at covering the Runaway Bride story or the John Edwards trial, and drawing unfounded conclusions as to what those outcomes might be, than she was at on-the-scene coverage.

"Watts? Who was Watts?" Mandy asked vacuously.

"It's what, not who," he whispered. "Look it up later."

At that moment Midland Chief of Police Hudson decided to take action. From all five cars officers appeared, all with drawn guns, and took up defensive positions behind their cars. Weapons trembling in their hands and sweating profusely under heavy flak jackets, the men of the Midland Police Department nervously waited for orders from their Chief. Most of them had never drawn a firearm from its holster outside of the protective confines of the police firing range in the basement of the station. They were a young, inexperienced, and very uneasy group.

Crouching beside his car, Hudson was conferring heatedly with his deputy. He took off his hat and wiped his forehead with his sleeve. "I said get the goddamn SWAT team over here—now, Tidwell—not tomorrow."

Tidwell answered timorously, "We don't have a SWAT team, Chief. We've never trained guys to do that. Remember? You asked for volunteers more than a year ago and no one stepped forward. You even threatened . . ."

"That's enough, Tidwell. Now let me think."

"Ah, Chief. Your hair . . .

Tidwell's toupee had been dislodged when he mopped his brow, and was balanced jauntily over his left ear. He adjusted it quickly as he looked nervously over both shoulders for inquisitive TV cameras. Satisfied that his rug adjustment had not been recorded for posterity, he returned to pondering the situation before him.

That process took a sufficient amount of time for the bikers to finish their dinner put their empty cups and plastic utensils into the paper bags and tidy up the bottom step of the bank. It was then that the Chief made his decision.

"You go over there, Tidwell, and tell them they better get their asses and their motorcycles out of here if they know what's good for them."

"Me, Chief?" His deputy answered uncertainly.

"You, Tidwell. And tell them we've got a dozen armed officers here, each one highly trained and experienced. If they don't pack up and get out of town peacefully, it'll be handcuffs and jail cells on the menu tonight."

"But sir, our jail couldn't hold . . ."

"You just tell 'em what I said, and sound like you mean it. They'll know who they're dealing with before I'm done with them."

Tidwell rose and left the security of the patrol car. He walked unsteadily towards a central cluster of bikers who were busily engaged in putting their trash into receptacles in front of the bank. He drew himself up to full height and addressed the one he hoped would be the leader. The man was large, fully bearded and sported a colorful tattoo with a banner wrapped around a knife. The banner read "Death Before Dishonor." Tidwell deflated visibly.

"I think it's time for you and your men to leave," he said, and appended an irresolute "please" to his request.

"Evening, officer," the man answered with a smile. "Why should we leave? We like it here. Don't we like it here, fellas?" he said turning to the men behind him, all of whom nodded and smiled agreeably through beards peppered with the morsels of Big Macs and Whoppers.

"You're disturbing the peace. Now please leave," Tidwell suggested, his voice completely lacking conviction.

"Only thing that's disturbing the peace is that helicopter and them reporters, far as I can see, officer. Weren't for them, this would be a mighty peaceful spot."

Tidwell scrambled for a response. "You're on private property, and you're disrupting access to a place of business," he said, knowing that he was on shaky ground.

"Didn't know concrete steps was private property, friend. And if we're stopping folks from getting into that bank," he gestured over his shoulder, "then it's the only bank I ever seen was open at seven at night. But just to be friendly, we'll move to the sidewalk and enjoy the evening, if that makes you feel better. Sure is nice out tonight, ain't it?" The biker turned his back on Tidwell and started to rejoin his friends.

The deputy looked desperately at the Chief, who grimaced and made an impatient whirling motion with his hand, which was easily interpreted as "get on with it."

He played his last card, knowing it was a loser. "Either you leave, or I'm afraid it's jail. Now please move along."

The man turned back to Tidwell, his eyes narrowed, his expression intimidating.

"Now you listen to me, little man. You go back and tell your boss that we'll leave when we goddamn well feel like it, and no sooner. And if you or any of your other MPD clowns decide to be heroes, you better fasten your seatbelts. No one's done nothin' illegal, no one's going to jail, and that's the way it is, plain and simple. And if anyone is dumb enough to come out from behind those cherry toppers with a drawn weapon, that will be taken as a threat and then the shit will hit the fan real fast." The man put a great deal of emphasis on the word "real."

"Some of us here," he continued, again gesturing at the men gathered behind him, this time his face more relaxed and almost smiling, "have had the need of legal assistance in the past—for one reason or another." The words were greeted with unrestrained guffaws from the other bikers. "I'll bet we know more lawyers than you know pimps. And if you like your job and your badge, you'll back off now, and let us go back to enjoying the evening like law-abiding citizens." Again laughter.

Tidwell left and returned to the chief, shoulders slumped, head lowered. He relayed the biker's message and waited for the inevitable explosion. But Hudson's only response was one of unusual restraint. After a moment he turned to the nearest TV camera and spoke directly to the commentator holding the microphone. Before he had said four words he was surrounded by a dozen other microphones, eager commentators and their attendant cameras.

"I'm pleased to report that we've reached a successful conclusion to what might have been a very dangerous situation. Deputy Tidwell relayed my demands to the bikers, and I'm pleased to say they accepted them in their entirety. They will leave shortly. I allowed them enough time to clean up the area and pack up their gear, and in a few moments they'll be gone. They only asked that the media leave. I'm afraid you make them nervous—understandably," he added with a feeble grin. "So if I could ask you folks to please clear the area, it would be a great help to all of us." He paused, and said to no one in particular. "And tell that goddamn chopper to get the hell out, too."

Meanwhile, Jay was buoyantly filling the air with mindless commentary while directing his Botox grin at the camera. "The police are leaving, Mandy. The show of force seems to have worked. The police have managed to resolve a very incendiary situation, and I'm sure our listeners will be glad to know we're in the hands of such a capable police force."

"They certainly proved their mettle tonight," crooned a revived Mandy. "They're heroes, no question about it, Jay. Each and every one of them is a hero." She subsided reluctantly as the cameraman indicated that the show was over and he was shutting down his equipment.

* * *

Louis and Sampson had been asked personally by Chief Hudson to return to the Midland Police Department for debriefing. They sat and listened impassively as Chavez and Lasansky again presented a summary of their conclusions in the cases of Sullivan and Sanjay. Although again among the missing, it was presumed that the Chief, awash in political ambition, was behind an effort to mend fences between the two departments. It was a meaningless exercise, and what they heard came as no surprise.

"Once again, these are the highlights." This time it was Lasansky who took center stage. He spoke in a monotone. "Sullivan's murderer is in custody, has been indicted, and the Assistant District Attorney feels we have a good case. The Chief likes our witness, and even if the accused is on the loony tunes side of things, the case is a good one. Best guess is that he'll try an insanity defense, but one of those hasn't worked since maybe the Sickles case over a hundred years ago.

"Sickles? Who was Sickles?" Sampson risked a question.

"Not a nice guy. He was a Union General during the Civil War who killed his wife. He claimed temporary insanity and an all-male jury acquitted him. We don't have a whole lot of those kinds of juries around these days." Lasansky chuckled at his own humor. "Anyway, this one's neatly wrapped and tied with a bow. The other one—the Hispanic guy who took about 10 pounds of bird shot in the head—that was a gang killing, no question.

You know how these Cubans and Columbians are. A disagreement over a drug delivery, rival gang killing—could be anything. That's the way they handle their disagreements. Something doesn't look copacetic to one of those guys and ten minutes later you've got yourself a stiff. So there we are. Cases closed, tied with a bow, and we appreciate your help. We couldn't have done it without you."

The last comment was both forced and dismissive, and made without eye contact. If the chief's aim was to mend fences, this one was a clean miss. Louis couldn't resist a rejoinder.

"Thanks a lot, but we don't want any credit for this one. You finished it off all by yourselves. As you say, wrapped up and tied with a bow. That package you've got wrapped up so neatly stinks like five-day-old fish, Lasansky. If I were you I wouldn't take a lot of pride in your results."

"Look what happens when you try to be nice." Lasansky's expression changed to a sneer. "The chief said to congratulate you, I have no idea for what. You didn't do squat. Now, you've been congratulated, just don't let the door hit you in the ass on the way out."

Louis rose from his chair. "You know, Barney Fife, you're gonna have serious separation anxiety without us around. But feel free to come see us anytime—anytime you want the crap kicked out of you, that is."

Sampson put his hand on his partner's shoulder. "Louis, there's nothing more we can do here. The Keystone Kops have everything under control." Sampson gently pushed Louis toward the exit from behind. Chavez rose quickly and went to the photograph on the wall, prepared to steady the Chief should it become necessary.

Instead, Louis loosed a parting broadside. "Oh, and say hi to Hudson. Tell him his rug looked great on the evening news. I really liked the jaunty angle look."

Lasansky took a step forward, but Sam firmly propelled Louis through the door. "Not worth the trouble, Louis. Let's go."

"They've probably got an innocent guy in jail, they're planning to railroad him and it's not worth the trouble? And the Hispanic thing—that was laughable and racist as hell. They're leaving a killer walking around out there because they're too lazy or too incompetent to do anything about it."

"No one's been sent to jail yet, and the other case isn't closed, no matter what they say. They can't close it 'til they chase down all the leads, and they're not even close to doing that. It'll unravel before it gets close to trial.

They just want us out of their hair and their cases, and unfortunately they have every right to send us packing. Our job is over."

"They just want to sweep the whole thing under the rug. It makes life easier when the next 911 call about a cat in a tree comes in," Louis spat out with disgust.

As they walked down the street, Sam decided to turn the conversation away from the Midland Police Department. "So, any truth to the rumor that you're taking a cruise with lady Kate?

Louis kept walking. "No truth to that at all. Where did you hear that nonsense?"

"From Kate."

Louis stopped and turned, facing his partner. "Listen, Sam, we're just friends is all. Friends take trips together all the time. It doesn't have to mean anything."

"Oh, I see. You're telling me separate cabins."

"I'm not telling you anything." Louis's mood seemed to be improving despite his best efforts to head it off.

"The ship's name is Love Boat, unless I miss my guess."

"O.K., Sam. I'll give you this much. It's a Disney Cruise, five days, out of Canaveral. It goes to Nassau and someplace called Castaway Cay. It's cheap, we're going dutch, and we both can use the time off. End of story—end of questions."

"That's plenty, Louis. I've got the picture. Calm seas, blue-green water, ocean breezes, dancing. Three or four drinks, then you pop the question, she says yes, sets the date and starts to plan the wedding details while you're trying to hustle her back to the cabin. At your advanced age, late at night with a snoot full of hooch, you'll have to hurry or your chances of hitting a home run are slim to none. Not that they're all that good anyway. Oh, and while you're at it, you better tell her I'm your best man. That's just the way it's going to be."

The animated conversation continued as two men walked into the heavy humidity of the Midland evening.

* * *

It was hot, the air was thick with moisture, and the air conditioner in the window howled unproductively. The small room was crowded with men in sweat-drenched tank tops and T-shirts drinking diet Cokes and eating Moon Pies. The heavy, sweet smell of the Moon Pies combined with the perspiration of twelve or fifteen men was more than sufficient to discourage any visitor from crossing the threshold of the door. The men themselves, bending attentively over their food, sweat dripping audibly on soiled note pads, seemed oblivious or indifferent to the pervasiveness of the stench hanging over the room.

Shylock stood before this sad and sodden congregation, screwed up his courage, lowered his voice and called the meeting of the Fountain of Life to order. One or two men looked up curiously, then returned to their Moon Pies. The remainder chewed and drank noisily, scarcely noticing Shylock's efforts to get their attention.

"Gentlemen, we have several important items of business to attend to. Nine, I believe we're expecting a report from you on your success re-establishing contact with the Posse." He nodded encouragingly at the man he had addressed as Nine.

"Bullshit, Shylock, and stop calling me Nine. You know my name."

"If we're going to revive our organization, we have to maintain discipline, Nine. Anonymity is the best way, you know that."

"I repeat, bullshit. All this secrecy is for nothing. Most of the guys in here are only here for the free Moon Pies and the drinks. You and Five are the only two in the room who take this stuff seriously, and I'm not so sure about him. You don't really think you can bring Texas to Riviera Beach, do you?"

Five sat listlessly in the corner, his white shirt stuck to his back and chest, his shirt collar open and his bow tie hanging limply from his collar. He was silent and lost in his own thoughts.

Shylock soldiered on. "All we need is a little more commitment and effort on all of our parts and . . ."

"All we need is a decent air conditioner," Nine interrupted. "And whoever came up with this name—Fountain of Life—must have been on something real strong. You want to talk about what we need, try this on. First a new air conditioner, then change the name, next get something better to eat and drink than Moon Pies and Cokes, and then maybe some of us will come to the next meeting. As a matter of fact, get some of that coke that doesn't come in a can and you may triple your audience." His words were greeted with a combination of muted cheers and murmurs of agreement from other members, whose mouths were too full to verbalize their approval.

Shylock had to admit that the new name, which had seemed like a fine idea when he and Five had moved to Florida, hadn't worked out so well.

He had read that it was a term associated with baptism, and the correlation between a new beginning and the re-birth of the organization had appealed to him. It also struck him as a fairly bland and innocuous name, one that would draw no attention should it by any chance be stumbled upon by law enforcement or the media.

The choice had, however, been nothing short of a disastrous one. A new member had indeed leaked the name, and Fountain of Life had been besieged with calls from prospective new members. Shylock had unwittingly chosen a name identical to that of a new but burgeoning evangelical sect located in Sebring, Florida.

The Fountain of Life in Sebring had a brief but storied history. Its pastor, John Nelson Canning, had strangled two elderly members of his congregation to death for their money and had been sentenced to life in prison. This fact, however, failed to discourage the great majority of his parishioners—quite the contrary. In the disgraced pastor's wake, the church had hired a replacement and was growing exponentially. By the time Shylock arrived in Riviera Beach, it had begun to spread its wings over a substantial portion of the southern quarter of the state.

Once news of Shylock's newly established organization leaked out, avid followers and perspective worshippers swarmed over Fountain of Life like fire ants. It was so bad that Shylock had been forced to change location of the meetings twice and to cut off all phone service. In retrospect he was forced to admit that a direct phone line might have been an exercise in bad judgment in the first place, but he was new to the job. Now they were stuck in a small room on the top floor of a run-down, third-rate office building that had been built well before central air conditioning had become both a fact and a necessity. But with the move, at least the assault of the avid had been curbed.

To make matters worse, it appeared that he might even be losing Five. When Stillman entered the room at the start of today's meeting, he shook his head, looked around and dolefully recited a line from 'Julius Caesar.'

"Are all they conquests, glories, triumphs, spoils,
Shrunk to this little measure?"

Shylock correctly presumed that Five was drawing an unflattering comparison between Fountain of Life and the once proud and powerful Group Twenty of Midland, Texas. He had looked around him at peeling paint and stained linoleum floors' and was flooded with memories of oriental carpets and polished mahogany. His confidence fell to a new low, and his renewed attempt to call the meeting to order seemed to be falling on deaf ears.

Unexpectedly, Five rose at that very moment and asked to make a formal motion. Shylock, sensing that some semblance of order was perhaps finally being restored, recognized him and leaned forward anxiously to hear the motion. Almost immediately he sat down heavily in his chair and listened to the motion in disbelief. Then, in a state of utter stupefaction, he sat in dazed silence as the motion passed unanimously. Stillman looked at him stolidly and dispassionately and, without objection, announced that the final meeting of the Fountain of Life was formally adjourned.

* * *

EPILOGUE

It was a matter of pure happenstance that I saw Sherwood once more following the events described in this book. It was several years later, and at the time I was in the recovery room at Reconstructive Surgery Center at Emory Healthcare in Atlanta. Sherwood walked in, just as tall and gangly as I remembered him, but otherwise a stranger. He was dressed in a blue blazer, a plaid necktie, white button-down shirt and dark grey trousers. The boots were gone, and in their place were black wing tip shoes. I looked furtively for a sign of white socks, but saw none. The Sherwood before me was a far more confident, self-assured version of the one I remembered. I spoke first.

"Sherwood, it's me. It's been a very long time." I reached out my hand to shake his. I was restricted to the wheelchair for the moment, and unable to rise and greet him properly.

He came closer and stared into my eyes. Everything else from my neck to the top of my cranium was wrapped in spiraling layers of bandages. "Is that really you?" he asked.

"It most certainly is," I assured him. "How've you been?"

"I'm fine, but are you all right?" he asked. "Were you in an accident or something?"

"Oh, no. I'm fine. I've just had a face-lift—actually my second face-lift. I'm just waiting to be picked up and taken home. You know, they won't let you out of these things once they get you in them," I said, tapping the arm of the wheelchair and trying to smile. "Lawsuits, or something."

"Two face-lifts? Why two face-lifts? You looked just fine the last time we saw each other."

"Well," I explained, "the first one didn't take. I have a certain look I'm going for-something between Dick Clark and Michael Jackson. I always liked Dick Clark's youth and Michael Jackson's chiseled features. I'm aiming for a combination of the two. After the first one I'm afraid I looked a whole lot like Morely Safer, so I decided I had to give it another shot. You know, cross your fingers." I tried my smile again, but not only was it painful, it was buried invisibly behind yards of gauze and tape. "What's a few stitches and six or eight weeks of recuperation in the long run. I sure don't want to die looking old. You understand, right?"

He didn't look like he understood.

"What happened to the top of your head?" He asked, completely off the subject.

Without the benefit of a mirror, I could only hazard a guess. "Hair transplant. I had it done just before my last facelift. Two more treatments and the doctors say I'll look just like Donald Trump." I attempted a muffled chuckle and leaned forward so that he could get a better look.

"Do you like it?" I asked.

Sherwood suddenly didn't look at all well. I decided to change the direction of the conversation.

"Why are you here?" I asked him. "If it's any of my business."

"Ears." He answered. "It seems my ears were holding me back, literally and figuratively. You know I left my concierge job three years ago and got a job as a representative for an electrical supply company. I'm in sales, and my boss suggested that the ears were a negative. You ever hear of an 'ear reduction'?"

"No," I answered. "I've heard of pretty much every other kind of reduction, but not the ears. Maybe that ought to be next on my list."

"I really didn't have a choice. It was the ears or the job, and the job pays well," he said with a resigned smile.

"Is this your first time?" I asked, solicitously.

"It is, and my last, I expect." He answered.

"Don't be so sure. You may get to like it."

Sherwood looked at me suspiciously. "Could I ask how old you are?"

"It's not how old you are, but how old you look." I smiled, or rather grimaced indiscernibly. "I'm shooting for the forty-five to fifty look. Dick Clark looked about fifty when he croaked, wouldn't you say?"

Sherwood looked even more uncomfortable and didn't answer. He muttered something about his appointment time and how late it was. Having been born with an innate sense that told me when others were uncomfortable with a subject, I moved quickly to another one. No doubt he was apprehensive about his upcoming surgery.

"Don't go yet, old friend. We've got some things to catch up on. Tell me about Archer, and Desmond. How are they and what are they up to now?"

Sherwood sat down and smiled as he reminisced. "The last time I saw those guys was at Raunchy's place, believe it or not. You remember Raunchy, don't you?"

"How could I forget? Raunchy was the one who referred to intimacy with his wife as 'emptying the magazine.'"

"That would be Raunch. Well, he threw what he called a potluck dinner for the bunch of us. He said he called it potluck because he hoped he'd get lucky and someone would bring some pot. Anyway, it gave us a chance to get together, and they all seem to be doing well. Raunchy got a gym membership and lost a bunch of weight. He wears his hair short, shaves every day and has become a deacon in a Pentecostal church. He's big into divine healing and eschatology. That's the belief in the imminent second coming, as he explained it to us."

I was secretly pleased that Sherwood had defined the word without prompting, having for some reason subconsciously fastened on the word 'scatology'.

"Desmond hasn't changed a bit," he continued. "Maybe a touch heavier, but still a formidable specimen. His Harley business boomed after the biking community heard about what happened in Midland. He became an immediate hero among bikers all across the south. Apparently buyers come from as far away as Virginia and Kentucky just to say they bought a bike from Desmond Brownlow's shop. Incidentally, he changed the name to 'Gator Motorcyclorama', and it's really taken off. He's been able to open two more huge sales outlets in Miami and Jacksonville, and he's made so much money he was able to buy a golf condominium at the Ocean Reef Club on Key Largo. He doesn't much like it there, but Claire does. I understand the other members aren't crazy about the fact that he rides his Harley around the club wearing his Gator Motorcycle Club T-shirt either. But he's still the same old Desmond."

"Wow. Desmond at the Ocean Reef Club. Another Marine made good, I guess. What about Archer?" I asked. "What is he up to now that all the excitement is over?"

"Archer is very involved in writing a book about the Civil War. I hear it's patterned after Michael Shaara's 'Killer Angels.' Apparently it's historical fiction. It's set at the Battle of Natural Bridge, and he follows the events with both fictional and real characters in the mix, just like Shaara's book. The last I heard he had gathered a great deal of information about both the Union and Rebel commanders, and was trying to decide if it was southern valor or Yankee stupidity that had the greater influence on the outcome of the battle. Given his background and regional biases, I'd put my money on southern valor."

"Any idea how much progress he's making?" I asked sympathetically.

"It's actually a bit scary. He's pretty obsessed with it, but that's his nature anyway. If you're sitting somewhere and talking with him he'll suddenly jump up in the middle of a conversation and say, 'I'll be right back. I've just had an idea.' I've even seen him come thundering out of the bathroom and rush to the computer without saying a word. An idea for his book, I guess, and he didn't want the bathroom to distract him. That's how involved he is."

"Archer doesn't 'thunder.'" I said needlessly.

"Well, you get the idea. Everyone who knows him will be relieved when he gets the book behind him and begins to lead a normal life again."

"I'm not sure what a normal life is for Archer, but how does he respond when people mention that to him, as I'm sure happens."

"He just smiles and says that the book keeps him out of the headlines and the singles bars."

"Please let them all know that I think of them often when you see them again. I really do miss them. Talk about characters. But what about you?

It's too bad you weren't able to uncover the whole story about the Confederate treasure train and what happened to it. After all, that's what got you involved in all this in the first place."

"Actually, I did track it down. At least I'm pretty sure I did. I've spent the better part of a year piecing all of this together. I'll admit a lot of it is still conjecture, and I don't really have any substantive proof yet. But if you add it all up, it makes a whole lot of sense—unfortunately." Sherwood added the last word and paused, looking rather subdued and pensive. He sat motionless for some time.

"Well? What is this conjecture of yours, Sherwood? What did you piece together?"

A nurse entered the room and walked up behind Sherwood, touching him lightly on the shoulder.

"They'll be ready for you in surgery in a few minutes, Mr. T . . ." She stopped and looked at Sherwood helplessly, waiting for support in pronouncing his last name.

"Too-all-a-tin." I volunteered helpfully.

She dutifully repeated the name and gave him an encouraging professional smile. "If you would follow me, please, we're going to give you something to relax you before your surgery."

Sherwood stood and spoke to me before leaving the room. "This isn't just thumbtacking the ears back, you know. The doctor says it's a lot of work—cutting, shaving, shaping—he's basically making me a pair of new ears."

"Some people have all the fun," I said and turned to the nurse. "Will he come back here before surgery? We haven't nearly finished our conversation."

"Yes sir, he will. We'll just be a few minutes." She flashed another brief, professional smile at me, then took Sherwood by the elbow and steered him from the room.

Sherwood returned twenty minutes later in a wheelchair with a peripheral IV drip in the back of his right hand. The drip was fed by a clear plastic bag of fluid mounted on a pole that was clamped to the back of his chair.

"Is that the good stuff?" I asked the nurse, indicating the bag of fluid. She looked at me sternly without answering and adjusted the blanket on Sherwood's lap.

"It sure feels like it," he said smiling, answering for her. When I looked at him I noticed that his eyes were unfocused and the eyelids were drooping appreciably. This was a giveaway to someone as experienced with these procedures as I that Sherwood was approaching a place where he couldn't be less interested in what they did to his ears. Having just left that very place, I'll admit to a brief moment of jealousy. The nurse was turning to leave the room.

"Excuse me," I said, "but isn't this the recovery room? Shouldn't Mr. Too-all-a-tin be in another area? A pre-surgery area or something?"

"We're renovating, sir, and we've had to combine the two." She looked around the room. "At least it's not crowded. It was hard to find a seat in here two days ago." She smiled professionally again and left the room, one of her white sneakers squeaking discordantly in the quiet room.

"Now, where were we before they stuck me in this thing?" he asked, gesturing absently in the general direction of his wheelchair, his words slurred.

"We were talking about the treasure and where it ended up. You indicated you had a pretty good idea what happened to it," I said, feeling that in his current state he might need a bit of background and updating.

Sherwood inspected his surroundings with excessive care—a slow, exaggerated caricature of surveillance. The waiting room was empty of patients and the nearest nurse was on the phone at a desk outside the entrance of the room. Apparently satisfied that we weren't in danger of being overheard, he looked at me conspiratorially, holding my eyes for a long moment. Then he said, "Are you sure you're ready for this?" The words had a challenging ring.

"Fire away," I answered, employing as casual a tone as possible in an effort to reduce the tension his words had occasioned.

Sherwood leaned forward and his voice dropped to a whisper. He spoke through a euphoric haze, but that notwithstanding his voice was strong and the clarity of his memory astonishing.

"I suppose it starts right here in Florida with our former Governor. You remember him, don't you?"

"There have been a number of them, Sherwood. Help me out here."

"The one with the very small male member," he answered, leaning still closer and almost whispering.

Memory jogged, I nodded.

"As you know, he was born in the very city which we made famous three years ago as the birthplace of 'The Great Motorcycle Incident'. He grew up there and eventually attended the University of Texas. And of course you know his father and his brother, either very well or too well, depending on your politics." He continued on without waiting for an answer. "Anyway, this former Governor and his wife have children, but this really only concerns his two male heirs." He stopped suddenly and wheeled himself closer to me. There was concern etched on his face. "This could get me in a lot of trouble if it gets out. No names here, you understand? It's safer that way."

His sense of secrecy seemed a bit excessive, but I decided to play along. "Sure, Sherwood—no names. That's fine."

"Right." The sedative was making him sound a bit like a garrulous drunk. I tried to look fascinated.

"His first son, let's call him P.G., was born in the late '70's, also in Midland. His youngest, we'll call him J.J. the second, was born five or six years after that." He paused and took a deep breath. Then his voice became softer even more secretive.

"P.G. earned a doctorate from the University of Texas after graduating from college. He is now in his mid-thirties—not so far from the age that a good many aspiring politicians begin their preparation for office. Now the youngest son, J.J. Secundo, is in business in Miami. He's a babe of about twenty-six or so, too young for the moment to be considered seriously for office, even here in Florida." His voice was tinged with sarcasm. Intensity seemed to be overpowering the effects of the sedative. "This is where it gets scary."

The sound of his voice was unsettling. I sensed an involuntary tightening of my sphincters. "I'm not sure I like where you're headed with this, Sherwood."

"You're going to like it even less," Sherwood replied "and if I'm right it gets scarier still. I mentioned that Secundo was too young for political office, didn't I?" He paused and wandered off his subject, no doubt under the influence of his IV. "I don't know. Given some of the people currently in office in this state, I suggest that nothing, including age, is a stretch in Florida politics. And I guess the same thing could be said about the state of Texas. When you think back on it, that whole Midland business is enough to give you the creeps, or hemorrhoids, or something."

I found myself hoping that his reference to sphincters was unintentional. He closed his eyes and rested for a moment. I decided not to disturb him, hoping he wouldn't doze off. Seconds later he opened his eyes again and smiled at me blankly. I decided to bring him back before the sedative carried him to a more distant and pleasant place.

"Let's get back to the subject. The family you were talking about . . ." He hushed me with a quick gesture as I was reaching for a name.

"No names, remember. No names, for God's sake." He regrouped for a moment and then continued. "Let me think for a minute." This took some time, and it was obvious that he was trying to create clarity out of the murk of his sedation. He suddenly sat up straighter.

"If you're ready, here goes. Group Twenty, as it was originally founded, was an alliance of very prosperous men with an agenda. As you know better than most, that agenda was to re-establish the objectives of the Confederacy politically and economically. I believe that the agenda has now been modified—revised if you like—in an attempt to maintain relevance. No more cotton and slavery, but the still aspirations remain strikingly similar. I believe their endgame has been modernized brilliantly. The objective of Group Twenty has now become to create enough confusion to allow a presidential candidate of their choosing to step in and re-establish control over that confusion. In other words, they are now attempting to clear a path for a future leader of the United States."

"I'm pretty sure I don't like where this is headed," I said. "I smell a conspiracy theory in the wind." Baptists in the woodpile came to mind spontaneously. I had lowered my voice and, as Sherwood had done, scanned the room for eavesdroppers.

"I used the word president in the singular," he continued. "Perhaps I should have used it in the plural. But for the moment let's go back a century or so. Let's just say, for the sake of argument, that the Confederate treasure was indeed used in the mid-1860's to promote the cause of the Confederacy. There is a fair amount of evidence to support this. If so, it most certainly had a powerful impact on Texas politics throughout the 19th century and it would follow that this could well be the case until the present day. You said as much in your book."

I was struggling to jump from one century to the next as well as to follow his logic, influenced as it was by the pre-operative tranquilizer. I had to admit that his ability to recall this information at all was remarkable. Then I reminded myself that this subject had been his passion for nearly a decade. There was really no need now for me to take the next step, but I did.

"Whoa, Sherwood. You're saying that Group Twenty—or whatever that bunch calls itself now, if they've managed to reinvent themselves—has been involved not only in a campaign against the government, but also in underwriting presidential campaigns." Once again scanning for the undetected, I whispered the next sentence. "And you're further suggesting that they're currently working in support of the campaign of a future president? Do I have that straight?" I tried gallantly to work my face into an expression of disbelief. The pain was incredible.

"Listen. You wrote the book, my friend, I didn't. That's exactly where all of this leads us." Sherwood's voice rose as he spoke and he uttered the word 'exactly' with such volume that the nurse at the desk craned her neck around the doorway to see if anyone was in trouble.

I tried to quiet him. "O.K." I said. "Then help me out here a bit, and not so loud. If I'm not way off base, you're about to link the Confederate treasure and Group Twenty specifically to a particular family. Please tell me I'm wrong."

"You're not wrong if I'm right." I struggled a bit to sort out his sentence.

"You'd better follow this through to its logical conclusion for me, if there is a logical one. I'm kind of hoping you're not saying what I think you're saying, and what I'm hearing isn't really what I'm hearing, but is the result of your sedative and the lingering effects of my anesthesia." My wording confused even me as it left my mouth. I decided my verbal impairment was due to that large, white, football-shaped pill they gave me shortly after my procedure had been finished.

"I think you know what I'm implying, but I'll state it clearly. Group Twenty has unofficially anointed a particular family as the country's answer to a monarchy."

He paused to let that sink in. I felt the pressing need for another large, white oblong pill. Without thinking I followed the large white pill image to its logical conclusion. "This is a pretty tough one to swallow, Sherwood," I cautioned. He continued as if he hadn't heard me.

"If we accept the premise that Group Twenty was working in support of this family—and I can't verify that the family is even aware of it for certain—then their short and long range plan would seem to be pretty clear. They're in the business of encouraging an angry, disillusioned citizenry to demand major changes within the government. Changes—not clearly defined changes, just changes." That seemed to trigger another lapse, and he took an oblique detour. "It's kind of like the Students for a Democratic Society in the '60's, if I remember correctly."

I explored my own memory of the '60's, and discovered they were well obscured in a haze of Acapulco Gold.

"In any event, in response to the need for change, they offer up a hard-nosed, no-nonsense candidate who promises to end the people's frustration, lower taxes, restrict the federal government, and so on and so on and so on."

"That sounds a bit familiar," I admitted.

"It should, for crying out loud. It's your book that led us here. And in the meantime Group Twenty employs a number of satellite bodies to work towards the same goal; convincing the voting public that the entire political system as it's constituted today is unworkable. If you have enough satellites, at least one of them is bound to take root and thrive. Plant the seeds, as they say. Are you making any connections here?" He posed the question as if the answer were obvious. It was. Nonetheless I played dumb.

"I don't suppose it would be the Green Party, or the Socialist Worker's Party?" He didn't even acknowledge my response.

"The Posse?" I suggested lamely. "Maybe the Occupiers?"

"Neither nor," he admonished. "Think. A well-financed, apparently grass-roots, vocal, appeal-to-the-people type message." He leaned back in his wheelchair, content that he had led me by the hand to the answer.

"Not the Tea Party," I protested, aware of how unconvincing my response sounded in the wake of his explanation.

"The Tea Party indeed. They certainly weren't part of an original plan. They're a new variation on an old theme. I'm not sure they're even aware of the role they're playing, but I don't think there's any doubt that Group Twenty is the wizard behind the curtain."

In spite of myself I liked his image of the wizard behind the curtain. "You're telling me that the Tea Party is actively engaged in a 'south shall rise again' movement'? Come on, Sherwood. Those folks aren't southerners. They're from all over."

"I'm not telling you that at all. I'm suggesting that Group Twenty recruited and groomed these people and set them on a mission to pursue certain goals. Use the right catchwords over and over and eventually you'll find yourself with a whole gaggle of disciples. Both teams use similar tactics, you know, and always have. To get the votes, employ any device that works. Stake out a position, dig your heels in and stir up your supporters. One side has a rabble-rouser who's demanding that his representatives sign an oath that they'll never agree to raise taxes. An oath, mind you, and of course that means no increase in taxes even if the country's going down the tubes. Meanwhile the other side boasts a congresswoman and her supporters who are all willing to let the bus go over a fiscal cliff if higher taxes aren't approved. That would lead to thousands of lost jobs and a drastically weakened economy when we least need it. And each side has considerable support from both partisan congressmen and its own voter bloc."

"That sounds a lot like a political doomsday machine—a kind of partisan scorched earth policy," I offered, impressed by the implications.

"More like playing Russian Roulette with the country. You can blame them all and you should, but that's not where we were headed with Group Twenty. They've exerted influence over the Tea Party, but so surreptitiously that even the members of the Party don't recognize it. Just think about what's happened during the last several years. All politicians from each party are terrified of making decisions that aren't sanctioned by their base. As a result the government is becoming effectively paralyzed. It simply has stopped working, blame whomever you wish. But in any case as a result one of the main goals of Group Twenty has been realized."

"And where exactly does this get Group Twenty? We started off talking about Jefferson Davis, remember? "I find that playing dumb comes naturally, and I was pretty sure I knew the answer.

"Where it gets them is well on the road to re-establishing a good many of the goals of the Confederacy, whether they realize it or not. And it also gets them a good deal closer to the presidency of the United States."

Sherwood sat back in his chair. I hadn't seen him look smug in a long time, but with his long arms folded in front of him and a self-assured smile on his face, ears and all, smug was the only word that came to mind.

"And those goals would be?" I asked, allowing myself to be led pliantly through the maze of his explanation.

"Freedom from federal oppression, a smaller central government, stronger states rights, and taxation were the four primary areas of disagreement that the South had with the Union before and during the war. Slavery, of course, but I've taken that out of the equation because it's no longer a feasible goal," he said as an aside. "Otherwise, you can see the parallels."

"You're saying that what we're seeing is an undercover operation to revive the Confederacy, and that it was organized and supported by Group Twenty using the Tea Party among others as a catalyst?" I asked, incredulous.

"That's simplifying matters nicely, but in so many words I am. These may not have been exactly the goals of the Confederacy in Jefferson Davis's time, but they sure look like an updated and modernized version of them. And I'm also saying that our Constitution and the Bill of Rights are looking pretty vulnerable right now as a result."

Still groggy from my surgery, I felt as if I'd been battered by a political cudgel. I thought about asking him if I could borrow his IV for a few minutes. "It's a long, long stretch, Sherwood. You might think about going into writing fiction."

"Is it now?" He answered easily. "Just think about some of the political messages being directed at the public on a daily basis. Any light bulbs going on? Reduce the size of the government, eliminate departments, lower income taxes, and improve states rights."

He ticked these off in a pleasant tone, but I still felt bludgeoned. "And where might we be headed now?" I asked wearily, wanting desperately to go home and sleep for several days. "You started all of this talking about our Governor with the little . . ."

He interrupted. "I'm getting back to that. As I said, my guess is that we're about to be faced with our own version of an hereditary monarchy."

"Are you sure that IV drip isn't doing the talking for you?" I asked hopefully.

"I feel fine. Just let me finish this up. For the sake of argument, let's say our former Governor becomes the next in line for the presidency, to be followed over the course of time by the rest of the dynasty—son P.J. and youngest son, Secundo. Are you with me?" he repeated again, and I told him I was, but wished I wasn't.

"Now go back a bit. For twelve of the last twenty years, a father and his son held the highest office in the country. If it came to pass . . ."

And it came to pass . . . I grimaced at the biblical terminology,

". . . we could quite possibly be faced with three successive, or nearly successive presidencies in one family in our not-so-distant future. The math works out quite well, actually. And if everything falls into place that could potentially add up to twenty-four more years of that family running this country in the early and middle years of the 21st century. You might throw in a four-year hiatus after either our former Governor or Secundo—just enough time to give someone else four years to screw things up. Then back to the game plan again. In any event there aren't many monarchies around that can boast that kind of record. There were six kings of England named George, I think, and this is getting pretty close."

I was quietly adding using my fingers. I was surprised that I only needed one hand. "You're about to tell me that this family is consciously involved in a conspiracy to insert themselves, one by one, into the presidency of the United States. Sorry, Sherwood, but I can't buy that."

"I'm not about to tell you anything of the sort. It would be nice and neat to say that the family sits by the fire in the evening drinking tea and planning bombings and assassinations. I don't think it's that simple. If they ever did exercise control over Group Twenty, they've probably lost it. Group Twenty is the proverbial horse that escaped before the barn door was locked. I think it's been feral and running wild for some time.

"O.K." I said. "For the sake of argument, let's say you're right about this. Now tell me that you single-handedly nipped this whole thing in the bud by what you did in Midland." Down deep I knew this was whistling in the dark.

"We may have slowed them down a bit," Sherwood said soberly, "but the money's still there, the ambition's still there, and a lot of the players are still around. As soon as a new configuration of Group Twenty gets its act together, they'll most likely be back in business. I'm afraid the only hope in the end is to rely on the intelligence of the voting public."

I hadn't heard more disheartening words since Sherwood had begun his recitation. I was reminded of Winston Churchill's words when he said, 'The best argument against democracy is a five minute conversation with the average voter.'

The nurse returned with the same gentle touch to Sherwood's shoulder. "We're ready, Mr. Twa . . ." She effectively swallowed the last two syllables. I interrupted.

"Just one minute, please. We're very old friends and if we could have just five more minutes."

"No more than five minutes. Just wheel yourself down the hall when you're ready, Mr . . ." She decided against the attempt this time. "I'll be in the third room on the right."

"And incidentally, do you by any chance have one or two of those white, football-shaped pills around? They certainly would help." She looked at me severely and again left without answering. Even lacking the added support of the oblong pill, I decided to ask Sherwood a question that had been troubling me since he began his explanation.

"Everybody, from Bowen on down, said they were following orders from a superior. Sounds a lot like Nazi Germany, doesn't it. Did you find any information as to who ultimately was pulling the strings of Group Twenty and the entire operation? Was it one of our former presidents?" I asked hopefully.

"Not the one nor the other," he answered without hesitation.

"Then it's our former Governor with the little thing." I was sure I was on solid ground here.

"Nope. You not even warm."

"Who, then?" I persisted. "Do you know?"

"I don't know, I think. I have no proof, just rumors and innuendo. If I tell you, give me your word you won't connect me in any way with this person or tell anyone that I gave you the name. This is a person far more formidable than any of those you've mentioned, and if either of us is connected with this, we could be in very, very serious trouble."

"I promise." I said immediately. "You're sure it's not one of the presidents?"

"Not a prayer," Sherwood said. And after taking a final, careful look around the room, he leaned forward and, sotto voce, whispered two chilling words in my ear.

"It's Barbara."

He reached out and shook my hand with great formality. Then, all elbows, arms and legs, propelled his wheelchair awkwardly down the hall to the third door on the right.

"Good luck with your ears." I called after him.

APPENDIX

APPENDIX 1—<u>BURPLE</u>

APPENDIX 2—WILLIAM GANNAWAY BROWNLOW, THE PARSON

APPENDIX 3—<u>DILLINGER</u>

APPENDIX 4—<u>TORPID</u>

APPENDIX 5—THE GREAT DICTATOR

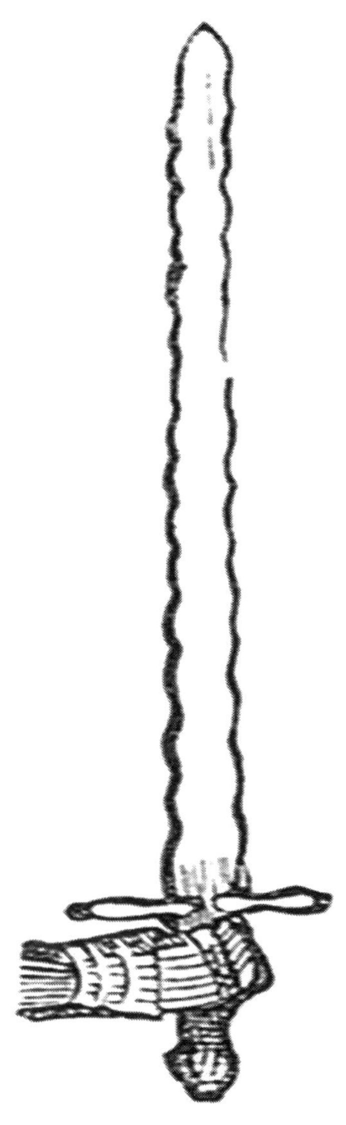

Fig. 127.—Flamberge

APPENDIX 6—FLAMMENSCHWERT

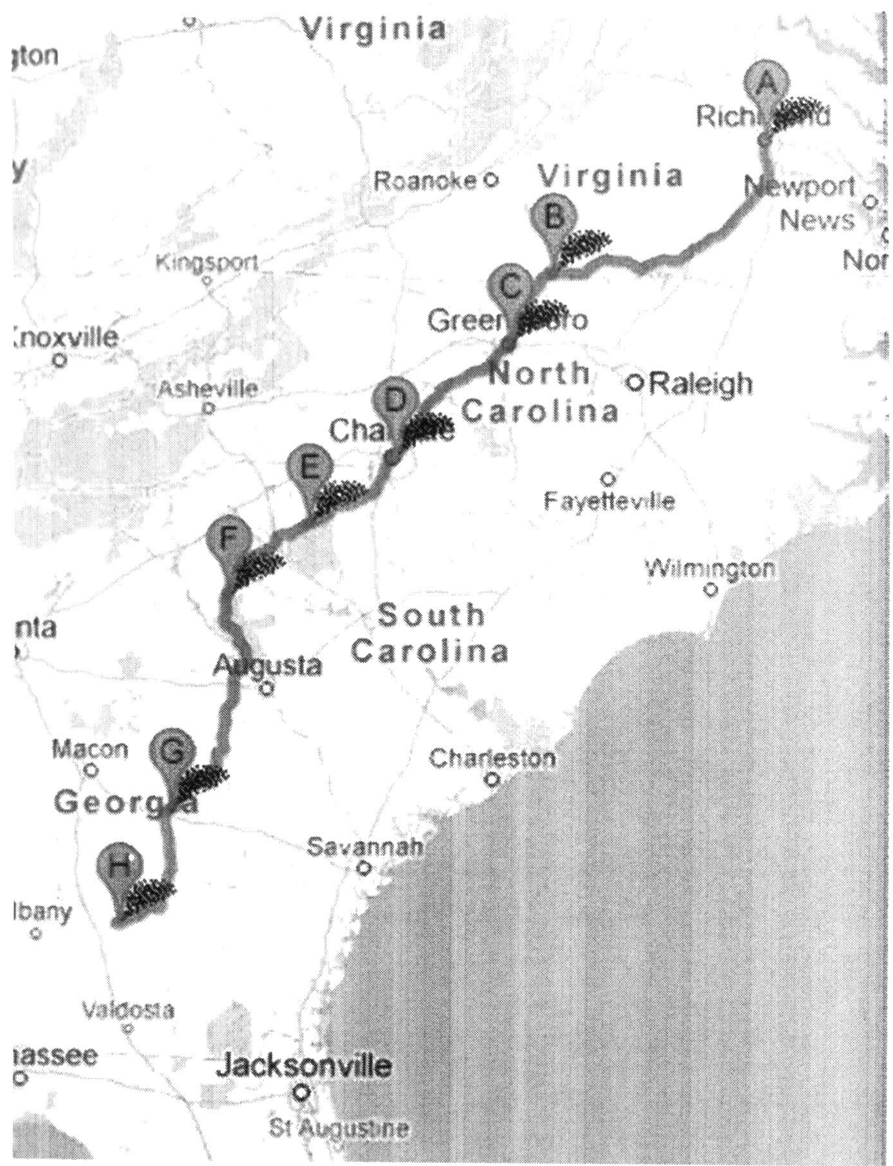

APPENDIX 7—<u>THE MAP</u>—See key below

A—Richmond, VA
B—Danville, VA
C—Greensboro, NC
D—Charlotte, NC
E—Union, SC
F—Abbeville, SC
G—Dublin, GA
H—Irwinville, GA

APPENDIX 8—<u>ERMEY</u>

APPENDIX 9 - METZGER

Ralph Metzger, captured by an unknown artist, October 2011

AUTHOR'S NOTE

Group Twenty was disbanded following what became known nationally as "the Great Motorcycle Incident" in Midland, Texas. Rumors persist that its structure and mission were briefly revived in Riviera Beach, Florida, greatly diminished in terms of both numbers and funding. Riviera Beach being ranked 13th in a list of the one hundred most dangerous cities in the United States, it would appear that the Group was attempting to establish a low profile organization in a high profile environment. They no longer called themselves Group Twenty, but changed the name to "Fountain of Life" in an effort to form an innocuous sounding, quasi-religious identity in the midst of so many innocuous sounding and quasi-religious organizations in the area. Unfortunately the name carried with it a far too evocative evangelical connotation. The organization's effort to hide behind religious skirts initially appeared to be working, but not in the way it might have been scripted. Fountain of Life was overwhelmed with phone calls from legions of ardent, needy, impassioned locals who were interested in joining a new evangelical mission. This acted as a catalyst to dry up the organization's limited funds and all but stop its recruiting efforts on every front. One can only imagine and sympathize with the dilemma faced when trying to recruit an effective, aggressive anti-government organization while awash in fervent, starry-eyed, evangelical aspirants.

Little is known as to what became of the Group's members with a few exceptions. J.D. Bowen stepped down from his position at the bank shortly after the Great Motorcycle Incident. He moved his family to the small, private neighborhood of Greenwood, a suburb on the outskirts of the city. When approached, he would acknowledge no connection with Group Twenty and refused to discuss his military record. From all reports a broken man, he became for all intents and purposes a recluse. His trips to downtown Midland became less and less frequent. It was said that he was able to distinguish between the sounds of various motorcycle engines, and that the throaty roar of a passing Harley Davidson would propel him into a state of near hysteria.

Shylock, after presiding over the collapse of The Fountain of Life, bought a small mobile home on the coast in Pinewood Park, just south of Riviera Beach. Soon thereafter Five moved in with him, and the two lived together in relative peace and seclusion for more than a year. Subsequently Shylock became active in an organization dedicated to preserving the current health care system in the country. He was instrumental in creating the organization's slogan; "Keep the Government out of Healthcare, but don't f . . . with my Medicare".

Curtis Sparrow, in fear of his life, fled to South Carolina where he eventually took refuge in local politics under the assumed name of Bobby Joe Byrd. Given the political eccentricities of the state, his past was neither questioned nor explored, and he was able to pass himself off as a longtime resident. Two years after his arrival Byrd was elected to the state legislature in a landslide after gaining the wholehearted and unconditional support of the Governor herself. He was subsequently forced to resign in disgrace, having been investigated and exposed by Leslie Stahl in her preparation for a 60 Minutes interview with the rising star of South Carolina politics.

Ralph Metzger was last known to be living semi-incognito in a small village in the Florida panhandle. He had no permanent address, and found it necessary to move frequently and furtively from one address to the next—and one bar to the next. Pursued by number of disgruntled clients, their lawyers and two private investigators, he somehow eluded detection, thanks in part to his altered appearance, which, it is reported, was for the worse. When last seen he had dyed his hair ash blonde and adopted an even more extravagant, eye-watering comb-over. He had also taken to leaving yet another button on his shirtfront undone, a contrivance that displayed even more lavish tufts of graying chest hair and had the effect of discouraging the approach of friends and strangers alike.

Henry Louis and Kate Smith were quietly married by Captain Luciano Tortorici of the 'Disney Magic' on the return trip from Castaway Cay. Upon hearing the news, Sampson Weeks at first threatened to quit his job and join the Peace Corps. Louis replied that the Peace Corps wouldn't have him. Contemplating the alternative of an expensive tuxedo rental and a destination wedding in Bermuda, Weeks relented. He agreed to continue working with Louis and Midland C.S.I. only on the condition that the couple's first child be given his first name.

The End

Made in the USA
Lexington, KY
20 May 2013